Nic

Nick Barlay is the author of
the underbelly of contempora
Zone and *Hooky Gear*. He has
contributed to short story a
appeared in many publications. He was born in London to Hungarian
refugee parents.

'It's both funny and melancholy . . . ultimately thought-provoking.
The language is vital, inventive, and this vitality and inventiveness
is itself a source of humour. The main character is complex, and he
evolves; he has a hinterland. You can feel how trapped he is, how
few choices he has in life after he made his first wrong choices. Also,
I feel this writer has thought about the country we live in and how
it got to be the way it is. I don't get this feeling from a lot of more
portentous novels that are around.'

Hilary Mantel on *Hooky Gear* in the *Guardian*

Also by Nick Barlay

Curvy Lovebox
Hooky Gear

Crumple Zone

Nick Barlay

SCEPTRE

First published in 2000 by Hodder & Stoughton
A division of Hodder Headline
A Sceptre Paperback

10 9 8 7 6 5 4 3 2

A CIP catalogue record for this title
is avaiable from the British Library

ISBN 978 0 340 74998 2

Printed and bound in Great Britain by
Clays Ltd, St Ives plc

Hodder and Stoughton
A division of Hodder Headline
338 Euston Road
London NW1 3BH

CRUMPLE ZONE

To Robin, Jan and the great Mrs Furstenberger

STANKY

killer stink in the house

Stanky have the whole place tagged. STANKY: BIG, it says on the Bevington Road public convenience. STANKY: FLYING 4, it says on the window of Ootie's Late Nite Store. STANKY: MASSIVE, it says in skull logo green on the firedoors of Trellick Tower, a concrete slab that looms over Golborne Road like a giant gravestone. And if you look up to the thirtieth floor of Trellick near where the walkway from the main block joins the stairwell, you'll see STANKY: CHONGA LOCO. My guess is as good as anyone's what that means.

Only thing I know is that all their tags and all the other versions of their tags like S:RY (STANKY: RUFF YOOT) have got the same characteristic: a colon. That colon, those two little dots, they're my contribution to *yoot* and *yoof* culture. I taught them that on one of the rare times the Stanky 4 bothered showing at school. They wanted tags with impact, tags that would blow the opposition out of the water. Tags that would stay on the walls of the old toilets at school. Well, it's given them an edge, and seeing their tags is the nearest most people get to seeing them at all, being as they are no more than a handful among a million truants.

So I'm always kind of surprised when I run into them anywhere. But today they *ain't just anywhere*. Today they've got real face.

1

They're standing – *hangin'* more like – bang on my home run. I mean, see the picture: half seven, sun setting on W11 and the summer term, and *there they be*, cool and big, living large in fresh trainers like they had daddy's standing order allowance *propping* up their lifestyle, like they were *straight-A guys* with careers mapped out all the way to the golden horizon. Instead of being the flakiest all-in under-sixteen bullshitters ever to skank off school and munch out on junk food.

As I'm approaching The Ridge, Big C and W, also known to parents and police as Ridgecroft, Clarke and Witter, they all look to their number one. Number one, who mostly responds to the name Stanky B but is down on the register at Kensal Grove as Burston, is way too busy to notice shit. He's backing his twelve stone of teenage protein nice and slow out of Golborne Kebabs and Burgers. He's unnaturally large in a yellow ski jacket, looming mean, and brandishing a leaky kebab:

—Hey you, *binnissman*: I ain't payin' for this cos it stink of poo. Get me? Look at that red smelly shit man. It's poo. Ain't takin' my peas for this. Look at it man: poo meat innit. *Killer stink in da house*. Get me? Nobody move nobody get hurt . . .

There's silence inside. Not even meek protest. Nothing. Burston hops out the store, holds up his free kebab and takes the biggest bite he can, then looks to his crew for acknowledgement. The boys fold with fake laughs, keel about with wailing street laughs that get right to the core of an enemy's ego. Diss 'em good. Tuff 'em down. Be first with the backchat. Then they're all banging and slapping fists with Burston, congratulating him on his *pioneering* sense of humour.

When Burston finally spots me I'm no more than twenty feet away, lugging my shoulder bag of books and marking. Suddenly, eight smirky eyes with insider knowledge are scoping me hard, which is really what the Stanky 4 like best. *Hangin' an' scopin'*. Only they should know better than to wrongside me on my home run, especially when all I want is to skin up a monster spliff, mark some delinquent drama projects, and kick back for the night. Burston shifts the food to one side of his mouth so that it swells out. Making sure I can hear, he drawls in a real showtime voice:

—Check Miss Thing boppin' down the street . . . One day she gonna be my ex. Y'na mean.

The Ridge and Big C fold over each other's shoulders, their faces screwed with hysterical laughter.

—Wicked, wicked, W's mumbling.

Burston pulls on his bumfluff whiskers, barely ten years younger and with a mouth too big for any age. I stop in front and give them one of my double-edged smiles, nice and sweet with the lips, nasty and sour with the eyes, a smile for which I'm famous and feared at Kensal Grove, a smile which has kept abuse and chair legs from flying in my direction. Burston clicks straight away and sticks out his chin trying to face me down. So I go:

—Say Burston: when you're absent you're meant to *stay* absent. Yet here you are, *feasting* on the fat, a real presence on the street and hey . . . dressed to kill . . .

Burston falls for it and puffs up like a designer pigeon. The Ridge slaps himself on his freckly orange forehead. Big C flips his wrist so that his thumb clicks. W copies both in turn. And all together again they fold laughing. So I go:

—What's the story? You just *had* to hang out here specially to see me right? And there I was hoping for another of your love letters . . .

Burston's jaw hits the pavement. His crew turn bug-eyed.

—Wha' you sayin'? I ain't never wrote you no love letter. I ain't—

—Don't explain. I understand . . .

I swing my bag on to my shoulder and I'm walking, sassing it up like a *schoolgirl*. It hits the spot. Burston takes a full three seconds to get a reaction together.

—Wha'? he goes stepping after me followed by numbers two, three and four. Wha' you dissin' me for in front of my homeboys? This is streetside now. This ain't no schoolyard.

—Burston, I say over my shoulder, you wouldn't know the difference.

3

—Needa would *you* innit, goes Burston throwing his free hand out at me then standing in front so I have to stop. You ain't even scoped them *poh-lice* boys down Trellick. Yeah workin' over your *own* yard.

Then he pauses, screwing his face with mock confusion, the corners of his mouth turned down.

—Or is they *up* Trellick? Ridge?

The Ridge has been trying to scratch his peepee which he cannot locate inside very baggy jeans. Now he's thinking up an answer. I can't help glancing over towards Trellick. Sure enough, past the bric-à-brac store, past the Lisboa café and the Moroccan Advice Centre both crowded with people looking for a way out, past the gutted salt fish and iced squid of Sisson's Seafood, and over the railway bridge past the lighters and matches man on his fold-out chair, there are a couple of bright white police vans, parked at odd angles, one still flashing blue, like they were props in a movie.

—It's go'a be *up* Trellick, says The Ridge with a sly bonehead smile. Things is goin' down *up* Trellick innit.

—Yeah, goes Burston looking at me then W, high up. Like around maybe floor number three oh innit . . .

—Could have been two nine, says W, could have been the roof terrace . . .

—Bus maybe ten fifteen hard stone stair *between* innit.

—Hundred per cent between boy, says W.

—Yeah, goes Burston, and we's all been wonderin': *wha' could be goin' down so high up Trellick between two nine and the roof terrace?* Innit . . .

—Yeah, says W, and like usual we ain't got no answer to wha' we been wonderin'. Innit crew.

—No answer, grins Big C stepping right in front and slouching down from six three to human size. But we got this *theory* . . .

And that's the cue for a four-way hysterical fold. I mean their laughter is so rehearsed you could dance to it. So ok, I'm thinking, they know where I live. But whether they're winding me up or trying to psyche me out I can't say. Either way, there's a teenage hysteric in my stomach doing step aerobics. It'd be useless to pick their brains about their *theory*. You couldn't torture it out of them. Information like that is power. They trade it. They use it to lever open people's heads and put the fear inside. For a second too long I don't know how to react. Act mean. Act tough. Smile honey sweet. Teachers always react. Most of them anyway. Should've been a maths teacher: *fuck with me and I'll kill you*. Ones and zeros. Keep the message simple.

In that second of hesitation, they see me, see everything I am, know everything I can say or can't, know even better than me what I will say. I have to come back at them with something, anything. It's always about last words.

—Burston: you better have a good excuse for not showing today . . .

Stanky clutch their guts and hold their breaths, their expressions frozen on the edge of the Almighty Fold. I walk off knowing full well I've just uttered the term's most pointless sentence. Burston throws it back at me, exaggerating my Manchester accent. So much for discipline. I'm ten steps away when their street laughs break. The wails ride high above the heads of grim, stubbly men slumped out in smokey groups, above shopping-laden old women arguing the price of dodgy toilet cleaner with shifty stallholders weighed down by 50ps, and above oily slicksters double-parked in tinted Mercs in front of the Jerico cake shop. Everyone seems to look up in an instant, searching the air for The Joke, then following the collective stare of the Flying 4 down the street . . . to me.

I have to make sure I stroll, not fast not slow, neither carefree nor uptight, just strolling strolling strolling till I'm well away, till everyone decides there are better things to figure than the mysteries of teenage humour. Besides, nobody's putting in requests for a punch line. Skanky fuckers.

Stanky M chalk up another mental victory, busting out with made-to-fit wisdom, big with untold streetside *Re*-speck, and smug as fourth years with sick notes that they *ain't never growin' up*.

The late sun washes orange over Trellick, marking out hundreds of windows. Red velour curtains flapping on floor twenty. Toothy

Nick Barlay

kid hanging a shoe out of the window ten floors below. Wideload mother in floral pink eating biscuits in front of the tele, corner of floor six. Trellick Tower in big red letters like an international hotel, like an international warning. And the *poh-lice* still flashing blue by the propped open fire door.

TRELLICK

the square one thing

I'm standing on the thirtieth floor on what might have been an average Thursday in late June looking at the trashed front door of my flat. There are marks round the lock, chips of wood on the floor, like someone's actually hacked through with an axe. Inside are three suited guys, the taller bearded, standing in the middle of the living room, hands pocketed, whistling Yankee Doodle. He glances in my direction just as he gets to macaroni. He raises his eyebrows at me, as if to say: *fancy joining in the chorus?* So, naturally the first words to pop into my jumbled head are: *who the fuck are you?* Only I say nothing. Or maybe I do. All I can hear is my heart. It's going so hard my eyelids are shuddering. There seems to be debris spread over the floor around his feet. My hand is in my bag. Deep down, under my regular stuff, is this canister of pepper spray that I got one time off a friend of my brother. He told me it could take out a cinema audience if the wind was right.

Whistler unpurses his lips and takes his right hand out of his pocket. With thumb and finger he curtains aside the bottom of his green M&S jacket to reveal, clipped to his grey polyester trousers, his shiny police badge.

—Detective Sergeant Mills. Grove CID, he says in this jerky

monotone like the words were on ticker tape punching out of his mouth. And you are?

My throat lumps up.

—Cee Harper. I live here.

I realise I'm about to be invited into my own place.

—'Fraid you've been burgled . . .

Not like I couldn't have figured that out for myself. Yet when I look past him properly, I go numb. Mills is still talking only I can't hear him. Something about a neighbour calling. I'm sort of aware of stepping over some dark spats of *goo* at the door and wondering if that's what other people's blood looks like. The front door's nothing compared to the wreck inside. Whole place has been turned over. Shit everywhere. My big cheese plant's broken near the root. Like it's been snapped off or trodden on. Black earth spreads in a trail to the windows.

Beneath the windows which run the length of the wall there's only a mass of stereo wires and disconnected cables, snaking to nowhere or knotted, useless. Everywhere there're gaps in the grand scheme. Nothing but space where CD, computer and stereo used to be. Speakers gone, outlined in dust. A blank rectangle of wall where the TV used to be. Records lying out of their sleeves like someone's used them for indoor frisbee. Including a couple of Dennie's old Charlie Mingus albums that he parked with Big Sis for safe-keeping along with his bass that better be in the cupboard.

Behind, a chair and coffee table lie turned over near the door. Cutlery leads out from the kitchen merging in with a pile of clothes from the bedroom. Everything, bra, crockery, bucket, furniture, seems to be on the move like a line of refugees escaping my life. Never realised I had so many separate things.

Mills turns slightly sideways, extending one arm towards me, the other into the room to usher me in. Very non-confrontational. The whole gesture's straight from the training manual under the section called *Bonding with Victims*. His two colleagues keep busy, one dusting for fingerprints, the other staring at the cracks in the ceiling like the prime suspect was Santa Claus. Mills I can feel looking. His mouth is moving, explaining something.

I'm scanning the floor, recognising familiar things in unfamiliar locations, listing it all in my head, all the missing things, then listing what I've got left, what they've left me with. I mean *all this now?* I mean I was coasting. It was the end of term, the big wind-down. I was coasting home. Time to breathe, time to think, make plans. I can't believe this now. The square one thing.

And all I can do is try to order the whole process of clearing up. Working out the time it's going to take for the knives, forks, spoons to be divided and sorted, the time it'll take for everything to get back to normal, and for the police to go. Most of all, I'm wondering how long before a big spliff fills the room with lush smoke and I can call it a day.

And that's the first thing that really gets to me, the thought that whoever was here found my stash in the small wooden cigar box on the bookshelf, thieved it, and is now standing somewhere smoking down my skunk. Like smiling to themselves and getting buzzed on my misery. Most of the books are off the shelves, scattered. No sign of the box. I mean taking my smoke would be just too fucking personal.

Can see Burston's face in front of me. The Ridge all sarky. Big C leery. Happy-go-lucky W happy with whatever mood's going. And I'm standing here with a Yankee Doodle cop who's now got his hand on my shoulder trying to get me to pay attention to him. I don't need this shit. Which I guess is something anyone can say about anything that doesn't quite square with their *world order*. Even so, I really don't. Finally I have to look at Mills.

— . . . Know it's a shock . . . But there's one or two things . . .

He starts moving towards the kitchen, treading carefully over lumps of black earth, making sure he doesn't disturb the wreckage. After all, now it's *my* wreckage. He keeps his eye on me in case I lapse back into a shocked silly stupor. Don't want to touch anything. I follow him, follow his exact steps, pulling down my black Wonderbra, yeah right, off the lamp shade then putting my bag down on top of it. Mills sees this but makes a polite show of ignoring it, scratching his chin instead, thoughtfully, like he was piecing it all together. He stops just inside the kitchen.

—Been a fair few burglaries last couple of weeks . . .

That makes me feel a lot better Millsy. Like we could *all go support group togevver innit.*

—Specially round the area . . . Golborne. Portobello. Normally it's been kids. You know, stomp the door down and go for cash and plastic . . .

—How d'you mean *normally* kids? Is all this slick professionals?

—Maybe, maybe not, says Mills coming on all crafty then nodding over to the far side of the kitchen. What d'you make of that . . .

At first I think he's commenting on two days' worth of washing up in the sink. Or the remnants of a dahl curry from Ootie's Late Niter, and a carton of mango juice leaking sticky yellow across the draining board that I don't even remember eating. But below the sink's a cupboard, and below that there's a large hole in the floor. It's circled by the imprint of the bucket that was there, a bucket that was never moved. You know, until now.

To create the hole, someone's obviously cut the lino, dead precise, then jacked up the floorboards. To get at something underneath. Something hidden. Which means the hole was made another time, earlier, before today. A hole in my floor to hide something. I'm about to glance at Mills and shrug. But he's a step ahead.

—Had the plumber in?

Mills scratches elsewhere this time, his head, along his half-inch silver-grey crew cut that he was probably born with and has probably scratched a million times in a million homes to hide his shitty sarcastic smirk. Mills can see I'm not exactly in the mood to play twenty dumb questions but goes ahead anyway.

—Now why would anyone do that?

—*I* have a clue? I mumble out, shrugging. I don't have a clue . . .

It doesn't seem to convince Mills despite the fact that it's the truth. Mills pulls on his ear lobe to cover a moment of silence. He's already a long way down some *theoretical road* towards a truth he already knows. He ain't gonna trust anything I come out with. Trying to sound truthful when you're telling the truth is not easy. Specially with Mills, who's most likely always taken other people's truth with a pinch of salt, who's always ready with a bit of sound advice, who double checks and double locks his whole life and gets great deals on double glazing. I can't help avoiding his eyes.

—Sure you don't keep anything down there?

—Course I'm sure. Wha'm I gonna keep down there?

—You tell me.

—I'm gonna tell *you*? What do *you* think I keep down there?

Mills pauses, sizing things up. I feel like Burston playing for time while brewing a good excuse. Mills reaches in his pocket. With thumb and forefinger, he pulls out a wooden cigar box. When I say *a cigar box*. Like fuckface opens it under my nose. Inside, wrapped in clingfilm, the way I left it, is a juicy green bud flecked with orange. I can smell it, almost taste it.

—Some more of this maybe . . .

—Oh please . . . Come on Sarg . . .

I don't know why I say it like that. It's one of those things you hear enough on television and just have to say the moment you get an opportunity. Better than the full *Sergeant* which sticks right in the throat. Silly rank anyway.

—Detective Sergeant, goes Mills *real patient* like it was a *listen and repeat* hour for exchange students.

Well there goes my job. First I get burgled. Then in a neat twist stitched up for an eighth. Less than an eighth. What's that? Nothing. Stanky get through an eighth just walking to school. Then another eighth to wind down after double biology. And then they're smokin' down eighths between passes during Wednesday afternoon football. At least they don't have CV's to worry about. Won't look too good on mine. I say nothing, expecting a reading from Mills' book of universal bullshit.

—Seems to me Miss Harper that whoever got in here knew what they were looking for and knew exactly where to look for it. The rest just looks like fun. I mean, they didn't come up for the view . . .

Too late, you said it, I'm thinking. Fun. I'd love to hear Mills explaining the difference between fun and crime.

—Well they got something didn't they. TV, stereo. And the rest ... Computer ... Left the answerphone. Wasn't big enough for them I guess. Then somehow they took all that stuff down *thirty floors* ...

Mills just stands there motionless.

—I don't know what's going on, I say giving out a little too much sincere exasperation. All I know is my place is stuffed and anything worth taking they've taken. But that doesn't include six tons of marijooani kept under the floorboards for all my chums with Parkinson's. Ok?

—You get on with people here?

What do I read in his eyes when he asks that? What people is he talking about?

—Not exactly united colours of Benetton but sure ... Get on with everyone I suppose. Why not?

—No grudges, arguments, spats with the neighbours?

—No. Why?

—What do you do for a living?

—Teacher. Part-time.

—Teaching ... ?

—Drama.

—So you're an actress ...

—Every Saturday night after a bottle of vodka. Otherwise I'm resting, as they say.

—My cousin's an actress. Does voice-overs. She was a barmaid in *Crimewatch* just recently. Reconstruction sort of thing. Funny that ...

—What with you being a policeman you mean, I go, getting more sarky, leery, facety and anything else I can work up.

—Where d'you teach?

—Kensal Grove.

—Boys?

—All of them.

—Live alone?

—Yep.

—No boyfriend?

—Come on, what is this?

—Anyone else use the place? Like a boyfriend. Or a girlfriend.

—Not to my knowledge.

—Anyone else have keys? Neighbours? Friend?

—Brother I suppose.

Regret it as soon as I say it. You can almost see the working part of Mills' brain working on this half of a half of nothing.

—And his name is . . . ?

—Dennie.

—And where is he?

—On holiday. Spain. Back next week or so . . .

—So he doesn't live here . . .

What to say? Always have to be careful with these type of questions because I never know D's exact arrangements with the DSS. Or mine for that matter.

—Sometimes stays here. Sometimes stays with friends. You know . . .

—No fixed address?

—In between fixed addresses.

—Well, goes Mills scratching his nose. That's it . . . Unless you have anything you want to mention . . .

I shrug, take a deep breath. When police take an interest in your stuff, everything takes on new meaning. All those bits of your life you figured you had covered suddenly look like gaping holes. And it's like there's violence in all my things, like violence has suddenly collected as dust in all the junk that ever cluttered my life. And you never get rid of that dust. It just circulates round, settles invisibly on one surface then another, and finds its way in everywhere. Like Burston. Come to that like Dennie since the first time he got arrested, *rousted* one rainy dawn on Moss Side with a roomful of bootlegs, a couple of bags of weed and a heavy duty water pistol to explain. And carry on explaining ever since.

Mills seems uncomfortable, shifting from one leg to the other, searching for the right word, thinking of a crime number, any number, filling a form, any form. Eventually, he passes me a form and goes:

—Insurance . . .

Deep silence. The word just hangs there like it was the abracadabra for the burglarised world. Or maybe he thinks I'm scamming the insurance. Only one flaw in that plot:

—What insurance?

Mills coughs a pointless cough, arranges his jacket, checks his tie, and looks round at his colleagues hovering in the background, keeping busy. Then he pulls out a card with his details on it, slips it into the stash box and hands it to me. I take it from him, big-time inner relief, managing a smile without either looking sheepish or like I suspect his motives. I mean, it's like he's dreaming a second. Like there's this whole thing going on. For a second he's in some deep fantasy about really saving someone, about the good life; some fantasy in which he sees our lives, mine and his, spread out before him, a vision of domestic bliss, a schoolboy flash of how it could all be if only school didn't exist. *All growed up* with his twinkie illuminating the end of the rainbow. Dream on.

—Worth thinking about insurance, he says heading vaguely towards the door. Worth changing the locks as well.

A lot of things are worth thinking about and worth changing. No doubt Mills has got a list somewhere, tucked up safe with other life-changing documents. He signals his chums. I usher them out. Suddenly we're all ballerinas tip-toeing on egg shells, trying to avoid touching anything and carefully stepping in turn over the dark stains by the door.

—Blood, nods one of them, his navel more or less winking at me from beneath his gut-stretched shirt.

—Don't expect immediate arrests or nationwide DNA testing, Mills adds doing his jokey best. But if there's anything else you think of . . .

—I'll be sure and call.

Mills gives me a parting look, a kind of cop versus suspect *I'll be back* look but maybe that's just me being para. Perhaps he expects me to snitch on the neighbourhood in return for letting me keep my *holy herb*.

The three wise men disappear into the open lift, experiencing one of the rare magical times when the lift is just there, open and waiting, and you don't have time to read a potboiler while ten baby mothers, four tattooed doleboys puffing rollies, a hundred and fifty bags of shopping, six killer dogs and thirty tooled up brats unload on floors six, seven, fifteen and twenty before the lift packs up on twenty-four.

It's when the doors close and the whole thing starts to clunk down, metal scraping and policeman grunts echoing in the shaft, that I start to get scared. Just standing there on the grey landing, nowhere in particular. I mean, like what next? What happens now? What do I do now? Where does my life go now?

Takes me a while even to turn round. Chrome lift. Grey stairwell. The crack in the wall that starts right here and runs through all the way down to the ground getting wider in the heat. Trellick'll split. Only doors hold the whole place together. Like the blue door of 161 with its sticky black numbers curling off. I imagine an eye in the peephole. A neighbour, smelly bastard called Dave, wears a vest, *gets on with all sorts* and *don't want no trouble*. My door, 160. The metal six has fallen off. It takes me even longer to walk back inside, stepping over what they say is blood. Not mine. Someone's.

One minute I'm standing in the middle of my place, the next face up to the corner window. Nothing's moved on. Below, far below, the alleys and narrow walkways that knot round Trellick suggest a million directions property could disappear. On one side the Grand Union Canal flows west towards Willesden Junction, away from yuppie balconies on the opposite bank laden with Ikea bullshit, window boxes, Japanese lanterns. On another side there's a scarred up chicken-wired basketball court like something out of *West Side Story*. Which I guess it is, only without the fake knives. Inside, it's a graffiti stand-off between *Stanky Fly*, *Honk Fonk* and some lone

Nick Barlay

Nubian activist: *My Bredrin, them that got beaten by police has got Staying Power.*

Going the other way is Golborne Road. You can see right along it to where it hooks on to Portobello. Same crowd shifting. Or not. Slumming trustafarians in their Goa chic and blonde dreds. Slumming trustafarians in Gucci slingbacks and Versace wraps. Arab men, Portuguese men, drinking black coffee, smoking Marlboros. Ootie smoking and haggling in front of his store with his cousin Amil. Bicycle bobby O'Hara, the laughing lawman, squeaking his way through toytown till his batteries run out or till the last crime is solved. Whichever comes first. And shadows, the dark fugitive shadows of Burston and his crew that seem to fall everywhere, get in everywhere.

High above in the electric blue red sky is a Philips airship, glowing with its message: *Let's make things better.* One day Stanky'll tag that too.

SABINE

check out the batty

Right now everything has to flow backwards. All things have to be put in reverse just to get back to the shit normal. Eventually I get the cigar box, skin one up which seems to take forever. Then I'm watching the smoke fill up the room. It replaces all smells of strangers, known and unknown, sweaty men whose cheap deodorant didn't last the shift.

I phone Sabine. Her recorded voice hollers back. This week she's a Mississippi riverboat queen. *Hi. It's Sabine. Leave a message and I'll be sure an' call y'all right back.* She could be anywhere. I tell her it's urgent. Which is not really a word Sabine's ever got to grips with. As I'm putting the receiver down it occurs that something else has gone: Dennie's mobile. I mean I look for it but it's definitely gone. Somebody's making calls to Rio by now. So I dial the number, just to whatever, see, hear. *Welcome to the Orange network* . . . I hang up.

Then, halfway to the bathroom, I just blub my head off. Like real big tears, *weeping* like a movie star, which, when it all starts, feels like something I've wanted to do since time. That's of course when Sabine calls back.

—What's up ba'? Heard the phone go but I was takin' a soak.

—Just come over, I tell her.

17

—You can't talk, she says, for some reason in a whisper, probably thinking I'm sounding weird because there's some guy here I'm trying to get rid of.

—It's not that . . . Been burgled . . .

—*No* . . . *Oh babes.* Wha' they take?

—What didn't they . . .

I go into a ten-minute rant, Sabine going *no, oh babes* after everything. Then when I say, for the third time, *I mean they broke the door an' everything*, Sabine goes:

—Hold tight babes. I'm flyin' over.

Sabine flies so fast she arrives a mere hour later. Well maybe not that long. I mean she's only driving from Harrow Road but she probably has to check two bars and a junglist dance first. No matter what the emergency, Sabine has to line up at least two dates before she does anything. Which makes being her friend like playing Russian Roulette: her date always has a best mate, a brother, a main man, a spar, a number one all-time buddy who'd just love to meet me. The only time she didn't have a whole Lonely Hearts column in tow was when she copped off with, shagged, and even went out with Dennie. But that was long ago and in any case didn't last half a dozen weekends.

The lift doors scrape apart and Sabine walks out and in through the still open front door. Look up all muss-eyed. Sabine's chirpy favourite *you'll never guess what* look's been exchanged for an *oh my God I don't believe it* face, alive with purple lippie, matching eye-shadow and a nuclear sunbed tan practically melting her purple Lycra cleavage. Sabine wakes me up like a supercharged cattle prod. She hugs me with a sorrowful *oh babes* and I'm about to boo hoo my face off all over again when I notice the guy.

He's kinda *lurking* on the threshold, trying to maintain a low profile through a gold-toothed grin and insect-eye shades. As for shell-suits they've been and gone but he's wearing his like he was signing albums at Virgin Megastore.

—Alrigh' inn'e? goes Sabine under her breath.

But she sees guy talk is the last thing on my list so she goes:

—He's gonna fix up the door. Hey Alvin . . . meet Cee. Cee Alvin. You can take the wraps off now Alv: you're inside.

Alv pushes his finger under the bridge and shifts the shades to the top of his head in a practised move. No doubt the revealing of his eyes improves his appearance almost a hundred per cent. But I'm thinking his disappearance would improve him the full whack.

—Alrigh' Cee . . .

Brief smile. Grin from him. Half a handshake. Handyman vibes.

—Not in so many words no but thanks f—

—No worries, says Alv going for his tools which he's left discreetly outside, I fix up the door easy. Barrel an' a chubb *fe dem sly teefs* . . .

Sabine scoops up an armful of clothes from the floor.

—You an' me clear up meantime, yeah? she twinkles as Alv comes back. An' then we can check out Slack Studio. There's some—

—Wha'? You want to go *out*? Now? To Dollis Hill?

—Yeah def. I know wha' it's like hon. You can't let it get to you. There's a do for some band. *Ticker* I think they're called. Or *Flipper* or summin. They just got a *pumpin' dance toon on the airwaves* an' all tha'. 'Sides I got a sitter in for Miles. We can go in a bit. Sort you out first. You need to go out trust me. I've been through this, you know tha'. If you stay in now you're just gonna get mega depressed. Let some steam out . . . Be ok ba'. Really. Do you g – *Oh my God.*

Sabine's just discovered some old knickers I didn't even remember I had and is holding them up to the light for inspection.

—Check out the batty on these . . . No way you're *this* big with your skinny arse. This is more me. Double cheeseburger. Fact this wouldn't even wear. Cee I swear my arse is gettin' bigger.

—So thass wha'm seein', goes Alv, I's thinkin' night had come innit.

I have to laugh. Sabine twangs the knickers over at Alv who responds with a burst of drill. I'm really trying to get in the swing.

—Sabine: where am I gonna go tonight? Look at this shit. It's out the question. I've got last day of term tomorrow as well.

Nick Barlay

—Cee's a *teacher*, Sabine says with a smile, casting out the word like it meant I'd been to outer space and back.

—You a *teacher*? goes Alv putting on a *blown away* face, chisel in hand.

—Mm. So what's with the *big surprise* Alv?

—If only I had a teacher like you way back, he grins. Y'na mean . . .

I glance at Sabine, and she in turn at Alv as she raises a thick-lined eyebrow and purses her lips which, to anyone who doesn't know Sabine, spells *watch your mouth or you die*.

—Just fix the door star . . .

—Easy, I'm workin' favours for no danger money, he says tapping the blood on the floor with the end of a screwdriver. *Bloodclaat*: somebody musta cu' 'emself good mashin' through the door innit . . .

—Yeah, I say, I guess they musta.

—Is righ' only somma them marks is on the *inside* like how—

—Alv, goes Sabine taking me by the arm, *work* don't talk.

She walks me into the middle of the chaos.

—Bastards innit, doin' all this. Used to be like this all the time when we's in Stockwell . . .

Which is where me and Sabine met three almost four years ago, Stockwell Road Estate, neighbours looking out for each other, helping each other, *that's when good neighbours become good friends*.

— . . . Then I spent three months up Broadwater and couldn't wait to get back, she goes, smiling as she picks up this old black and white barber-shop photo of Dennie that got him free haircuts for a year. Police been?

—And gone. They reckoned I had a Colombian drugs haul under the floorboards.

—Did you?

—Did I?

—Have any gear under the floorboards . . .

—Sabine . . . I had two spliffs'-worth in a tin. Fuckin' hell. They

20

took the TV, my computer – which I only just fucking paid for –
stereo. Lo—

—Honey come on all that stuff's totally gettable trust me.

—Handyman's gonna fix that too? I say under my breath.

We look over at Alv. He glances up but says nothing, just chisels
and grins and chisels some more.

—Wha'ever . . . You can have my old CD player an' speakers for
a start. They weren't exactly *unhooky* when I got 'em. An' there's
always some, you know, *useful geezer* at Slack. Like Georgio. *Big
G*, goes Sabine mimicking a man scratching his crotch. You know
him already no? Georgio Georgianou? No?

—Yeah kind of . . .

—Trust me you'd remember. Great name, shit personality. Anyway,
Dennie knows him. So, she shrugs putting a hand on my face, you
know . . . *sorted.*

—Yeah I know, I say taking her hand, only I've got my end-of-term
sermon tomorrow about what not to do in the summer holidays.
Which is more or less everything worth doing as far as the posses,
the crews and the *homeboys* are concerned. *J'na mean babes* . . . ?

—Yeah I'm just tryina help. You do need to get out. You can't let
'em run your life . . . The teefs I'm talkin' abou'. I thought you'd
want to get out that's all. See the lights . . .

—Slack Studio's the lights?

—Well, goes Sabine, so it ain't the Hippodrome on a Saturday night
but what's the choice? The Bull Bar?

—No way on *earth* I'm gonna go there, shouts Alv. An' I'm sayin'
that *verily* y'na mean . . .

—See? I mean I just thought, you know . . .

—I know, I say, planting a big kiss on her smooth cheek. I
know . . . I'm sorry . . .

I'm tired by now and caving in fast. We start to clear up and
I'm moving on auto reverse back and fourth along the regular
routes from living room to bedroom when I get a mental image
of Dennie's bass stashed in the bedroom cupboard. Slide the door.
Nothing there except Dennie's old trainers among my shoes and

best outfits. Nothing guitar-shaped. Not even the space where it was. Dennie will grieve plenty for that space when he gets back. But why did they slide the door closed? I mean after taking it?

Sabine's sweeping, tidying up, ordering it all up. Half hour, we're done. Misery all the same. Ugly. Sabine's checking her angles in the bathroom mirror. I'm standing behind and holding up mine for her to look at, not that there's even half Sabine's story going on, especially not in my low-key school clothes. We make *Essex girl on the pull* faces – or more like *Stockwell girls* – which Sabine has a definite gift for mainly because she's permanently on the pull. Me, I'm just there to help her figure an escape from whoever she's pulled. Anyway, there's some mild hysterics for Alv to gawp at, shake his head at, carry on working to.

Don't really want to leave. Or see people. Especially the twilight zone musicians at Slack, the wannabe *gangsta rap* stars, and all the trash always carried in their slipstream. I'll breathe again after the term's done. And Sabine's right. I can't, don't want to let it get to me. In any case, Sabine's baby mother arrangements cannot be resisted. Once the sitter's sorted, which is most likely Sabine's mum, she just has to go out and stay out as long as she can, using anyone, any excuse, not to go home when she's supposed to.

Alv slams a couple of nails into the kitchen floor. I put the bucket back in place over the scars. He even cleans up the blood and finishes on schedule with the door, swinging two keys for each lock into my hand.

—Death row max securi'y now innit. Swee'. A bent stick for the Devil an' new keys for a new life. Isaiah sixteen.

—Thanks Alvin, I go. If you say so.

ALVIN'S CAR

simple an' righteous

So anyway, about ten or after, we're in Alvin's car on our way to Dollis Hill with me having agreed to more or less everything. Whatever that is. Only when Sabine says about anything not to worry and to leave it with her, you know you're going to end up somewhere way beyond predicting. Like Alvin's car.

He doesn't so much open the doors of his BMW 5.3 XRQZi fuel-injected fuckmobile as pull them aside like silk sheets. Oh so smooth. Sabine goes front and I get in the back while Alv does a good impression of a boy playing with his fave toy, kicking a tyre, examining a pinpoint of paintwork, running a vain middle finger across the top of the rear-view as if slicking down an eyebrow, then steering out of his slot with his index. Oh the power. Alv's power smells of carpet shampoo.

The radio's tuned to some pirate station like Towerblock FM and there's a phone-in karaoke going with *two gigglin' fannies from Shepherd's Bush* – as Sabine puts it – singing along to *Voulez-vous coucher avec moi ce soir?* The two of them get right into it, clicking along and making plenty of eye contact. Window down, Alvin drives as if he knows everyone on every street and grins left and right like he's about to pull over for a quick chirp. Truth is, he doesn't actually know anyone and some people, still

23

out and about, *hangin' an' scopin'*, leer back like they mean it.

He drives up Kensal Road, over the Grand Union and stops, engine running, outside the Seven-Eleven like he was about to make a move on the place. He wouldn't be the first. The Seven-Eleven is the nearest thing to night life on the Harrow Road and Alvin's warming to it. He jumps out and sticks his head back in:

—Want some sips for the way?

Sabine puts in an order for one of those little vodka cocktail things that schoolkids hide in their pockets and single mums stash in their prams. I give Alvin a fiver for some chicken tikka sandwiches and a chocolate milkshake.

—You ok hon? goes Sabine shifting round.

—Sure sure, I smile back, glad that my face is in shadow.

—*Hope my Mum ain't listenin'*, goes one of the Fannies before DJ Surfboy cuts her off with a jingle then a burst of *well constructed drum an' bass*.

—Ain't growin' one are you? goes Sabine.

—Triplets. Now I can't remember if it was Crispin, Quentin or Snoop Doggy Dog . . .

—Serious girl I mean chicken tikka an' chocolate milkshake—

—Are *you* serious? I haven't even been with anyone since I dunno. Just feel like making myself sick.

—You can do it more quicker with a few of them vodkas. An' unless you ain't been updatin' me on the latest it was since Steve the stockbroker innit.

—Thanks for that memory.

—Wha'ppen to him?

—Sure I told you.

—No way ba'. I'm like a computer chip when it comes to them typea details. I mean he was all sorted no?

—Joking sweetheart.

—So run i' by me again.

—Drifted apart over breakfast.

—Happens hon.

—Yeah only we *started* on different planets. Told you about him sure I did . . .

—Only tha' he was wedged up.

—Loaded. Owned a massive, family-size ego. Pillow talk with him . . . I mean, I'd rather sit in front of the whole of 4c with a gag in my mouth.

—You're just way too choosy. An' chicken tikka an' chocolate milkshake *definitely* ain't righ'.

Meanwhile, over at the Seven-Eleven, Alv is making good his escape, bag in hand. Sabine reaches for my hand:

—Be ok trust me, she says spreading warmth like central heating for the soul.

—*Nuff foolishness*, booms Surfboy, *Let's be singin' out to the Christian massive here on Soldiers of Christ FM. Six-oh-six two-oh-eight-four gets you through. We got Jonah reachin' in from the Westway. Hello Jonah: you havin' a whale of a time innit* . . .

Alvin eases in just as Jonah's dredging up the words *You are the sunshine of my life* . . . Sabine gives him the wide-eye.

—Wha'? goes Alv arranging himself in the seat and passing round the food and drink.

—How you explainin' Soldiers of Christ FM Alvin?

—I'm a Christian innit, says Alv pulling off into the backstreets with a stage-managed manoeuvre but more than a bit put out.

—I didn't know you was Christian.

—I didn't know you was baby mother.

—Whass wrong with bein' a mum?

—Whass wrong with bein' a Christian? *A time shall come when every tongue shall confess Jesus Christ is Lord.*

—Yeah? goes Sabine with a full-on eyebrow. Well nobody's fessin' up tonigh' thass for sure . . .

Alv weaves in and out of some loose traffic while he works hard to keep his cool. Sabine checks me in the back. Alv just thinks she's checking him.

—Don't keep givin' me that look, he goes which just gets Sabine's eyebrow back to where it was. Leas' I ain't Pentecostal. My sister's goin' Pentecostal. Told her untold time she's crazy. The outfits alone is gonna set you back a ransom. Break you. Na mean. I told her: stick with the Methodists. Simple an' righteous an' a Peach Canei for the road . . .

Alv grins, takes a pull on his Peach Canei and sighs with pleasure. Him and Sabine find some middle ground talking about great pirate DJs they have known. The passing street lights blink me back into another stupor, depressed, whatever. Not knowing where I want to be, how I came to be here.

Last spring or so, at the beginning of term, I started writing. This. Because I ended up having to. Gave them what I thought would be the last word in projects, writing up events from *real life*. Their *own unfolding stories*. Their *personal histories*. Department head loved it. Tickled her silly. *Let them tell it like it is*, she said. *Stoopid cunt*, they would've said. I should've said.

Thing is, it was out of hand from the off. Burston – or one of them – straight away came back with: *How we gonna write abou' real life miss? We's at school innit. This shit cannot be real.* And somebody else went: *You do it miss. You write summin real an' we'll think abou' i'.* And somebody else went: *Write abou' your love life miss.* Then all hell.

After two seconds I was at the negotiating table just to keep the peace. Only the table had two screwy legs – both on my side. I was weak and that was Monday. By Friday, I was producing; *they* were producing. And since real life for them was *when something bad happens*, the domestics, the beatings, the robberies, the drugs, the bad sex just poured out. I had trouble keeping up. Mum was up North; Dennie wasn't getting arrested fast enough. He just wasn't living *large* enough. I was *out-realed*.

Now burgled. With *them pesky kids* walking around thinking: *that'll give the bitch summin to wri' abou' innit.* Couldn't tell the cops they were there. Not yet anyway. Not ever probably. Besides, it's real life. Real life drama. *Summin to say innit.* Feel like I've spent most of my life being shouted down so I guess I should have plenty to say.

But from me there's a big long silence, voice unheard, thoughts in the back of my head, long way from spoken, still further from heard, a million miles from listened to, nowhere near respected, and only ever obeyed by death-threatened, dozy, mashed, Wednesday afternoon teenage fuckers.

A time shall come when every tongue, especially mine, gets to blow one back. Glory be. Sabine was right though about the chicken tikka and chocolate milkshake.

SLACK

bitches, whores, cyclists

—Dez two typesa people in this world, goes Georgio Georgianou in a voice that's chain-smoker deep, crackpipe in one hand and mini blowtorch in the other. Dez *Bruvvers* . . . an' dez *Geezers* . . .

Everyone goes silent while G incinerates his rock, his sweaty, black-ringed eyes on full beam like nothing existed except flame, cocaine and personal paradise. Me, Sabine and Alvin have just piled into the pool room at Slack Studios, a smoky hole with a head-scrape ceiling at the centre of a world with only *two typesa people*. This is Musoland, one of those mythical places where young musicians go to get hip and take off, and where older ones come back to to get loaded and give up. They usually pass each other on one of the six staircases leading in and out of fly-toilet studios and rehearsal rooms. Stuck behind two skips, next to a wormy timberyard and backing on to Dollis Hill Tube, Slack ain't exactly a filling station on the highway to MTV.

Everyone's waiting for the rest of G's theory of life, that's if his chunky yellow cheeks don't explode first from the crack smoke he's swallowed down, jaws set, curly black hair greased, Rottweiler pecs taut inside an even yellower *World Dance* T-shirt. Sabine's description on the way in was note perfect. And I should've turned round there and then and cabbed it home.

29

—So wha' 'bou' bitches an' whores G?

That's Sabine talking, mental as usual and all eyebrow. G looks her up and down, from her slick hennaed hair to her painted platformed toes. And begins to boil inside. His eyes seem to water, even kind of vibrate. While G's taking *nuvver hit* on his peace pipe, Sabine gives me an eyebrow like to say *here's that geezer – or bruvver more like – I told you about*. Truth is, I also heard about him from Dennie, and what Sabine mentioned with a pinch of salt or a quick smirk, Dennie muttered to the wind in a voice that didn't want to be heard, and if heard forgotten, known *and* denied like every good secret. Like he was scared of him or something: Georgio G, the guy with an office two floors up, the guy who'd be sending Dennie a memo any day. Maybe already had.

There's more drum an' bass pumped in from one of the studios.

—Ain't tha' the Mindbendz? goes someone's girlfriend in a tight blue T-shirt with *Stupid Slut* written on it in silver dust.

—Nah Sonic Lekky and the Poodle Perms innit, goes Sabine.

—You wha'? mumbles Stupid Slut pulling on a tress of poodle perm.

Sabine blanks her.

—So wha' 'bou' *bitches an' whores* G?

Sabine's got her neck jutted out three feet in G's face like one way or another she's gonna get her answer. She's playing her big night out game, playing Alv and G with a whole set of looks, glances and smiles. I'm the back-up, sinking down into depression. For the moment G's more or less disappeared. What's left of him is looking through her. Fact, he's looking through us too, through the people, through the wall, through the world, through everything then beyond, like some prophet about to make sense of smoke. After whatever seconds, with everyone listening out for signs of the holy ghost and a half-word of wisdom, G goes:

—Who?

—Ah man, Alv laughs, you'd remember *who* if there was one

of 'em all kuffed up an' baby oiled in the back of your car innit.

—Make it three of 'em.

—*Three?* Why three?

—One for you, goes G, eyes laughing, the rest of him now aimed at Heaven as he lifts off.

Alv's been got good with that gag and shakes his head. There's applause from Stupid Slut, her permanently grinning boyfriend and galfriend and a round of *wicked*.

—Mista Georgio Non-*sense*, may Jah in's mercy recom-*pense*, goes Alv in full-tilt downtown Kingston JA.

—Ain't no way Jah gonna recompense me. Ah go'a steal it from the cunt y'na mean.

—Innit bruv, some gangster in a Nike hood shouts to wails of laughter.

—So Alv, says G from his personal Planet Rock very very far away, Is you a *Bruvver?* Or a *Geezer?*

—Ain't one or other G, says Alv trying to figure G's next step. I's simple an' righteous. A Christian. The JC of NW10. The—

—Yeah, oh me too me too, goes G turning up the volume. Ah'm so Christian Samaritans come to me for a fistfuck. Ah'm so Christian Christ come to me for healin'. I'm so Christian Sista Wendy's got her gums round ma cock hopin' one day Ah give her lovechild. INNIT.

Everyone's creasing, folding, keeling about, making a big show of knowing the difference between Alvin's *lame duck Christian act* and G's *supercharged crackhead rap*. Everyone except me. Too much like school ten years on. Twenty or so people are stretched out on the floor, squatting on chairs or jack-knifed on tables, breaking off into their own chat, commenting on the action, or saying *wicked* to cover themselves just in case anyone accuses them of missing something smart. Whatever you want to call it.

—Gi's y'pipe Georgio, goes the Hood.

—First you gimme nuvver dose.

This cannot be denied him. Hood places a rock in the bowl

which G burns before passing on the pipe and blowtorch, blowing smoke into the grey air as he reaches full personality output:

—Bitches an' whores is different yeah, he says like he was being interviewed on his equal opps for a teaching job. One way or uvver dey's all *bints*, only *whore* bints give it up easy an' *bitch* bints dey don't. Bruvvers an' Geezers yeah, dey's different. Dey even die different defs. High-speed, low-speed innit. Bruvvers die high speed. Geezers get chibbed. Iss all about who can and who can't innit. Like Bruvvers you *can* burgle wiv. Geezers you go'a watch close like dey was four-eyed cyclists with suits an' crash helmets givin' it noncey hand signals round Hyde Park. Geezers like you Alv.

—Who you callin' a cyclist?

—Noncey wheels just like a Geezer innit. Righ' *malakas*.

—I ain't no geezer.

—More geezer den bruvver.

—Nice little boil-in-the-bag idea G. Must be real pleased with yourself comin' up with goods like tha'.

—Up to a point.

—Only up to a point? goes Alv all sarky and looking round for support.

—Yeah, cos to be hundred per cent pleased Ah'd haveta be God. An' Ah'm short on the basics.

—No. Such as?

—Such as Ah'd haveta be in all places all the time. Ah get around but Ah can still only rob one gaff at a time. Wha' 'bou' you Alv? Show us some hand signals.

—Fuck off Georgio. Ain't listenin' to this . . .

—Come on Alv baby gi's a fuckin' signal, says G sticking his left arm out and shuffling after it, staring Alv in the face the whole time. Come on Alv, come—

—Yo G, easy on the guy you'll get slayed by a pissed thunderbolt, shouts Gaj heavy-breathing his way through all the little people with his fifteen or so stone.

—Ain't pissed, mutters Alv.

With a big bruisy paw round his shoulder and thrusting a saxophone in his face, Gaj leads Georgio a few steps away, sparks up two Bensons and puts one in G's mouth, gibbering under his breath.

Gaj I've seen before, round mine, with Dennie, on the way out of course as I was coming in one evening. Dennie said he was in the Israeli army, a paratrooper who plays a flute. Weird, like there's too much air going on in his life. Plays like G talks, too fast and too many notes. I know because Dennie played me tapes of jams probably recorded right here at Slack, complete with breaks where the guys are discussing the joys of household ammonia and the best way to wash rocks. Gaj – on account of his love for his gadget, his flute – is firing off crap jokes in between trying to sell the saxophone.

—Got stung by a bee last night . . . charged me twenty-five pounds for a pot of honey . . . Laugh sweetheart, goes Gaj brushing his wiry-haired little beard in some girl's face. An' trust me cos this sax is the ultimate sax on the circuit.

—Iss who? Dass the hookiest fuckin' sax off of dat dumb cunt Dennie. Look at dat banged silly piecea brass. Who gonna give dollars for dat?

—You stoopid Cyp you're messin' up my pitch.

—Listen to fluteboy. Dat's wha' happens when you go filchin' up Hampstead. All of dem in Hampstead play summin or uvver innit so you end up wiv loadsa fuckin' violins to shift. An' you, you're sellin' a hooky dented up sax dat you teefed firstplace off of a dumb cunt who teefed it firstplace off—

—Dennie *knows* man. He's a *mensch*. He's a *player*.

—You told me he blew out y'gig.

—Ain't till next week *schlembo*. I'm talkin' about his *goods*. He *knows* his goods. Ask his sister.

—Geezer couldn't sell Travelcards in a rush hour. He work wiv us two time he don't know *nish*. He's a cunt. Ask his sister . . . Who's his sister?

—That's his sister right there you *stoopid* Cyp.

33

Georgio glances back, feigning surprise but really not giving a fuck who or what he's talking at, to or about. Checks me out first like a bint asking him for a wrap of disco powder up the Plastic Coconut in Tottenham. Like *how she gonna sort me? Wha' the bitch got for me?* Then comes a different look, a full-on face-down, like a fifth year without the rules to hold him back, a kind of *you're just food in my pond* look. *Splash too much and you're dinner.* And Dennie's *worked* with him? Wonder if he's ever been round for tea. G's mouth twitches. I want to smack him like he's all the leery creeps I've never laid hands on. Sabine steps in like a referee.

—Georgio Cee.

—Yeah?

—Cee got robbed, goes Sabine out of the blue, like the fact really needed worldwide broadcast.

—Yeah? Well maffact Ah was wiv ma muvver on the night in question watchin' Chuck Norris action video, goes G inspecting a gold-ringed sausage of a finger.

—Yeah an' me I was watchin' *him an' his mother* on the night in question, goes Gaj.

—You was fuckin' where dreamer?

—Me I—

—The night, Sabine interrupts, was tonight . . .

—Yeah? Well Ah got vanloada tutti frutti alibis with chocolate chips. How many was you after?

Sabine's eyebrow wants to carry this thing to its limit for reasons I wouldn't want to guess. All I know is by now I'm totally pissed off with her. Out of the corner of my eye I can see Hoodsy holding out Georgio's pipe. Georgio doesn't notice it with Gaj and Sabine jabbering in his ear. I could reach it easily and as I think of this there's a click in my head, can't explain, a knowledge of the thing I will do. Sabine with a superflirt smile:

—So it wasn't you then G . . . ?

—Dunno, goes G eye to eye with her, cock poking out from crotch-crumpled Armani jeans. Where she live?

G reaches for the pipe.

—Trellick, I go, taking it from practically under his nose.

—Trellick? says G looking at the pipe like I had his dick in my hand, is a fuckin' ruin.

He's wondering what I'm going to do. So am I. So is Sabine. Like: I have the pipe so I could do all the talking. Tell him what I really think and so forth. Only there's another little rock sitting in the small metal bowl, tubed down into water and out again to the mouthpiece. Just the fact of it, the possibility of it, kind of pushes everything else into the background. And I know it's like *fuck it, I will do this*. Why? Because my pen ran out. Why? Because.

Hood's hand comes into view with the blowtorch. I'm aware of a look between him and G. Him and probably everybody. Silence. I just put the pipe to my lips, wait for fire, pull gently when it comes, till the water fills with white smoke. Around me silence. I look into the smoke wondering what's in it, *what the burglar saw*. Then I suck it all out, all the way and hold it in, hold it down, just like that in front of everyone, especially Alv and Sabine who I know are looking at me like I was a crazy bitch they never met before and I don't care because my thoughts are on King of Dipsticks Georgio G and his five-hundred-watt amplified gob. I hold the smoke down and more down till it's good and gone and when this massive heat sweats my head, numbs my cheeks, runs all the way through me and finally lifts me out of my shoes, I go:

—What did you say?

—Babes, goes Sabine, then turning to G, She's upset that's all . . .

That's all? G knows I'm reacting to things that are history, buried with dinosaurs, and just ignores it. What do I mean anyhow? What was I gonna argue about? Dennie?

—Trellick, he goes looking straight at me, is a *fuckin' ruin* like Ah say. *Nobody* rob Trellick less you been fated to live der. An' if you live in it y'gonna *burn* it sooner'n rob it y'na mean. Only people live in dem typea places is muzzies an' pervs. A muzzie prophet once said the Muslim man seek out ruins for illegal drinkin' an' all typsea *activity*. Na mean. Trellick's fulla muzzies. An' whores. An' hooky gear. An' cunts like Dennie. An' if troof be told *blood begets blood*. Which mean if *he* need a slappin' down so's his *poutana* sister. His *crackwhore* sister.

Beautiful. At least you can't kill an evening that's already dead. So *troof be told* there's fuck all to lose.

—Georgio, you ever written bedtime poems for children?

G's about to answer but the sound of the pipe shattering on the floor as I let go of it shuts him right up. G looks at Gaj looks at G looks at the glassy floor looks at Gaj looks at me and so on.

—Fuckin' 'ell, goes G.

—Fuckin' 'ell, goes Gaj.

Fuckin' 'ell, everyone's thinking, as I walk out with Sabine obliged to tow behind and Alv obliged to strut behind like Mr Christian Soldier with turned cheeks and clenched fists. Funny thing, at first we can't find the right staircase and actually have to half walk back past the crowd that has yet to take a lead from Georgio G as to what to do. Or think. Mental mutterings of *bitch this bitch that* no doubt, but so what. Maybe G thinks it's all part of a sexy little game every type of bint plays, has to play, can't resist playing, with the superstar. Before swooning in his arms.

So anyway, we're out. I think Sabine's shocked. Alv drives us back. I think he's shocked. Me I'm in the front this time with the window down, bare arm in the slipstream like a hand signal, feeling fucking great. In a way. The conversation goes something like this:

Great night out. Cee I didn't know it was gonna be like tha'. Him a snake innit, can't tell which way he gonna move, ain't got no respeck dissin my wheels. Wha' d'you smoke that thing for Cee? You telling me you never have? Babes that thing'll make you mad. Babes I don't care. May Jah recompense. Alvin shush, babes you shoulda sweet-talked him. Sweet-talked *who*? Shouldna got wound up you know wha' Dennie's like. Do I? Hon, Georgio can business for you he didn't mean nothin'. *Neeva did I j'na mean.* Babes wha'm I gonna say?

What can she say? Then I'm back home still ranting or is it

blubbing in my head, lights in my eyes, the sour medicine juicing my mouth. I turn both locks first from outside then again from in. New locks for a new life. Wish it was that obvious. But all there is inside is night.

NIGHT

a dark place

Night in Trellick among the stars and gasping wind and freak noise is a scream from a place you could never find, is a smell that settles round a sleeping nostril from where who knows. Night in Trellick is a draught of shadows rippling out of farty arseholes. Night in Trellick is two hundred farts meeting in the stairwell to compare. Night in Trellick is a roach tap-dancing on a pipe behind a wall, on a draining board, then stood vertical still, its feelers feeling the whole of it, the whole motion of night. Night in Trellick is nothing but motion. Like the whole building sways in winter storms and that feeling, the feeling of the building moving, seems to stay long after, well into summer, like a physical feeling of a thing long gone that has moved you. Some people get sick from it. Like being moved inside and out from it. Nights when you hear retching it could be the drink, the drugs the general state of people or some motion sickness that gets to you at night and stays by day. Sometimes I wake up citylight orange and dizzy from clouds. Sometimes from smoke. Sometimes from the general state of things and people. The cracks widen in the heat, running from roof to basement and webbing out all over with only loose-fitted carpets to hold the concrete in and cups of tea on little tables that could go either way. I thank the moving stars *there ain't no lard batty* living on the roof who'd crush me by falling too soon. I mean, if the ceiling goes I go. I mean, if it all turns up in outer space I'd've seen it all already in dreams.

I mean, one night one ordinary moving night when alone and even silent the stairwell will fall away and leave spaceship Trellick to lift off like G, windows aimed at Heaven. And believe me who'd care. I mean, we'd fly over Golborne Road dumping crap furniture and tins of beans that most of the population stockpiles in case of war. We'd shit on Portobello and puke on the Harrow Road. We'd burn Harlesden and drop the lift on Dollis Hill. And at times like that to be a guy like Georgio would *sure be sumfink* cos I'd spunk all down Notting Hill and other bodily fluids could *go to science innit* or be used to fill the cracks. Tonight of all nights just ain't a good night to be hearing personal dramas filtering through and up to the thirtieth. Tonight of all nights is not a good night to be talking in appreciation of my home. Tonight of all nights when robbed and anxious and mad on crack and with myself for being sucked in and suckered by a fuckermother is not a good night, as good deepnights go, to be thinking at all. And I would really let one go from my lungs but the thing that keeps it in is the motion sickness. And the thought that there's already enough of the noise like a drip-feed of pain from out the moving walls.

But I want I need. When sometimes I stand at the window with the window open I feel like being sucked out or sure just jumping. That's when for some reason I think about the guys I have brought here or who have brought me and how all these things ended as they began, with me screaming them out silently because they belong even less here than me. Which is saying something. I mean I could do with *one of them guys* now to stand in the door *like* a door and let me sleep. But the crack and the *sly teefs* and Dennie's mobile which is somewhere as mobis generally are will not say yes to SLUMBER. My head hits the pillow more than once like to say: this is it this time, no sickness no motion no fuck-ups just sleep. Dennie and his mobile, on holiday in two directions. Somewhere, he's sleeping and not giving two !! for sister. I will never tell him how off my tree I get because then I could never tell him not to get off his the way he does.

But anyway when sometimes I've brought guys back here or they me it's like there's never just us but Trellick and its people in there with us coming through the pipes and floors and even out one window in another whether open or not. Just the way air moves round big structures like hot gas round Big Georgio. The pages flutter in the still night like they were chatting back and they are I know because nothing else is. If I could hear what these pages had to say they would sound like Dennie on peak rate. They'd be chirping instructions at light speed. Impossible tasks like the labours of Hercules and *borrow me a ten* thrown in.

A thief. And a *dumb cunt*. He thinks I don't know. And I don't, I know. I don't want to know.

With those guys, the trail of mister rights, who came in and went out and then had to wait for a lift or give up and walk down just to go and keep going, stairs or no stairs, smells or no smells, freak noise or no noise, there were good times. In this place with or without all things there were good times. But in the still at this time whatever time I wonder how I come down off this pillow how I come down off this fucking pillow and how it would all come down.

Perhaps easy as three bored cops in a lift each staring at a patch of floor or wall or ceiling that is the same patch of floor or wall or ceiling night or day or whatever season and you can rely on it. And in the lift with its same patches just being the same patches the G button would glow red like a hope. And life would be just echoes of someone else's. Not mine.

J'na mean. Safe. Bruvvers an' Geezers innit. Bitches an' Whores. Innit. Wicked. Yeah.

Finally, in the dead of it, with G's fingers inside me yeah I know I mean mine, my legs trembling, everything explodes.

41

Anyway. Whatever. A moment of silence. And in the silence I just want more.

You can say one thing for crack. But then you could say another thing. You could say I stepped in a dark place. You could say that.

OOTIE'S LATE NITER

mister double oh zero

Ootie's Late Niter in the early morning is a place that proves the saying *shit happens*. In Ootie's case, it happened only hours before. Wrappers, bottles and beer cans on the floor courtesy of the punters; boozy sleep smell from Ootie's still clothed body emerging from behind the counter bidi already smoking in his mouth; beer or puke or some body thing God knows on the pavement. But hey, it's the corner shop. And Ootie, in ropey jogging pants and flappy sandals, bristling up the black silver outgrowth on his face, is no less than the keeper of my breakfast.

—Now she arrive, he says, full-frontal smile, teeth brown as his pants, brown face of wrinkly milkskin, breath fragranced with Thunderbird or who knows what *Hindi moonshine* or, most likely, Haddows Scottish sherry at two seventy-eight a bottle.

—Alright? I go reaching for a Ribena and a bottle of water from the cooler just to get my head together.

—No, says Ootie, smile disappearing. All my life I work for increment. All I get is excrement.

—Know the feeling, I go having heard this line once or twice from him.

—No Cee, this time . . . I mean. I mean I have to say last night you know . . . your brother—

43

—You saw Dennie?

—How many brothers you have? he goes holding his arms out until I have to manage a smile.

But I'm too blown away by this. *He's supposed to be in Spain.* I repeat ten times. *He is not supposed to be here.* I repeat ten times. He's supposed to be doing the whatever, the *Luton to Alicante* routine. A holiday. On holiday. With some girl. *Nathalie* or something. Hairdresser in some pubic weave emporium round here. Or something. Don't know her and never met her. Supposed to be gone till next week. What did he say? *I'll be duckin' out the UK for a couple of weeks, take care of my bass yeah?* Sure send a postcard and bring some golden sand . . . Ootie's waiting for me to pay attention. Now I'm waiting for the story.

—So he—

—So he come by . . . Pick up your *top selection*, he grins straining at the eyes. I have your top selection ready waiting, you know, usual, one pint semi-skimmed, Kelloggs Crunchy Nut, Müller chocolate dessert, one litre Sunshine guava juice, one Cousin Amil dahl curry, two packets Wrigley Extra and one packet king-size blue Rizla. You know? In the bag? Ready.

—And?

—And he say *oh hi Oots* – you know he say *Oots?* Piss me off. *Oots*, he say it rhyme good with *roots*. So this time he say *hi Oots just picking up Cee's stuff.* Ok, ok so I get the bag, wait for the money. You know? He say you know what he say? He say *put it on her tab* . . . I say Cee don't have tab, don't need tab. He say *well put it on mine.* I say Dennie what tab? I say you can't keep asking for money. Dennie say *who's asking for money?* I say if you didn't ask you wouldn't be Dennie. He say *if you didn't say no you wouldn't be Ootie.* Can't believe . . . I mean bloody unfair after all he owe me . . .

Ootie gives me space to react only to butt in. Have to play the game all the same.

—Listen I—

—No no but then worse. *Lot worse.* Listen this: he see the *till open* and he make *grab*, you know, like *jump-over bandit star* on *Crimewatch* bideo. Sixty pound. Three time twenty pound. *Sixty pound* . . . On *bideo*, says Ootie pointing to the camera high up behind him next to dusty bottles of whiskey.

Fuck. If it wasn't for the slump after the crack I'd have the energy to panic. Maybe crack gives you the energy to panic. I try to think what to say. Put some coins on the counter. Then some woman, face like a baked potato, comes in trailing a cigarette, a kid and a dog, four distinct smells in a line and moving slowly towards the dairy products.

—I'll take care of it. I promise. I'll talk to him . . .

Sound phoney enough? Like a million parents say that to a million teachers about the million genetic fuck-ups they park in classrooms all day, every day. But what can I say? He *is* somewhere. Like back in London. Like back in the area. Blazing a twisted trail. And must have been at mine some time yesterday. Ootie's explaining:

—. . . I say nothing to police, nobody Cee. But what – *Hey no please*, goes Ootie finally noticing the life forms before they've gone too far.

The woman mumbles *sorry*, sends the kid out with dog and cigarette or the other way round no difference they all seem to be smoking. By now Ootie's pretty wound up.

—I mean who I am? Ootie mister double oh zero, smile now pay later? *Thanks Oots* he say *'preciate it big time. Easy man* he say. Easy? Big time? He borrow cash money, live the life. I go Neasden, pray for the afterlife.

Give him my best sympathetic look. Not difficult. I lost a wedge more than sixty. He's waiting for a reaction.

—And you're saying this was yesterday yeah?

—How many yesterdays? goes Ootie shrugging, trying to grin, lighting another bidi from a paper wrap.

I nod, agree, sure, whatever. As long as the *whatever* includes a one-way ticket out of my life with computer, TV, stereo thrown in.

45

Nick Barlay

—Ok, I say like I've been saying to everything. Ok, don't sweat, I'll—
—Inchoo just told us *no smoking*, says the woman all queued up behind me, basket of chunky chunk shite for her animal.
—No *dogging*, goes Ootie. No dogs in. Already enough dogs in ...

SKOOL INNIT

miss looks shit

My head's still all over but that doesn't matter. I feel some sort of bra rash coming on in an unusual place, round the sides not underneath, and keep wanting to pull on the straps. But that doesn't matter either. It never matters how I feel on my way to Skool or how stressed I am or if there's an arrow going from ear to ear. It never matters because the moment I go through the gate, a ten-foot, clunky, concrete-scraping railing, I get hyper aware. A psychic self-preservation thing. Comes from doing too much supply teaching I guess, being like a sheriff riding into a new one-horse town every day. And that feeling, once it gets hold, never leaves.

It's a walk from the gate to the staff room, behind Maths and Science. Check my pigeon-hole. There's a letter and some memo-type things I stuff in my bag. Then on to the classroom used for Drama in Block C, usually smelling of boiled dinner because of the big steamy silver duct sticking out of the dining hall to the left. Makes a lot of people sick that steam, and a lot of sick-notes are dreamed up just walking through it.

But last day nobody needs a note. The last day's loose and baggy as they come, even though it finishes at noon. It's the day when everyone takes risks and the risk-takers risk everything. Which

Nick Barlay

gets many people unnaturally happy. They realise that whatever shit goes down they don't have to face the facts or clean up the mess till the leaves fall. Like everything goes out the window on the last day. Last year it was a third-year called Barrett, hung by his ankles out of History on the second floor.

This year's got a special twist to it: a weapons amnesty. The build-up started two weeks ago after a staff meeting. Well, we met and were informed by Mrs Rhubarb Crumble (nobody queue-jumps to lick her arse) that there'd be this amnesty, like it or lump it, makes no difference, *just sell it to the kids* bullshit. *It's for their own good*. Police officer showed them full-colour pictures of victims. The rest was down to us: *So hands up anyone with lethal weapons* . . . Yeah right.

To front the *scheme* (and she always calls the answers to her menopausal nightmares *schemes*), Rhubarb came up with a few catchy slogans, easy for the kids to remember, you know, to help it all sink in. Guess this one's the version for scouts and guides:

CUT THE BLADE BEFORE IT CUTS YOU

Version for posses and gangs:

IF YOU'RE SHARP YOU DON'T NEED A KNIFE

And the killer:

DAGGERS ARE FOR LAGGERS

These just confirmed what some of us, at least me and anyone under sixteen, have known all along, that Rhubarb's body has been taken over by extra-terrestrials. The proof of this is in the worst move of all: she gets caretaker Stanley, like he's the neutral United Nations' observer, to collect the weapons in a bin outside

48

his office. Soon as the bin goes out with one of the signs, he gets a new name for himself, the all too predictable *Stanley Knife*. Sure, Stanley collects a few knives, and forks, a plastic Uzi and some boiled dinner (which could easily count as lethal).

Then his bin mysteriously explodes. A sugar bomb in an empty tin of baked beans, according to police. *Where do they get this type of knowledge?* the great Roob asked. *Where do they learn?* Good questions. But the people, they ain't saying fuck all.

So the amnesty degenerates fast into a *general* amnesty, you know, *justice for the Kensal four hundred* kind of thing. The professional truants, the real pros who usually turn up to register then walk out around ten, jump back in for afternoon register, then disappear again, don't even bother to turn up. Like full stop. Anyone sees them and asks them – if I see them and do anything as crazy as ask them – they just go:

—*Wha'y'gonna do fishfanny?*

Or:

—*Get wiv it bitch you get stabbed up.*

What am I gonna do, arrest them for ripping off a kebab? For threatening behaviour? For *bad language? J'na mean?* But that doesn't mean I lose it in front of them. There are too many people, so many stories of teachers losing it, like *completely*, shouting, screaming, getting physical, storming out. Somehow, and looking back I don't really know how, I let them know or least they came to know that I wouldn't get mad I'd get even. And word gets round. Like people can get reputations for nothing, just for the *way* they're talked about.

And the clothes. And hair. Did I say about the clothes and hair? A lot of it is about being right for your clothes and having a hairdo that's tough to criticise. Otherwise they'll take you apart. The staff room's full of people who've been taken apart, heads sliced down the middle like laboratory locusts by teams of teenage ninja psychologists.

Geography teacher, Geoff Maynard, in his thirties but stuck in the Seventies with a feather-cut and a show-stopping line in stripey rugby shirts. Leaky Beetle with a sticker: *Humberside says no to nuclear waste.* Nuff respeck Geoff baby, you might as well drink petrol and chain-smoke.

Or Samantha Day, English, scent like tear-gas, make-up like a Hawaiian sunset, short black skirts, black tights, tight tops, Moschino gold-buckle shoes, chandeliers on her ears, a toilet chain round her neck and a ravaged bird's nest on her head. No comment. Or William *call me Bill* Marsh with his DMs like a cop, schplatty walk to match, and a ho-hum *you can trust me* seafaring beard. I mean come on.

Then there's this other woman, friendly enough but keeps herself to herself, black wavy hair pulled back in a safe *don't fuck with me* bun. Black eyes, no make-up on pale brown skin, couple of bracelets, personal trinket sort of thing, nose pierced with a gold stud, white Levis, dark blue silk shirt outside, big collar, plain black loafers. Cool, no curves, I think that's me. Nothing you could put a finger on. Nothing that would make anyone say *oh Cee Harper, the one with a basketball for a head, thighs like a speed-skater, smells like she tried all the free samples in this month's* Cosmo ... Or *Cee Harper the drop-dead gorgeous drama queen, larger than life* ... Or *Cee Harper she should get her hair fixed, get new clothes, get a life the crusty splosher* ... No, nothing anyone could put a finger on. Well, apart from the nickname: *Harpic*, germ-buster.

Here I am like I am in corridors buzzing with shouts, laughs, high-pitched abuse, low-profile exits and entrances, doors slamming, feet scraping, teachers all grinning like the secret of happiness had junk-mailed itself into their morning post. I notice everything and don't notice a fucking thing. Until, that is, I turn in the classroom. By which time it's too late. BANG. Like the *joint's smoking*. Like there's *eighty per cent* attendance? No way. For what? Not only that, dead silence.

Everyone's occupied with some complicated business: Big C sprawled across three spare chairs at the back, tapping on a desktop to whatever's in his earphones; Albigheri lost in the moving squares of his Gameboy; The Ridge nibbling on his nails with love like he was getting them ready for Crufts; Karmesh talking secret business on his mobile; Mintera working on a chin spot; the Anson brothers gambling, Burston trying to disconnect the central heating; Witter doing a bit of what everyone else is doing. The rest, backs of heads, heads down, like it never happened, couldn't have happened. Vague smell of cigarette.

Then I see what this is all about, the only type of thing that makes classroom friends out of sworn enemies. Hanging, drawing-pinned, from the middle of the board, the whiteboard, is a pair of black panties. Mine I just know it. The match to the top half left hanging from the light. So fucking mine in fact they speak my name. Computer, TV, stereo. And underwear. Wave of blinding anger.

The sort of thing I've prepared myself for in a hundred dingy nightmares, body in a white-knuckled cold sweat, legs in some *lethal* position half-remembered from a self-defence course. I'm like: ENTER JUDGE HARPIC. Zero tolerance. Now there's a beautiful insane phrase. *Zero tolerance* is what got Telman beaten to a pulp. This was at another school. Got beaten to a pulp because they or who couldn't, didn't, would not tolerate his what? His grin. They beat him for grinning.

I mean way back ex-boyfriend Nas – great guy in a lot of ways, no really – he grinned all the time. Like a what? Like a gimp. Seriously irritating, having someone grinning when, especially when, you're *life-threatening serious*. Grinned at everything. Grinned himself into being dumped as a grinner. Yeah ok, cruel, it was, maybe. But people on the way in to my life shouldn't grin too much. Too obviously suspicious. But Telman – his first name was what? – Telman was just an average boy with an average grin who, like most of us, even Nas, expected an average return on his grin. Like *no violence*. Like going home with the property he came with. Instead, Telman got beaten to a pulp two feet outside the gate or half a mile what's the difference. Couldn't grin after that. Who could? And now I feel the same as them. I mean the same as the people who beat Telman.

51

—Miss looks shit innit, says Snigger Number One (James Anson) to his brother.

I'm walking towards the board. I'm saying things, usual things, a whole list of usual things.

—Like she been lyin' awake vexed up, says Snigger Number Two (brother Jonathan Anson).

And they crease up. Fold left and right. And I'm at the board. And I'm looking at the board, close enough to write on it, smell of marker solvent from the surface, just me and this blankness, this split second of aloneness that every teacher experiences, back turned to the class, like *suicidally* turned, looking away, with nobody looking at them, nobody looking into their eyes. Almost peaceful. I mean in that moment you can almost forget who's behind you. Only the way I see it, the more of these moments you have the shorter your career.

I pull them down. Definitely the match for a certain bra. And with it comes all the stuff about who did what to whom, about where Burston was on the night of whatever, about what to say or do now. And I'm turning. With this thing, my thing, in my hand, held like, like what? Like a board-wipe. All this is seconds, barely. All this is no time at all. All this time I'm thinking: hold it down, no way you're caving in to this, no way. All this time I'm thinking about Geoff Maynard's dinner-time favourite, his big story, the story of how he walked into this classroom one day – this was at another school, of course – and there was this girl at the front, by the board, on her knees, her mouth round some boy's dick, gobbling it like no tomorrow, the class cheering her on. I mean, you know, what did *he* say, big Geoff? What did *his* face look like? That's the part of the story he never reaches. Still alive, though, sort of, to tell it.

Against my better judgement or any judgement, I glance at Burston. Hand over mouth, plaster on his finger, leaving a trail of clues like a cartoon cat. He's looking straight at me. And you know what I'm like? I'm like: it never happened. I'm like:

—Very funny guys. I guess this is down to the Most Wanted crew . . .

That's what I say. It gets more than a few laughs. The laughs do the rounds and get funnier. Big joke. Being shocked or something is just a matter of decision. Maybe the *outrage* would come easier if I was married with two kids and knew for sure what's what. But I'm not and there's only me. The thing goes under my bag.

Now I'm not exactly a *settle down and turn to page thirty-eight* kind of teacher. But that's exactly what I say next to get their attention. And they're all like *Wha'? Wha' she say? Wha' book miss? Wha' page? She say settle down? Miss wha' we s'posed to be doin'? We ain't workin' today. You said free lesson. It's traditional innit. You said we was gonna* . . .

Once they realise they've been had, they're all pointing, accusing each other of falling for it. Then it's gone, all gone and forgotten in a hail of abuse.

—You should give them panties to Hammond. Goes with his bra.

—Wha' you sayin'?

—I'm sayin' you're distressin' everyone with your chest. Miss, how come he don't wear no bra? He should be made to wear one innit.

—So should you titty bwai.

—Issall them sandwiches you eat wrapped in clingfilm cos the clingfilm's got *female hormones* in it. Was on TV. One sandwich an' he's growin' titties like Rhubarb.

—Yeah man, Rhubarb's go'a wear duffel bags over each one innit. Tellin' you boy, her chest is a *crumple zone*.

—Jus' like Hammond.

—Wha' you sayin'?

And so on, more or less, until I tell them to shut up ten times and for some reason the tenth time works, cuts into a split second of silence. Then the ritual of moving furniture. The tables move like dodgems. The chairs get surfed across the room. Anything that isn't welded to the floor, and let's face it what is, starts to move at speed nowhere in particular, especially other people's bags. This is all part of the lesson plan, oh sure it is. Create a space for the end-of-term *gangsta drama* – the people's choice. Their choice.

We had a vote on whose project was going to get done. And guess what, in the end, after much consideration, like after five seconds, the vote went to Personality of the Year, the one, the only, Stanky B, *El Presidente*. Trouble is B, being B, *ain't got no project*. Why? *Cos I don't do dem fings.* Cool. That's ok. No problem we'll work around it. Like we'll all work *together* on this one.

Result: Stanky B, *righteous gangsta boy* from the wrong side of town, wants to muscle in on the right side. But there's a big slimy cop in the way. Plus all the usual bits of *LAPD corruption telemovie* McPlot thrown in, bit of *Norf Lundn nutter*, bit of *smack my bitch up*, and a bit of their older brothers or cousins who *know people righ'* . . .

Same old this same old that. So I say to B, like why not play someone *other than yourself*, and someone can play you no? Suddenly everyone's going *yeah miss yeah* and volunteering to play B's part. And B's so high on everyone pecking each other to play him, that he gives the Big Nod, goes *safe*. Everyone nods back. *Wicked*, they go. Great. B looks round, *nice an' easy*. After way too much consideration, he chooses. So who's he choose? The chosen one's Hammond, the kid at the real end of the pecking order. Hammond's the one, the only one, the one chosen by B to play B.

Check the bully psychology: B chooses to play the weakest, the fattest, the slimiest. He knows that that will only make the weaker look weaker. And Hammond, being Hammond, could never turn in a convincing B. H would just make the real B look more real, *bigger* real. H is *gonna large up B* just being H. The rest take their cue from B. They're all thinking *yeah laugh at Hammond*, same old laughs but good laughs, easy laughs. Right? Wrong. Wrong because Hammond, ham-face, sweat-pig, pig-face, with his *distressin' chest*, a shirt-splitting lifebelt between tits and balls, Hammond *oh ma God* Hammond just happens to be the closest thing to smart this side of the Chemistry department.

When I say Hammond's smart, it's not a *long-term think of your future* sort of smart. More like *spontaneous survival* smart. I mean Hammond has to play B which is a tall order and he knows it. So he comes up with this: he plays B sitting on the toilet, making crucial gangsta calls on his mobi. First everyone's folding about as Hammond mimes out pulling his trousers then his pants down, then lowering himself on to the toilet. In their minds, they all see Hammond's rolls spilling out of his Y-fronts and spreading through the room like deadly jelly. So they're all pulling disgusted faces, *argh miss you gonna 'low this to continue?*

Then as Hammond starts tapping numbers into the phone and everyone realises he really is the man, they begin to make the subtle mental shift to seeing B, sitting there, daks round his ankles, all of him exposed to the world, and looking tough as baby-boo on his potty. It kills them. Kills me.

I'm saying all this because for a second, inside, I feel like I'm ahead, that I have secret things going for me, that in the end it'll all work out, that it will work out. All I'm saying to myself is situations, they're never clear, never just one thing. Things do turn.

They surely do. Because seconds later (in what is the pretty fucking obvious when you think about it *highlight* to all this) Hammond forgets the plot, the characters, the toilet and the fact that his trousers are supposed to be down, and just lays into B before B can lay into him. It's over before it starts but Hammond's got a nose-bleed by the time I can do anything and is off to the real toilet dripping all over. I get a thump, a definite hit in the back. None of us of course can tell who's done what to whom.

I mean I could write all the stuff that comes out of a teacher's mouth at this point but it makes me cringe just thinking about it. Although most people are just having a great time with their prankster gangster roles. But it's not the point anyway. It's what I catch Ridgecroft saying to Burston that's the point:

—She gonna tuff you down. Jus' like with Davis innit.

—She ain't gonna do nuffink cos she'll get the P innit.

—Yeah too many witnesses. Davis didn't stand no chance. Girls fight more worse than boys. Shoulda got the B for def.

—Nah man, the P. The Push . . .

—Ain't the P or the B. It's the E, goes Witter, the Big E.

—Maybe this time she'll get the P, the B *and* the Big E, goes Ridgecroft.

They've been saving this stuff. Been building up like a fat chin spot waiting to go off. The emergency lesson plan kicks in which always has to be different but not too different in case anyone thinks they've scored a victory by *making* teacher change. Any case, they know nothing about Davis except what Davis has told them. But who needs proof when it comes to a good story? And Davis I bet's been pasting on the brutality. And yes it was at this school. It was here right here. Thing is I did what I did before it became like *policy*. Not *policy* right, but good as. More like *acceptable* when before it had been *wholly unacceptable*, according to the memos steaming out of Rhubarb's rear duct.

Proof or no, and definitely no witnesses, I still got suspended. But they couldn't make it stick because it was Davis's word against mine. And he's the one I slapped. Plus he'd been excluded on a previous occasion for violent behaviour. And then the *policy* thing, well, that helped to iron it all out, sweep it all under and so on. The policy thing came from one of the unions. They came up with this phrase that makes Rhubarb's top selection look biblical by comparison. But it was a phrase she connected with straight off, like *made-to-wear*. This was it:

BASH AND DASH

Meaning: if absolutely necessary it's ok to hit one of them then run like fuck. And not just hit anywhere. They came up with some special targets. Like the elbow, the knee and, get this, the little finger. Unbelievable. Seriously unbelievable. Like do what to their elbows, knees and little fingers? Like how do you trap someone's little finger? And even if you've trapped it, what are you supposed to do to it? Have a chat with its parents I guess.

Anyway, whatever. By then I'd already done it. And it wasn't the knee or the elbow or little finger. It was the mouth. A good slap in the mouth. More than a good slap. I could say that Davis deserved all that and so much more for what he did to me but big deal, he knows that and so's everyone else. The thing is, I didn't report it. My first instinct was to deal with the situation, then look for witnesses. When there weren't any I just carried on and nobody except Davis was any the wiser. And he was a whole lot wiser with his fat lip.

I still got suspended because I didn't say the right things when asked about it though what those things would have been I don't know. She didn't like the way I sat there. She didn't like my attitude. She questioned my clothes. She looked at me trying to pick on something but it was the look itself that seemed to pick on everything, detail by detail. Still suspended me the bitch, *pending her own investigations.*

The way it works is like bookings in football, as Geoff Maynard explained one coffee break around that time. *In other words, two and you're off.* I only got one, I said, and I'm off straight away. *Very dodgy refereeing decision,* said Geoff. *Just have to run with it. That's football.* Yeah right. A game about a lot of people all together with no fan segregation or crowd control and not much change in their behaviour from event to event. *That's skool innit.* Oi ref ya fuckin' cunt.

If it wasn't for the last day, knowing it's over, I'd be happy to fall apart. I don't know any more. I really don't. Anyway, whatever. Reality is, Hammond's nose has bled before on a regular basis for no apparent reason, over his books, on the playground, over someone else's books. And so on. So that's easy to pass off. Thump in the back? Sore but no damage. Not like Davis *grabbin' me up*, as they say. More like a thump you can ignore without looking like you're asking for more.

And with the class, well, you know, sure there are the nice ones, the polite ones, the caring and cheerful ones, the ones who hand in their homework and ask you how you are and what you're going to do in the holidays and like listening to your stuff. I could talk about them, how uplifting it truly is and all that. How I get that Jean Brodie feeling every morning. That mission feeling, that *crème de la crème* vibe. No, truth be told, more like that *Richard Dadier* feeling, the one where he's just fine as long as he's saving just one kid. Like as long as *just* one *just* makes it out of the Blackboard Jungle, boxes clever out of the ghetto, springs up and out into the bright new day, well Good Ole Rick, why, *he's just fine*. Sometimes I do wonder about crowd control. But in the end, fuck knows, I'm happy to let them, all of them, anticipate the bell by ten minutes. Which I know is *wholly unacceptable* and easily long enough for the apocalypse. But I mean, it's better than falling apart.

HOME TIME

we's all bunnin' round my cousin's

Home time comes just after final assembly. First time I notice the sun. It comes through into the hall in long shafts, all this dust spiralling in it. Most people're fidgeting like mad, shirt sleeves rolled up, sweating and scratching. All this dust is bits of people, flakes of people, all jumbled and spiralling together. The biggest flake, Rhubarb, makes her speech. It's about League Tables and building on reputations. Only the sound of a distant snore interrupts her but that's dealt with by Rog Poole, physical fitness instructor and part-time Gestapo enthusiast. Then some prize-giving, applause, more prize-giving, more applause, and back to the staff room for a bottle of wine, expressions of relief, heart-rending goodbyes.

I'm more or less out when I'm cornered by Samantha Day's hairdo. She says I'm lucky not to have to do parents' evening and destroy my popularity in an hour, not to mention answering the same stupid question from stupid mums and stupid dads for three hours. Question: *Does Jimmy do his homework?* Answer: *How should I know what he does at home?*

I tell her she'll be in my thoughts always. She laughs and I tell her to have a good summer. She laughs again and says:

—I'll certainly do my utmost.

I hate that word *utmost*. Hundred per cent fake. In any case,

nobody ever really does their utmost. They just do their utmost
to make it look that way. Then she goes:

—Well I'll see you at Geoff's no doubt . . .

Oh, right. Turns out Geoff's having a do for his thirty-three-
and-a-third. I must have just stuffed the invite in my bag.

—Yes, I say, should be a laugh . . .

So I'm doing my utmost to avoid Geoff on the way out in
case I have to promise anything. Take the long way round to
the gate through Geography, knowing he won't be there by now.
Trouble is, Geoff's already at the gate, chirping to Stan. I have to
admit I'm actually *sneaking* past through a crowd of kids who're
giving someone or other a light stoning. The Ridge is shouting
from behind:

—We's all bunnin' round my cousin's.

Geoff turns, sees me, we grin. Funny thing right, the moment I
see him I want to tell him everything. Obviously for the sympathy,
I know. Run to daddy. Have a good cry. Feel sick. I can't say
anything. Say what anyway? I was burgled, Burston's got a big
mouth and someone pinned my knickers to the board and I think
it was Burston because he seems to know something about me
getting burgled and and and and and.

Then what if he asks some dumb question, some question like:
You're sure they were your, er, knickers? Oh fuck off. Or he might say:
Burston? Well Burston's been on report for more or less everything else.
Then he'd give me the list: arguing; swearing; aggressive behaviour;
being late; destroying two books . . . And all together now we'd do
the Big *that's life* Shrug. Whatever. Geoff's going:

—*Bunning*, Ridgecroft? That's a new one on me . . .

—Gonna cane some skunk sir. To celebrate, y'na mean. Stretch
myself by the canal an' *chill*.

—Y'ain't s'posed to say dem fings, goes Witter.

When sir grins, it inspires someone else to go:

—Ridge's cousin's a drug baron.

—Well at least he'll get one honest reference then, goes Geoff,
which is pretty funny really.

—Just like Miss Harper's bruvver innit, goes Burston, which is less funny.

—That's enough, goes Geoff grinning even more then turning to me. They'll say anything to wind you up. Brothers, cousins, *mothers* . . . Thank God they can go missing legitimately for the next three months . . .

True enough. I look at him and by the time I've nodded, grinned back and moved close enough to respond in like *a positive way* to his nasal hair, I've made a decision: I'm saying nothing. Double oh zero nothing. I mean he'll say what in the end? He'll give me some cheery old bumble on load of thirty-three-and-a-third bollocks about how life is. Besides, the opportunity's gone. He's already selling me his party.

—Got the old Labour and Social Club in Acton. Food, disco, bit of a boogie . . .

He paddles his hands in front of him like he was searching for a teaspoon in some grim bowl of washing up.

—Might even do a few of my own songs . . .

He leaves a big pregnant space – I hate it when people leave big pregnant spaces – so I sort of have to say:

—Oh, I didn't know you wrote songs . . .

And he goes:

—I've got a few concept albums in me ha ha. But I might just do covers on the night. See you there? *Eight till late* . . . It'll be a friendly crowd. Bit mad. And the first drink's free . . .

How could I refuse? I reply. *You couldn't*, he says. I promise him I'll be there, I really will. And I'm out into the street that's crowded with heated holiday-makers all keen to play the last gag, just one more wind-up, one more laugh before they make off in groups, gangs, posses, on their own or in parental cars like mobile caves into which tiny people disappear, lost for months. Some of them anyway. Burston, leaning at forty-five degrees against a lamp-post, squinting, sun on his puffy smooth dark face, shirt unbuttoned to the navel but still wearing his tie, shouts the last words:

—Nice one miss. It's been real.

Nick Barlay

Mighty real. I smile and wave, say nothing. Walk off with the shambling crowd until I'm alone, back on my route. *Which reminds me,* she said casually to herself . . . My knickers go into a bin down the street or up some other street. What I mean is, I can't take them home. Don't think anyone would. I mean who would take them home? Even Sharon Stone would dump them. She'd dump them for sure. And it would look like an empowerment thing. She'd make it look that way. That's the way she'd play it. Can you imagine her playing it any other way? So I'm walking and I'm like *yeah right, really, an empowerment thing* . . . Call me Sharon.

COFFEE-COLOURED KID

he don't know how much milk he's got

Meet Sabine in a café down Golborne where the white metal tables are too hot to touch. She's in a micro mini at two three in the pm, lips, wraps, rings like a movie star. Miles is under control and gorgeous like a designer *bébé*, sweet-dreaming in his pushchair. She's sharing a table with a couple of Portobello music-biz types, peroxide spikes, combat trousers, trainers like rubber dinghies and more logo than a racing car. Between oh so funked-out yawns the bigger of them's saying:

—Nice name *Miles*. Is that cos you're into Miles Davis?

—No, goes Sabine, it's to remind me of his dad.

—Wha' like *Miles Senior an' Junior* typea thing?

—No, it's cos his dad's *miles away*. Just where I want him.

Once they get the punch line they repeat it a couple of times to let Sabine know how much they like her humour. Then the conversation's on to *you live round here?* I get an orange juice and a pastry and another Coke for Sabine which she tops up with her own supply. After introductions Sabine soon gets them talking about, guess what, some record they're producing, some track, some deal, some white label etc etc.

Reaching in my bag for my cigarettes I come out with unread memos, Geoff's *party till you drop* invite and, with a sudden kind

63

Nick Barlay

of doom-laden suddenness, the letter that was with them. It's unstamped, unaddressed, just my initials on it in capitals. Not school post for sure. A different piece of post altogether. So I know it's to do with Dennie even before I open it. He must have delivered it by hand today, this morning, earlier than anyone. Except Stan. It's not only to do with, as it turns out, but from.

I reach in a second time and get a cigarette. Little Biz lights it with a fake Zippo that he snaps open and alight like that Japanese Elvis fan in *Mystery Train. Whoa baby.* Manage a wince. He flips the lighter shut and holsters it. Big Biz has got a flyer on the table and is inviting Sabine to some DJ club-night thing. Sabine's nodding, and I'm nodding too but opening the envelope, unfolding the badly folded paper and straight away recognising the writing. The same glance is enough to tell me this ain't exactly open-heart long-distance pen-pal stuff to be read slowly in a warm bath all aglow in spiritual candlelight. I mean here's what Dennie's pulled together in writing like weird Aztec hieroglyphics:

Dear big sis, I'll be dropping out of site for a bit. Dont worry. Its complicated. Be in touch. Love D.

First thing I'm doing is mentally correcting the spelling. Then I read it a load more times to see if there's anything between the lines. But it's typical D. Typical, that is, of the sort of thing he'd *say*. Dennie's never written any kind of letter in his life, far as I know. Certainly never to me, even if this qualifies as a letter and merits a sealed envelope which, let's face the harsh facts honeybunch, it doesn't.

Big Biz and Little Biz are stubbing out, standing up, yawning, stretching. One of them leaves a business card (with a big logo) on the table, nearer Sabine than me but he casts an eye in my direction, like to say *this is for you too*. Sabine gives them full beam.

—It'll be a slammin' nigh', guaranteed, says Big Biz with Little Biz going *yeah yeah righ' slammin'* just behind him.

64

Then they're sloping off down Golborne, loose and baggy as a whole summer. Sabine's got her cheeks sucked in.

—Don't understand you babes. Why you cold-shoulderin' everyone?

Which is a nice way of saying I'm an uptight bitch, which is how she'd say it about some uptight bitch who wasn't really a friend. Great. So I'm an uptight bitch. I'll get Geoff to compose a song. Maybe that is how I am. Maybe it is. How I am right now anyway, so I tell myself.

I get all defensive and tell Sabine what happened at school, the whole morning, complete with knickers. Or without. It doesn't sound right though. It all comes out less emotional than it should. I think it's because I'm too depressed to get emotional. Although Sabine'd say she was never too depressed to get emotional. But when you get depressed the first thing you feel shit about is all the positive stuff. I mean everything good becomes shit. Then you get more depressed, so depressed you really think you couldn't get more depressed, and that, that is when all the really shit things seem to get, incredibly, *less* shitty. I mean you realise you're so far down that even your shit isn't good enough to be the *worst* shit. It's just average shit. At least if you had the best shit you'd have good reason to get depressed. But with average shit you don't. And that, that's really depressing.

Sabine listens – not to this shit but the school shit – and puts on some really genuine sympathy but I'm too depressed to believe it. After some *oh babes*, she goes:

—Well, at least no knickers is good for thrush.

And I go:

—What, so I have to get thrush to make it all worth while?

—Yeah, she goes, I'll get those two spikey bods back. Give you a dose.

Yeah right there is a funny side to depression even if it is thrush. And I do laugh which is a big relief. Only then she goes:

—But seriously hon, you know, you shouldn't be so *anal* ... Y'na mean.

Anal. Now there's a word. Like straight out of a magazine thing on analysing your best friends. Is she a) shaped like a bottom; b) smelly like a bottom or c) generally anal? But she could be right about that too. I'm an uptight anal bitch. Hate that word. *Anal*, I mean. *Uptight* and *bitch* I can live with. No really. Words like that come armour-plated and I can live with being. For the meantime anyway.

—Sabine, I'm going through a shitload right now, I say which is more or less totally feeble.

—Oh please babes come on, goes Sabine, eyebrow practically arrowed at the blue above. It goes back more further innit. I mean come on hon . . .

—I'm worried about Dennie now, I go which is even more than totally feeble, pathetic, and Sabine knows it straight off and actually *snaps* back:

—He'll show up at the gig.

—I'm not sure he will, not from this, I go showing her the letter like it really was proof of something.

Sabine takes it and squints over it which is the only time she looks less than beautiful.

—When did you get this?

—When? Like today, this morning. At school.

It's the way she asks, like it doesn't quite square with something she knows.

—Sabine. Have you talked to Dennie?

Pregnant pause of a very unnatural kind between friends.

—Have you?

Sabine says no but she's not telling the truth. One hand's turning rings on the other's fingers. Round and round. I put my hand on hers but she pulls it away.

—He'll be at the gig . . . Stop worryin' 'bou' everythin'. Just chill babes.

—Did he go to Spain?

After another second or so of saying nothing, Sabine takes off her sunglasses with a sigh like she was auditioning for a new series of *Dallas*. Usually this would just crack me up.

—All he said was – an' this was at least a week ago – just tha' he – I mean *they* – him an' Nathalie – were gonna go then they weren't gonna go.
—So they didn't go right?
—S'pose not.
—Which is a *no* yeah?
—Yeah.
—Well how come . . . Why didn't you just say so?

After another second and another question it all, well, some more of it, comes out. Sabine tells me that *no they didn't go*, that Dennie joked about going round the M25 instead. *Carshalton's beautiful this time of year.* But he said *to keep it quiet for a little while* for reasons she doesn't know. Then Sabine says that some time later Nathalie calls her because she'd seen the number in Dennie's address book and knew the name, knew they'd gone out together. And Nathalie's *distraught*. That's the word Sabine uses. *She was distraught abou' i' y'na mean babes.* I tell her I haven't got a clue what she means. So then she tells me Nathalie said Dennie was in some kind of trouble and that she, Nathalie, didn't know what to do and that she, Nathalie, wanted to call *me* but couldn't cos she didn't know what she, Nathalie, *should* do. So I ask Sabine what she, Nathalie, *should* have done about what? First Sabine says she doesn't know. Then, when I ask what *kind* of trouble this has to do with, she bites my head off.

—Babes you think I know tha'? I don't know an' I don't wanna know. Dennie's got a *loada* problems. Wake up hon.
—Like? I ask, wanting just to hear one real, specific thing out of this *loada problems*.
—Like for instance, she goes, he's got an *identity crisis*.

Oh girl does my heart sink hearing that phrase.
—Haven't we all.
—No, actually. I don't.

Oh girl oh boy. After another second I ask her what she means about D having an *identity crisis*, swallowing hard to get the words out. And eventually she gives this whole big thing about Dennie, so big it seems to add another ten floors to a skyscraper of crap. What she says is this. She says: *Dennie's got this coffee-coloured kid thing goin' on and wants to be more blacker than he actually is.* She says being mixed race she can feel this. I could tell her mum and dad are Moroccan Jews. *Sephardi*, like a bit dark, *caffe latte if you will.* Well dad *was*, he's dead, and I only ever saw him in photos anyway. But, I mean, it's the same thing. And that, that's the whole *coffee-coloured thing.*

Like I could tell her all this but Sabine knows it since time anyway. She kind of reads my thoughts and says *Jews and Black people is all One Race whichever way you look at it and in any case that's not the point.* Well what is, I go. The point is, she says, *Dennie's tryin' to be someone he ain't.* Which is to say like some *super-smoov LA homeboy* or *gangsta rappa* or like some homegrown *roughneck soldier* straight off the Grove front line. She says *Dennie don't know how much milk he's got* and that it's *gonna get him in serious trouble.* If it hasn't already.

Don't I know this? Maybe not in these words. I do know Sabine could tell me something more, a lot more, like one of the million missing links, but that's when Miles wakes up and goes right into a major holler. Sabine stuffs his bottle in his mouth, ok not *stuffs* but a little too hard anyway, which makes him holler worse. Then she realises the stuffing was really meant for me and starts to feel guilty.

So she gives in, hugs him, hugs me, tells me she loves me. She says she's sorry about keeping stupid secrets. And didn't mean what she said about me being anal. And she's sorry she didn't get Nathalie's number but Dennie'll show up at the gig and I can give him an earful then. And will I come over later for a bite cos Alvin and a friend are swinging by? So I say I love her too and what's a word like *anal* between friends? And sure I'll come. And we smoke a little spliff which Sabine has as we walk down Golborne. Two gals and two tokes of skunk in the bright sun and we're all over the place giggling, especially at this red-faced fat boy, corner of Southam, who's breathing heavily while balanced on one foot and trying to pull gum off the opposite sole, then he's *distraught* as the gum sticks, strings and loops all over his shoe. Sabine's laughing as she turns off to hers.

—La'er babes.

Wave back and walk towards Trellick with all these things milling around like Dennie's homeboy act which is so true and Burston, whose act is pretty good, and Giant Georgio Georgianou who doesn't really act at all because he's a natural bastard that even Richard *I'm going to save one of them if it's the last thing I do* Dadier would give up on. Everything seems to spread itself loose and baggy in my mind and the sun keeps shining and there's nothing I can do except mumble more to myself than Sabine:

—La'er sweetheart.

GEORGIO GEORGIANOU

you think I'm funny?

I get back late from Sabine's, maybe around one, pretty cabbaged, drunk enough for Alv to drive me back the ten-minute walk with his *number one*, the super-silent Ray, in tow. The lift takes an hour to make it down from the upper twenties by which time my head's spinning.

—Easy Cee, once you're in the lift your life's your own y'na mean, goes Alv holding up his hands.

Manage a *thanks Alv* as the doors close. I've barely finished fucking around with my new keys, dropping them twice, missing the holes three times and so on, then hearing signs of life from Smelly Dave's flat, getting in, swinging the door shut, too loud, I've barely got in when lo and behold a knock. Figuring it's Silent Ray who's had a late rush of wind or Alv remembering he'd forgotten to tell me how much he wishes he had a teacher like me, I open up. But it's neither of them. It's Grinning Georgio Georgianou, scrubbed and slicked ugly, holding a massive TV in his pumped arms like a whole dead lion he's just dragged in from the jungle. Like *hi honey I'm ho-ome*.

—Where shall I stick it? he booms. Don't answer, I'll find a place.

—Hey . . . Hey, I say like an over-Martinied Sixties' crooner as he takes a mighty step forward.

There's a warning scrape from behind Smelly's door that I hardly hear what with the reverberations of Georgio G's voice.

—Come on issa present innit. Ah was on one the uvver nigh'. Mattafack so's you . . . Come on ain't standin' here wiv a hooky zom box all nigh' . . .

An act of will straightens me out.

—Look there's no way you're coming in with that.

—Ain't tha' hooky . . .

—I don't care—

Smelly's door opens, is more like wrenched open, door-chain swinging, knocking.

—Oi. Know what time it is?

—Way past yours grandpa, goes G taking another step.

Me and Smelly exchange a long look, long enough for both of us to know we could really hate each other if we knew each other better. Anyway, if this isn't a cue for an entrance I don't know what is so I step back and he steps in eyeballing Smelly the whole way. For a moment I wonder if Smelly Dave saw anything, told the police anything. Probably did see; probably didn't tell. Our doors almost shut at the same time but I stop, leaving mine open. Alv's words – *him a snake* – ring in my head. By the end of the evening, you never know, Smelly Dave could be a real friend. Looking at Gargoylianou I'm nauseous enough without remembering some second-long fantasy. How he even made it that far I don't know. Some people shouldn't even be allowed near fantasyland. Let alone allowed in.

—So you hangin' wiv d'geezer wha' died for us all? he goes, searching for a place to set down the TV.

—Who?

—Alv. JC of NW hundred an' nine.

—Alv? What's it to you? How d'you know where I live anyway?

—Was written in shit on a dead whore's arse . . . Jus' kiddin'. She wasn't really a whore.

—Very funny.

—You fink Ah'm funny? *Hey: you think I'm funny?* Who d'you—

—Yeah Georgio that's really terrific. Whassisface from—

—*Goodfellas.* Joe—

—Joe Pesci. Right . . . So what's he, your role model?

—Mattafack yeah. He kills me.

—Kills most people doesn't he. Rest he just damages with car doors.

—Very funny. Now where d'you wan' i'?

Bottom-draw innuendo aside, answering a question like this is the same as saying yes to the TV. Expensive-looking item with speakers either side of the screen, built-in video and a remote thing taped on top. What to do? There's no way I can keep the thing or even leave it here too long. Like *he'll have something on me*, isn't that the line. And in return I do what?

—I told you. I don't want it.

He puts it down on the floor anyway, right there, not in a corner where you could forget about it but in the way where I won't be able to ignore it, and will at some point have to move it, *handle stolen property*. I can hear Sabine saying *just chill out babes, it's only a TV.* He looks all round the place, more like searches it, before looking at me.

—So, he goes.

—So, I go.

—Ah don't expect a blow.

—Glad to hear it darling.

—Darlin'? he laughs, Dass a seriously horny word . . .

I don't say anything, wishing I had Sabine's eyebrow control.

—Uvverand . . . could murder a brew.

—Murder who?

—Come on, lovely cup tea.

—Tea? You wouldn't look right sipping tea.

—Be surprised.

I just want to flop by now but yeah right that could be giving out the wrong kind of signal. So I'm shifting from one leg to the other and back, waiting by the door. Meantime, he's wandered over to the windows in short fat steps. He says something, like everyone says something, about the view, about the way the town looks so small and you feel so high, almost like you own the place, almost like it's your town. Really. Then he says something about the heat, fans his shirt, loose white shirt with ironed creases sharp along the sleeves, then looks at the window frames, runs a finger down one, then stands there kind of smirking, waiting. I know he's trying to intimidate, to scare, to show he's the one who could do anything, if he wanted.

—You wanna stand round all night looking at the decor. What's this about? Why d'you come here? Really.

—Wha' like *really* really?

I shift again. He shrugs.

—Just checkin'.

—*Checkin'*? What like just *generally* sort of checking? Or more like fittings and fixtures, gas appliances—

—See if some nonce'd been up here workin'.

—*Some nonce?* What're you talking about? Doing what? How come you're so interested anyway? Your *manor* is it or something?

—Or summin. Get the tea on an' Ah'll tell ya.

—I don't fuckin' wanna know tell you the truth *Georgio*.

—Yeah you do. You could do wiv a bi' of a buzz.

—Oh yeah? Well I'm alrigh' now for excitement. *I've got me tele.* So if it's ok with you . . .

—Supposin' i' ain't . . .

—Wha' you gonna do? *Slap me up?*

—Nah . . . Only really slap people up—

—When you need to?

—Nah, when Ah'm drinkin'. Rocks is different.

—Right right sure . . . Well, Georgio, since you *ain't gonna slap me up*, it's been nice. Tea an' biccies another time . . .

He stands there, looking round, finally at me again, low forehead creased like a crap T-shirt, sniffs once, teeth grinding a bit, maybe crack, maybe amphetamine stress, maybe he's a bit of a drama queen himself, kind of big on self-importance, ugly big, gangster big, *you ain't gonna do nuffink* big. Feel all this steam rising in me then he mumbles:

—No way you's burgled . . .

I stand there taking this in, saying nothing, too drunk for my face to change much or betray anything anyway. He looks at the damage to the door.

—No way you's—

—So you said Guv. Or is it more like a *takes one to know one* sort of thing?

—Helps na mean.

—Whatever you're gonna say, say it.

—Calm down . . . Don' wanna disturb Bedtime Billy next door innit.

He wanders a few steps looking around and stroking the bristle on the back of his neck, then talking more to himself than me.

—Even if dey's finkin' she's doin' insurance scam dey ain't gonna be interested. Y'na mean. Wiv a straigh' pull dey ain't even gonna press on a ballpoint. Innit. Tellin' ya righ', your gear, it never went down no firty floor an' out. *Nobody* rob Trellick 'less dey live in it. An' if dey's serious deyda come in froo dem windows wiv a rope from up d'roof innit. Ah worked like da' *hundred* time. Bu' troof be tol' iss too noncey. You don't get A Cats dressed like the Milk Tray man an' Ah should know. See dese marks? Here inside the door yeah? Was dey—

—No. After.

—See'm sayin? An' PC Mugsy musta seen it. An' the only reason dey ain't askin' is cos iss just forms innit. An' legwork.

—You still haven't told me what—

—You know uvver people live in Trellick? Din the pigs say nuffink 'bou' witnesses?

I look at him a couple of seconds, then go:

—What's it to you? What's your big story?

—Ma big story? Ah could talk all night an' maybe someday Ah will . . . Bu' it ain't abou' me. Iss y'bruvver iss abou'. Innit. See he's

75

been a bit silly. He's go'a come froo wiv some serious shells. Like by last week y'na mean. Only nobody seen the stoopid *malakas* . . .

Fold my arms. Glance at the still open door. What do I say now? Just stand there. Shrug.

—If you think you're gonna get a handout—

—Wha'm finkin' yeah, is his sister's a well dodgy bitch who's coverin' up for him.

—Really?

—Really. An' she won't even put the kettle on.

—Covering what up?

—Slippy bruvver of yours has already done six months Scrubs innit. Now here's his skinny sister, his—

—Save it for your girlfriend . . . What're you saying he's supposed to owe?

He shrugs with his eyebrows.

—Bou' twenny-five . . .

—What're you talking about? You're saying twenty-five—

—Grand, yeah, he goes, then in Joe Pesci style, *Like twenny-five large* . . .

—Bullshit.

—Well Ah don't break legs for twenny-five squids.

—So he owes *you* then?

—Someone . . .

—You're sure it's not you, *tough guy*?

—Ah'm the nice one y'na mean. Ah sip tea.

Touché, I'm thinking, stepping back to the door and opening it fully. Time for goodnight. He knows it too and comes to the door. *Nice one* that he is, he writes his mobile number on the wall by the door, and leaves with the really over-the-top *someone's gonna want sortin'*. Maybe it's the drink but I don't feel scared or anything. After one shock, the next has to be easier. But the numbers I cannot believe. Like I can't believe Dennie's run up anything like that. Maybe he does owe here and there. Ootie a few quid. Call it a hundred. Whatever. Call it whatever. But twenty-five grand has just never passed in or out or sideways through Dennie's life. It just never has.

After he's gone I smoke half a spliff, can't help dialling Dennie's mobile number. The Orange network is still as welcoming as ever. Then I stare out across the spatter of night lights in the black orange city wondering if each light is an unpaid debt and each dark a debt collected. Which is seriously cringey as images go. But the big bad wolf's been at the door, inside the door, right here inside. I mean I've seen the movies, listened to schoolfuls of excited cops and robbers and I could say I've heard it all. Just like most people, like most of us, I've heard it, pretty much, all. But that says nothing about what I'm going to do.

It's too hot to sleep on or in bed so with the windows wide I don't move from the sofa. Just stare out at the black orange city, glassy lights rolling, flickering, and I wait for the dawn to come up, little by little, like a certainty, like a known thing, like the dawning of the fact that Dennie's lost his fucking marbles, has gone beyond himself, in some way, some way I don't even really know. And that scares me, turns me cold. I fear for him.

DENNIE AND ME

same bone structure, they said

Nas, my ex, he used to go to the Lisboa and get croissants for breakfast. He had this like *French thing*. I mean he worked over there for some company, *France Télétronique* or something. Anyway, it led to a French breakfast experience which he couldn't get out of his system. Also French lunch, dinner, sex, cigarettes, culture and so on as it goes. The other stuff I don't get sentimental about but his croissant delivery, that was good. Probably the best. And I miss it. That's the first thing that occurred to me when I woke up sweaty and stiff on the very un-orthopaedic sofa, squinting at the bright blue-yellow day.

In fact I only thought of Nas first thing because I had this dream about hairdressers. Nas used to spend more time doing his hair than is healthy for a human. So did Dennie. They did have nice hair, thick and black, but they used to have more lotions, oils, creams and conditioners for it than Sabine. And, like Sabine, they managed one way or another to make use of them all. Anyway, in this dream I'm at the hairdresser having my hair fixed to look like Samantha Day. Right, more nightmare than dream. Nas, he's there too, standing behind me going: *trust me it'll make you look more French, like really really sexy*. Gee thanks. So I'm glancing at the girl fixing my hair. And the girl is Nathalie. I mean I don't know it's her, don't even know what she looks like, but it's just the feeling in the dream, that it's her. But the bit that woke me up is when I'm looking in the mirror and seeing not my face but Dennie's. Like Dennie's face instead of mine. I mean people often said we looked alike. *Same bone structure*, they said. Same black eyes, same strong straight nose and wide lips. But Dennie had something extra. Everything was a shade darker, richer, and with him all the bits we had in common seemed to go better with all the bits we didn't. He was beautiful.

We used to get the coach down from Manchester. Mum used to take me and Dennie down to the West End, me and mum for clothes and stuff. Dennie would go round music shops. Later, by the time we left Mank, we were both decided: I wanted to be an actress; he wanted to be a musician. I ended up doing *community theatre*; he ended up doing scabby weddings in Stanmore and Kenton and places. Well not so scabby since he sometimes skanked enough smoked salmon and cake to last a month. I went an even longer way round and got into teaching drama, was a star two, three, four days a week. Dennie went from one band to the next, getting better all the time, doing sessions, being a star too. He could play, people said so, and he was in demand. He looked the part, stopped combing his hair, got into funky twists. We looked out for each other. I was the older one, with a responsible job, whatever. He could be the artist, go on benders, look total shit and still look good, play the muso, hang out with some crew or other. Drugs, sure. Dodgy people, sure. You knew, I mean I knew, I did know that he was doing his *certain different runnings*, as he'd say. Leaving stuff round mine in bags to pick up *in a few days*. Moving in, moving out, turning up late and crashing out. Hanging out with guys like Gaj. *He's solid, he's my spar*. Dennie you knew, I knew, took risks. *Fun-loving criminal*. That's how it started. That's how it starts. Teenage game. Because looking back, *fuck* looking back. I could have given a speech but by then I was sliding myself. I was the one who needed speeches. As Dennie's women got dumber and dirtier, my boyfriends got straighter and sillier. In fact Dennie started hating my boyfriends about the same time I did.

Then Sabine. I mean from the beginning Sabine had an endless supply of brothers and sisters and cousins for both of us. *Endless supply* well ok more like a wide choice of the equally fucking bad. And then sure, they went out, her and Dennie. Stormy, very stormy. But I didn't mind. Truth is, I liked it. I was single then too and it wasn't like I lost a brother or a best friend. I didn't. I actually kind of gained two totally unreliable parents. Didn't last long that feeling. Or their relationship. Made me feel like going back to Mank, spending time with Mum. But she'd been busy too and had met this guy, tall, late fifties, Jamaican but white, white but Jamaican, like his *accent*, that was the thing that blew everyone away. You'd look at him three times, check his mouth long and hard but his stuff still didn't sound right. I mean he'd lean back, look at the ceiling, and say stuff like: *Few prospect fe dem modern yoot.* And: *Blod ticker den water.* And his favourite line: *Me cyaan believe it.* Dennie went up for a weekend with Sabine round the same time and they came back all slack-jawed. Back here we took the piss bad, even though the guy was totally on the level, natural, nice and everything. Like there's kids, especially at school, white kids, who have I guess what Sabine would call an *identity crisis*, like Burston once told Ridgecroft: *You been wigger-fied innit.*

Anyway, whatever. Dennie and Sabine split. Or more like stopped having sex. *We're still amicable*, they both said like they were starring in a crap sequel to Punch and Judy. But they were. We had a crowd of people round us. Sabine's phone directory of brothers, sisters, cousins; Dennie's fun-loving criminals; my actor-waiter-twilight-supply-teacher types. That was when things were good and I didn't think too much about how I was sliding into shit one way and Dennie another. Like he was out there somewhere, operating. *Guy's largin' i'*, Gaj had said. *Whass wrong wi' tha'?* Nothing. Until, that is, Dennie's three, not six, months in Scrubs. AV 6204. They transferred him, just before his release was due and for no apparent reason, to the floating poodle parlour in Portland harbour. Me Sabine and Nas went down to pick him up in Nas's car, made a day of it. Freedom-on-Sea. Photo of me and Dennie and Dennie's washbag. But somehow the fun had gone. Maybe I should've made my speeches then.

Bit by bit, more lately really, we'd seen less of each other. Not like before. I think we were kind of finding each other depressing. Or maybe Dennie found me that way. Or maybe he had more to keep quiet about than talk about. And it occurs to me first thing, after the croissants, the hairdresser, the dream, the looking back, that I've been thinking about Dennie in the past tense. I mean the gig is what, five days away. I can't wait that long. I can't wait five days to see him, to do something, though what I'd do I don't know. But I can't and that's what starts me thinking about Nathalie, about finding her which is the obvious thing. She's a hairdresser, so I remember Dennie saying, and she works round here. But what does that mean? The *Yellow Pages* have got stacks listed. When I start thinking about the possibilities, the ifs and buts and bullshit, I start to get mega depressed.

I mean there was some story on the news just a while back about a student, a backpacker, who went off to the Himalayas to find himself or whatever. Went off walking. And lost himself. I mean disappeared like *completely*. No call, no sign, no battered postcard, nothing. So then his father, after doing what he could from here, making calls to Kathmandu or wherever, went out there after him, retracing his son's steps, what he *thought* were his sons steps because he didn't even know that for sure. He just went from village to village with a photograph. Like he walked from place to place with an out-of-date picture of his grinning son. Days turned to weeks turned to months. I mean, you know, the sheer fucking loneliness of it. They never said whether he'd succeeded in finding him. There was no Kleenex-sponsored airport reunion that I can remember.

Anyway, whatever. I'm working myself up. Take a shower and call up, well, I'm about to call Sabine but then realise it's only half eight. The holiday vibe hasn't exactly kicked in yet. But thinking about school leads to a whole load of other things. Burston. Supposing I talk to him? I could find out his home address. I know where all that stuff is kept, all the records, registers, don't even have to access any database, and I could get Stan to let me in, could tell him I've left something urgent behind, doesn't even have to be urgent, just a smile will do, a big smile that's all. But what would I say to him, Burston? Can't even play teacher when *school's out for summer*. He'd laugh in my face.

Likewise the police. Types like Mills'd make everything worse. They'll do nothing after being a bit patronising, *gently* patronising which is even more of a fuck-off. Or they'll decide Dennie's public enemy number one, ask questions I can't answer because I don't know or because I do. And there's always the gig. He'll show up there. He'll be there. He will. I'm so sure of this I make a list of hairdressers, including the ones I know of, and stand in front of Trellick feeling a total arsehole: woman with list.

Then I remember something: Georgio looking over my shoulder the whole time towards the kitchen. He wanted tea? So I go back up, back in, through to the kitchen, straight to the bucket, move it, look around in the hole. Nothing. *Feel* around in the hole. Muss and filth of the sort that's pretty fucking predictable under the floorboards. Nothing. No used tenners, traces, flakes, cakes of cocaine, weed stalks or seeds or whatever. The hole only says that there *was* something there. Why not money, drugs or both? Why stop there? Sure why not Dennie had a gun down there, a big ugly *blow-your-head-off* gun ... The door of the cupboard was shut, his bass was gone. The burglar took the bass then carefully shut the door of the cupboard, taking even bigger care to throw some underwear about. Make it look like what? Like *fun*.

All this takes me back to the entrance of Trellick with a stupid fucking list in my hand. In a cop thriller you'd cut to Cee Harper *getting key lead on Nathalie*. Cut to Cee Harper in her Mercedes soft-top (top down) en route to hairdresser's along scenic river drive. Cut to close-up of Nathalie explaining everything. Instead I'm back upstairs, examining this old black and white of Dennie

83

taken for a barber's window. Him with funky twists, looking tough, with a bit of sidelight showing bone structure, and the thin scar across his eyebrow that happened cycling when he was about six but that became a designer accessory for some people. I bet Dennie looked as good on his mugshots. But being stuck in a barber's window is something that would mash up most people's reputations. Didn't faze Dennie though. He went for the mystery prize: a year's free cuts.

The picture's got a label on the back with the details of the place. Phone's engaged. Scenic canal walk to Harrow Road. I'm wearing my groovy orange T-shirt which was a real inspiration about an hour ago but which just makes me feel like going home and changing and I hate that feeling. Anyway, whatever. The point is the barber, some snippety little bastard with a mouldy left ear, goes *oh yeah him*, when I mention Dennie. Says *yeah, Dennie, seem to remember he still owes me a coupla quid*. And Nathalie? *Who? Nah don' 'ave birds in here. The old boys don' like it*. Just for the sake of being leery, I go: So what did you have Dennie's face up here for? He goes: *The pictures was all my son-in-law's idea, daft git*.

This is definitely not my line of work. So I sort of mope around, buy some cigarettes, which I haven't done in a long time, ten Silk Cuts like a wine bar splosher, sit on a bench on the canal tow-path, smoke one of them, which I haven't done in even longer. But in the sun it feels ok, no, what am I saying, it feels fucking great, just like old times, holy even, the smoke, like I'm going back to an old comfort zone that I should never have left in the first place. I almost decide to take up smoking again. I mean, I am kind of committed to the other nine anyway.

An empty plastic bag, with blue and white stripes like you get in convenience stores, floats by. That's a really sad sight: empty plastic bag floating down the Grand Union. They're even sadder when you see them in trees. Like a gust takes them up and they get hooked on a branch for more or less ever. One time, when I dropped in to see Dennie on Moss Side, on this estate where he lived for about eight months, we saw this guy with a long pole and he was trying to pick all these empty plastic bags out of the trees round the buildings. Dennie said he'd flipped about a month before, slagging off everyone on the estate, the Council, all the kids, all the adolescents, all the dog-owners and so on, but mainly the Council, about the bags. Then he'd chilled out a bit, sort of settled down to his task, picking the bags out, one by one, muttering shit to himself the whole time. But the wind was pretty bad that autumn. And it's not as if anyone was about to run out of bags. Dennie said the guy must've banged his head in an accident, said he was obsessed and couldn't understand how people let themselves get like that, like obsessed with one thing, thinking one thing, doing one thing. I said the guy just woke up one morning and knew what he had to do.

Then I get restless again and swing by Sabine's on the way back to mine. For help. It's Alv who opens the door. He's in a suit that would straighten out the worst blasphemers and have them on their knees crying *praise the Lord*. Yeah that kind of suit. I say:
—Alv, you look dynamite. What you selling?
—Helpin' a brother sell a stocka mobis na mean, he says eyes smiling. Wha' brings you into the ligh' at this hour? You's on holiday innit?
—Early bird catches the worm.
—Don't believe the hype. Tellin' you 'Bine's still ou' cold. I mean *iced* bwoy . . .

Then Alv looks down at Miles who's more puree than face. He's on the floor laughing to himself with a puddle of drool forming on the carpet.
—Been like tryin'—
—I can tell, I say stepping inside.

Alv gives me a helpless glance as he's getting his personal effects together, gold bracelet, watch like a doorknob, wallet, pager, Filofax, mobile, keychain and so on, by the end of which his suit's all out of shape. He mumbles over his shoulder:
—Some girl rang for you. Like *late* last night. Soun—
—For me?

85

—Yeah 'Bine took it. Number's on the phone ting, he points with his chin.

Takes me a while to locate the *phone ting*. Like Sabine's place is stuffed, like a car boot sale waiting to happen, which in a way it is, that and a market stall under the flyover on Saturdays. I trail the phone line through piles of second-hand clothes, toys, boxes, kitchenware and soft furnishings to the receiver. From there finding the pad's pretty easy. On it, blotched in red wine, could be Ribena, there's a number with the letter N underneath. Seek, and sooner or later someone'll tap you on the back. I start dialling.

—I'm out, goes Alv a bit sheepish. I mean Miles with you yeah? I mean, I ain't gonna be the one to wake—

—Sure Alv go slay 'em.

—*Respeck*, he smiles. Owe you one.

—Call it quits.

The number's ringing. After a couple of rings someone picks up. There's a sharp crackle: *Crsch hair centre how can I help you?* I ask for Nathalie. Whoever it is, some guy, shouts for Nathalie. Second later, she's on the line.

—Hello.

—It's Cee. Dennie's—

—You got my, um, message?

Well yes, I'm thinking, though she doesn't give me time to answer.

—Um, I don't mean to ... Well I know we've never ... Um. Could we sort of meet. Um, I mean ... I'm just a bit ... worried.

—Makes two of us.

—Um, listen, can't really talk now. I, um, just wanted to ask ...

—Yes ...

—Um, have you seen Dennie?

Yeah right. Like my end of the conversation's pretty obvious after that. I mean I still tell her we can hook up. I still tell her that. In a way I want to see her even more now. Anyway, whatever. She tells me she's the one locking up today and could we, um, maybe um, meet around five um thirty. I say ok even though five thirty's a piss-off kind of working person's time and *I'm on holiday innit*. Added to that she seems to know three things less than nothing. Anyway, so much for playing the detective.

BOSCO'S HAIR CENTRE

rastaman twist up his dred day by day

After having a good try at being Miles's primary carer, then talking Sabine out of her persistent vegetative state, I'm back home marking, trying to get some of it out of the way and trying not to think about Nathalie. I should really go down the dole office and sign on but that's even more depressing than the pile of projects on the table with more stains than words. I phone up a bunch of people. I mean when you've had a *bad experience*, you phone most of the people in your address book. With a good one, you phone mum.

Whatever. What I'm trying to say is, *later that same day* I'm up the top end of Portobello where it leaks into Notting Hill. Bosco's Hair Centre is an air-conditioned, mock black marble, white basin, lifestyle magazine type of place staffed by *hair designers*, dressed in black, who've all got more highlights than *Match of the Day*. Ha ha. That's not my line – one of the customers is saying something like that to the aftershave-drenched *male grooming commercial* who's finger-primping her sun-kissed locks.

I'm early. Hairdriers are still blasting out, water's trickling, electric shavers are whining, general chatter. Just in front of Johnnie Primp is a reception desk with no one behind it so I just stand there for a second, looking, trying to guess which one of the hair designers is Nathalie, which one Dennie'd go for. There's a West Indian girl, body like Naomi, face like a car crash. Next to her's a Latino girl who's really tall, ribby, kind of haunted, kind of beautiful. Sweeping up's a small, round, cutesy type hauling Double-Ds, big dark eyes, big dark hair, big red lips. I mean, you kind of know why they all made the grade at Bosco's, it's just that none of them's really Dennie's type. But then again, even our own *types* come as a big surprise. Especially over cornflakes.

Anyway, I ask the guy for Nathalie. He points behind him like he's doing backstroke and calls her at the same time. Moment later, Nathalie puts her head round the door of the back office.

—Someone for you Nats, says the guy.

Nats shoots him a nervous smile, more of a wince, catches my eye and comes over, head down. She's also in black, with a tight zip-top hour-glassing her chest, black high-heeled ankle boots squeezing out her little bottom. All I see's her head till she's practically in front of me. When she lifts her head she's really close, like *rush-hour-Tube* close. She's very pretty, small blue eyes looking everywhere but at me, tiny nose, eyebrows sculpted, hair slicked into a ponytail, small mouth frosted purple, whole face symmetrical like some landscape garden, max eighteen nineteen. She's talking, saying something about closing soon, five minutes, and would I mind waiting. I find myself focusing not on what she's saying but the way she's saying it. Like a deer out of the opening of *Tarzan* that's heard this gut-knotting yell and is caught in that split second before blind panic. And she passes this vibe straight to me, like one deer to another sort of thing. I go no, no problem, and sit down on the low, leathery couch by the window.

Johnnie Primp's got some story going about some old Portobello Rastafarian, *you know, the one who came in here that time, sat down, wouldn't leave?* Cutesy, Ribby and Naomi all laugh and go *oh yeah* like it's the big in-joke. So Johnnie's going: *well I passed him the other day in front of Europa Food so I sort of smiled and said hello, as you do, and he turns to me and says, he says, hey mon wha' you barin' dem teet fe? So I say I'm from the hairdresser's, remember? Telling you girls, wrong thing to say. He goes to me he goes, Rastaman don't go 'airdresser. Rastaman twist op his dred day by day.* Johnnie laughs with his head thrown back. The girls all laugh again, making sure to share their laughs by turning to each other, noses crinkled. And everybody does an imitation of the imitation of the old Rasta.

After five ten minutes and a few pings on the cash register, goodbyes and so on, the place is empty, silent, apart from Nathalie doing duties, switching lights off. Then she comes and sits next to me like we're going to talk right here but straight away her vibe gets worse. Like the conversation needs another setting. So I suggest going for a coffee. Nathalie locks up, alarms the place, and we walk down Notting Hill. Working dress codes're all screwed up on a sweaty afternoon. The whole puffy red-faced town's in shorts and sandals. Elbows everywhere sticking out of car windows. Hairy, freckly, bruised, flabby, brown, sunburned raw, black and shiny, ugly stumps pointing sideways, elbows made for one thing, for elbowing, for giving someone in the way, anyone, the Big E. Anyway. Small talk. Like I ask her how long she's been a hairdresser. She says *I'm just a receptionist but I'm gonna do my training and everything.* Whatever. She kicks a dog by accident and makes it yelp. The owner's somewhere at the end of a long leash several people away and doesn't notice. Dog's ok about it too, too busy following one of a million bad smells. It's Nathalie who can't let go of the thing, half-smiles of embarrassed apology on her hot face and even more para after.

Eventually, in a corner of a café on Notting Hill, some place that's not too busy or anything, waitress smoking and has to make coffee for us from scratch, Nathalie stops shredding her serviette long enough to look at me for a split second. She takes a breath, looks all over the place again followed by another split-second glance, focuses on a stain on my T-shirt, gift from Miles, then says: *Um . . . I just, I just want you to know it's not about the money.*

Which is actually kind of a relief, the fact that it could have been about *the money* but isn't. Looking at the top of her head, I'm thinking of something to say. I mean, so Dennie's overdrawn with Girlfriend Bank plc. Among others. I'm wondering if I have to act surprised. Like demand the balance sheet. But who cares? I mean, after all, who does care? A few round figures here and there. Just a few ball-park zeros, *twenty-five large*, a pension, a mortgage, a couple of life-savings. So? So instead I'm lighting a cigarette and can feel Nathalie looking at me, waiting for a reaction or a prompt or something.

—I mean I don't want it back or anything like that. I mean I trust him. *Totally*. I mean I love him. I'm not um, I'm not saying anything like that . . .

—What then? I go, offering a cigarette to which she shakes her head.

—I just, well, wanna know if he's, um, ok . . .

—Thing is, what makes you think he isn't?

—It's just, she says, eyes blipping all over the place, It's just um, like *everything*. I mean um I know he's a record producer and everything and he's really busy and he um *knows* all sorts of people. Important people. I mean Dennie said he meets a lot of pop stars. Like the Spice Girls. He—

—The Spice Girls?

—Yes he's um *remixing* some of their songs, like um *drum an' bass* sort of thing . . .

—Oh . . .

—Mm. And he actually said I had um, well, a really nice voice . . .

—You do, sure you do.

—But he said I had no character.

—No character? Like—

—Cos of the way I don't um *look* him in the eyes. He said people who don't look people in the eyes have no character . . . I, um . . . Do you think I have no character?

—No. No. Course not. It—

The waitress brings the coffees and I'm suddenly thinking if she's listening to all this. She's the sort of waitress who judges people not by their faces or politeness but by the amount they spend and the mess they make. She's got us sized up as low on spend, big on mess. Anyway, I say thanks, then take hold of Nathalie's hand before it reaches her cup. Same time I'm making sure I keep my voice down.

—I . . . It took a lot of *character* to phone up like you did . . . Really. I – Look . . . What makes you think he's in trouble?

—Well because of what happened . . . I mean, one time about, can't remember . . . But, um, sort of since. I mean—

—What happened one time?

—Well he – We were out – He got um, sort of beaten up I mean not really—

—*Beaten up?*

—No not *beaten up* no. Just um I mean I don't want to get you worried—

—Oh please . . . Nathalie . . . Look, just tell me what happened.

—Someone just hit him. Was gonna stab him but some other people held him back.

—Who was gonna stab who? Who hit him?

—Um, this guy. Wouldn't recognise him or anything.

—No sure . . . And this guy, the one you wouldn't recognise, he was gonna stab Dennie?

—No Dennie was gonna . . . but . . . he didn't . . .

—Go on . . .

—Um, well, Dennie and me, I mean and some other people, friends, we were at the Bull Bar, you know, up—

—Yeah sure . . .

—Anyway, um, I mean we go to quite a few places round there, round here I mean, Market Bar and . . . Well, Dennie always pays. I mean, for *everyone*. Buys everyone Es, sometimes coke. Um, I mean I'm not really into all that, drugs an' stuff, not really, just for a laugh, maybe, like, *at the weekend*. But I mean, um, Dennie often pays for everyone, like my two friends and me that time, he paid for all of us *and* gave the, um, *bouncer* something, a tenner, or something, for nothing really, just the way he is. Says he does it *for the service* . . . Everyone respects him. You know what I mean?

—Sure. Sure definitely. So go back to what—

—Well, um, that time, this was after we'd come out of the bar, the Bull Bar this was, it was a Saturday I think, like a few weeks ago, um, maybe even a month . . . Time – I mean, anyway . . . Um, we were coming out, we were twenty feet away, just walking, away, going home, we'd just come out and this um, guy, this guy comes up to him, says something, sort of *warns* him, and um, just sort of *hits* him, Dennie. I mean, in the face, and sort of slashes him—

—*Slashes* him? His face?

—No no it wasn't serious it was more his . . . arm. Um, it *was* his arm. I mean um, there was blood and everything but it was more of a scratch, um, I'm, it healed. Really really quickly. He wasn't *hurt*. Not really. Not at all. Not um, in the end.

—Right ok . . . ok. Nathalie, what did this guy—

—I don't know. Um. I really don't. It just all happened—

—So fast sure . . . But you don't—

—No. No . . . It was just some bloke, some—

—Wearing like what?

—Well, it was, it was *dark*. Everything happened in a second. You know? Um, I mean, there was a name—

—A *name*? What—

—Mentioned. But there was a lot of noise . . .

—Sure you could hardly hear . . . But can, I mean, a name like what?

—Well, sort of heard . . . Um, sounded like . . . *soap*? Or something but—

—Soap . . .

—Yes and ever since—

—No no wait a second wait . . . This *name* was mentioned how? Like you remem—

—No . . . No can't um . . . Can't remember much we were all off our faces. *Just a bit.* You know . . .

—Yeah yeah. Sure. Um, so ever since . . . ?

—Um, well, ever since, Dennie's been acting . . . more *distant*? Um, scared? I suppose you'd say, in a way.

—What would *you* say?

—Um, he said it was about business. Like about him being um *successful* and people getting jealous. That happens.

—Right . . .

—It all builds up, goes Nathalie starting on another serviette. The pressure I mean. You have to um, *cope with stress*. It happens bit by bit.

—Yes it does. You're right . . . But what would *you* say it was about, that night?

—Me? Um, I don't—

—Fuck's sake . . . Look, Nathalie . . . Honey. I hate to be the one to break it to you but Dennie's never produced a fucking record in his fucking life. And sure, you've got a great voice and everything but whoever's gonna make you a star, I mean, don't count on Dennie changing his name to Jim'll Fixit. You know? Like this thing yeah, *whatever* this thing has to do with, has fuck all to do with the *Spice Girls*. Dippy, Lippy, Pissy Spice or the rest. Right? . . . Right?

—Um, I—

—What did this *guy* look like?

—I don't—

—Yes you fucking do. You say you're worried—

—I don't I promise I don't . . . I really don't . . .

She looks straight at me for perhaps the first time and the look says *please don't ask because I'm too scared to tell*. For a second time I'm aware that we've been getting louder and the waitress hasn't been getting any busier.

—Ok . . . Look. I'm sorry and . . . Why – I mean . . . What, if anything, can you tell me? Why're you telling me this now? Like why did you wait a month or whatever to tell me this?

—I didn't. Um, I mean it was the state he was in—

—When? You saw him?

—He called. A few days ago. Maybe like a week or – Um, I—

—This was before you called Sabine?

95

—Yes. Um. It was after he, he wanted, well *needed*, some cash so I met him and—

—Do you know where he might be?

—No. No really. I'd um, tell you if I could. I would . . . I would really. He didn't leave his new number. If I knew I'd tell you. I mean, you're his sister. I just—

—His what?

—Well you're his—

—No, before. You said his *new* number?

—He's . . . His . . . Um, I mean, he got a new phone and I – Um, like, *people're always running me down too easy.* That's what he said. So—

—But he didn't leave it, the number?

—No I—

—And he hasn't called you since?

—No. I um, no. That's what I mean. He—

—Wait wait . . . Wait. What do you mean a *new* phone? What happened to the old phone? I mean I don't have a mobile . . .

—Well, um, he just left the old one. With me I mean. Said it'd be easier to um, *avoid people.* You know? Like I said. Like Dennie said. I mean I haven't *used* it or anything if that's what you're thinking. I haven't touched it. I promise. Really. I, you know, I'm just um *keeping* it for him.

—Yeah yeah no I understand . . . So where is it, the phone?

—Um well, thing is, you see I shouldn't. I said—

—Nathalie . . . Where's the phone?

—It's, um, back at Bosco's. It's safe. In reception. I promise I haven't been using it or anything.

—Can we go back and get it?

—I can't—

—Look to be honest Nats, fuck what Dennie told you—

—No it's, it's not that it's . . . I don't have the *key*, the *master* key, for the alarm. I can only—

—Tomorrow?

—Um, well tomorr—

—Look, I'll come first thing yeah? Ok?

—Um, well, tomorrow's Sunday.

—Oh. Shit. Well, Monday then.

—Um, ok . . .

Holy mother. I pay, give the waitress a dirty look before she can give me one. I sort of hug Nathalie outside, remind her twice that I'll be there first thing Monday. Exchange numbers. I honestly don't want her to go away upset, which is pretty funny really because the truth is, first thing I feel's this huge urge to slap her silly right there in the street. *Glass the bitch y'na mean.* Rude Girl style. Like *stab her up.* Then I kind of realise what I really feel which is sorry, sorry for *poor little idiot girl.* That's her, not me. But the problem, the big problem, with feeling sorry for Nats is that there's no way round feeling seriously fucking pissed off with Dennie. To say the least and I don't want to say the words. Anyway, whatever, with not just him but the way of him. The whole way of it. I mean the way it happens, the way it builds up. Bit by bit. Twisted up day by day. By fucking day. And then some.

SATURDAY NIGHT

it's alright

There are several messages when I get back. People return calls
straight away to cross *condolences* off their list of things to do. One
of the messages is from Jodie saying *how awful* and *how terrible* it is
to be burgled, how sorry she is, and how her *inner child is lighting a
mental candle* for me. Really. I mean, Jodie, actress turned new-age
waitress fuck-up, set up a theatre company last year so that she
could star in her own show. She applied for a grant from the local
authority for this play she'd written about an *inner city single woman
with exotic dreams but no prospects*. She got the grant and, with any
money left over from the launch party, went on holiday. Before
the truth dawned on the grants committee, Jodie had like *modified
the subject matter to incorporate multicultural women's issues*. In other
words *single woman with exotic dreams goes to Goa and gets tranced*.
But in the end, grant and theatre company aside, the whole thing
was about a single woman with no prospects who gets pregnant.
That's more or less what happened to her in India, apart from a
suntan. Cut a long story, she says she's *been meaning to phone for
ages and now's a good time*. Pause in the message, then she adds, *not
for you, obviously* . . . Anyway, she's *having a little birthday stroke
reunion drink thing* with some of the other losers involved in the
ill-fated Tranced Out. I mean the play had one and a half shows

at Kensal Road Community Centre, the half because the audience
was there but Jodie wasn't. Eventually the official question about
the budget was asked, so Jodie did the only thing she could do by
that time which was to plead pregnancy. And when the officials,
men mostly, asked why she hadn't finished the performances, she
came out with the awesome response: *oh for God's sake, closure's
such a male thing*.

Since then she's kept her head down, even though the first and
last performance wasn't that bad. I mean we did it. Got favours
from anyone we could. Even Dennie helped out. Me, I played the
trance-dancer who gives Jodie her first E. Yeah right. Maybe I
just want to take my mind off things or maybe secretly I've got
ambitions to revive this classic. Whichever. I'm regretting it as
soon as I step through the doors of the Slice on Kilburn Lane
around nine, still chewing a piece of gum which I've forgotten to
ditch before going in.

The Slice is the kind of place that draws people who wake
up in the morning and can't decide whether they live in Kensal
Green, Queen's Park or Ladbroke Grove. Jodie, sitting in a group
of six or so and talking in the sort of musical notes you get at the
tinkly end of a piano, is one of those people. She talks herself up
to the up-and-coming Queen's Park; she slums herself back down
to Credibility Grove. She's also one of those women who screams
woo woo from somewhere deep inside, especially in public places,
just to make an occasion of her life. I mean, bottom line, she's
the sort of actress who spends most of her time rehearsing being
an actress.

As she backs off from her welcoming clinch, she flicks back
her straggly blonde, part bleached, part braided, part beaded hair
and goes:
—Wooo.

When the ringing in my ears is over I remember, one by one,
all the things I couldn't stand about her. Apart from the *woo woo*.
Actually it's more *coochie coo* as it turns out since her first major
topic is her adorable six-month-old daughter, Joliette, who's at

home with her adorable born-again trance-dancer builder, Jake, the guy she met in Ibiza after ditching the trance-dancer who'd made her pregnant in Goa. Jake, the one from Ibiza, is *like totally accepting* and adores Joliette and is *totally into her genetic destiny*. Whatever the fuck that means.

All this Jodie's telling not just me but the others. Judging by their aching grins, they've heard the story of the three Js before. There's Emma and Rhiannon who also made it into the Tranced Out hall of fame, Emma as *artistic director*, Rhiannon as *choreographic designer*. And to look at them now ... I mean, just a couple of mobile phone owners from Kensington who like taking turns to stand up, flick their hair, wander round, stand outside the door, flick their hair, wander about some more, the whole time with the phone on one ear, finger in the other, stars in their own little soap: Mobile Babes. The others, an Ian, who's gone to get drinks, an Ellen, who tells me like I've got a hearing problem that Ian's her boyfriend, and a Marcus. Never met any of them although this guy Marcus is cute with his number one cut, bit red blond but a face that's clean and bright and flushed from the sun. I get a vibe off him even before I've sat down. And halfway through the day I even started getting into my orange T-shirt again. By nine we've kind of *rebonded*, especially with help from a cropped Levis jacket and a vibe off some guy I don't mind getting a vibe off.

The weird thing though, I mean, I've sat in this place before in this kind of group fancying that kind of guy. The even weirder thing is that Dennie's gig is here next Tuesday night. And that's maybe the reason I'm here, like three nights early, waiting for my life to wind back to where it was or fast forward to where it should be. Anyway, whatever. Ian's back, other conversations have started and Jodie's moved on to one of her shit-hot favourite topics: the DSS.

—Oh come on Ian, she's going, looking at me like we both know Ian's a dummy. You can talk about *New Labour* all you like but *everyone* does it. The whole like *rave* generation, a whole generation, no two, *at least* two, of people. I mean the dole, it's *pocket money darling*, beer money, buzz money, everyone knows that. Get a council flat, move in with boyfriend down the road and sublet, claim benefit, child benefit, whatever. And then there's your job. You know? Play the game and the game is *so easy* it's *crazy*. *Pièce de pissé*, as they say. God even that sleazy bitch Henrietta, the one with that flat in Notting Hill. Cee, remember? The party? *That* party? Woooo remember that? That was a fucking wicked party. Thanks to us I mean. *Totally* mental. I mean Henrietta she's got a *split-level lifestyle darling* with that *bath stroke jacuzzi stroke swimming pool*. And *Le Creuset* pans that've never even had tinned splodge in them doing fuck all on her reconditioned Aga. *And* she's on social *and* she has about two grand a month from *daddy stroke standing order*. Least I've got *Jake stroke fucking way out genius* when it comes to getting things sorted. You know? Not to mention anything to do with other people's credit cards. Woo. Darling. I could tell you scams. Like I mean if we got burgled Jake'd make Norwich Union poo in their premium-padded pants. *Poo in their premium-padded pants*. That's good isn't it. D'you like that one? But no, he would. He'd find a way. Seriously girl. Like recently we've had about four sets of three-piece suites, like *top-of-the-range* stuff, that Jake fixed up on the drip, you know, HP or something. After you don't pay for like three four months they send you letters and stuff and eventually repo it. But so what? You've trashed it by then. Thing is, people *want* to give you stuff. They *want* you to have the credit cards. And if they want to throw cheques at you once a fortnight, well why the fuck not? But with people like Henrietta, you know what I mean ... There's a limit.

—There is? I go, my grin beginning to ache. What is it?

—I actually meant her *credit* limit. Woo. Like *daddy stroke standing order* kind of lost it a while back to *step-mother stroke fuck off and get a job*. But Hennie's well sussed. Now she's got her standing order, her dole 'n' housing, weekends in Val d'Isère *and* her job. Last five months we've been on shifts together at the Bull Bar, so I should know. Top of everything, can you

believe it, she's *really tight with coke*. D'you want a little toot
in a sec?
—Nah I'm ok.
—Sure? she shrugs. Telling you though, the Bull Bar's *so mad*. You
should come – oh God *Dennie*, he's *brilliant*. He comes down there
loads. You must've seen him in his *big night out* gear. Walks in,
silk shirt, gold necklace, a whole *hareem* in tow, and every time we
see him we're all like *guess who won the lottery?* Still really friendly
though. Very *buddy buddy* with Fergal, the manager. I mean, *forget*
Tranced Out. He's gone a long way from being *transport consultant*.
Right? Wooo. He's *mystery money man*. You know? So what's he
up to these days? Really. And *don't* say community theatre.
—Oh he's set himself up as a pimp in Chinatown and says he's
gonna take Bayswater back from the Colombians.
—*Cray-zee*, goes Jodie pretty uncertainly.
—He's got a gig here Tuesday.
—Here yeah? I'll have to come down ... So he's got into the
music thing full-time now?
—Kind of. Truth is Jodie, you probably know more than me.
—Well I'll tell you this: Dennie's *really generous* with coke.

She looks at me like this is going to make me feel good. Then
goes *woo* to kind of bridge the huge fucking hole that's opened
up in the monologue. Then goes:
—Like working in that place, *so* much coke ends up on me I
finish the shift looking like Joliette after a talc sesh ...

She leaves a space like a panto horse for me to laugh into.
Only I don't. I can't. So she laughs for me.
—Woo, sure you don't want a line?
—Nah really, I'm ok.
—Where's the groove spirit girl? Where's your soul? Saturday
night. *It's alright innit.*
—I know but—
—Actually I try to lay off during the week but *you* try dealing
with all that baby stuff without a little *organic energiser*. You know?
That's what Jake calls it. Wooo baby. Come on ...

She looks at the Mobile Babes in that girly secrety way, like *let's all go to the loo together*. And they do. Traipse off in a line, the two Babes looking round over everyone's heads, like *yes we're looking for someone but no way is it you*. Phoney bints. Then it's me and Marcus and Ian 'n' Ellen. Ian 'n' Ellen're like cold warring it with some of the hammiest body language in W10. Like no looks just *awareness* of each other's presence. Too complicated to figure out. So me and Marcus exchange our first meaningful look.

And in no time at all he asks me his first meaningful question: *so how d'you know Jodie then?* So I put my chewing gum into the ashtray and tell him we met on a Buddhist Chanting weekend. And he goes, completely straight, *I've always wanted to go on one of those. Like Buddhism's supposed to be a really happening thing . . .* What can you say to that? So I go: Oh it is, it's really happening, are you into chanting? That shuts him right up but I don't know why I'm being so whatever, ironic, when only a couple of minutes ago . . . So I smile and tell him it was a joke. And his face cracks up and goes redder than it was, and it was, like I say, a stop light anyway. So then I give him a warm, squinty, twinkly, beamy kind of look, *à la* Sabine, and say:

—So where do you know Jodie from?

—Well me an' Jake go back a long way . . .

Hate it when people say that. I mean, anything but a long way. Too late, he's started, he'll finish.

— . . . First met in Ibiza. Bit mental both of us. We were gonna set up a bar, with like *food*, all vegetarian, music, chill-out zone, our own cocktails. Had recipes an' everything. But it never happened. Went on six-month benders both of us. We were mad for it. Had a really good time though. *Rave till you're stretchered.* You know? We wanted to keep that whole thing going back here . . .

—Right . . . So what happened . . . ?

—Well, we were both living South, so we got this sound system together an' started putting on raves an' stuff. Round Deptford an' Peckham. Like *Spirit of Ibiza* vibe. But like South London firms kept coming down an' fucking everything up. Getting heavy. Threats an' everything. So like me an' Jake eventually thought *enough's enough*. You know?

—What you just took them out?

—Fuck no, no way, goes Marcus panicking, no way. No. We were only in it for the laughs. You know? I mean no way I was gonna risk ten psychos with baseball bats on my case. Or worse . . . And there is a lot worse. You know?

—I know, I've done Buddhist chanting.

—Yeah right, he smiles. No mercy them Buddhist chanters . . .

So he's got some humour I'm thinking as Jodie, Emma and Rhiannon traipse back, all of them acting *casual secret* but Jodie over-doing the sniffing like she was dress-rehearsing for a Lemsip ad. They all sit down, Emma and Rhiannon with their bodies *draped* over the backs of their chairs, legs kind of spread like they're trying to prove they're still warm from the best sex of their lives, anybody's lives. First thing Jodie says:

—What's that guy staring at you for?

Nobody knows who she's talking to but she says it really loudly, suddenly, big sex machine of a grin on her face. Everyone turns towards where she's looking.

—Been standing there a while staring right at you Cee. What an ape. Eyeing you up. I think you're in there, she laughs. Wooo. Go for it girl . . .

My reaction is to turn away from Georgio soon as I spot him near the doors, arm on a ledge, smoking, staring, not drinking, alone in the hot, smoky crowd, like there, waiting, silent in the noise. My reaction tells everyone I know him.

—Didn't think he was your type.

—He's not.

—You don't have to say anything darling. We all make mistakes, only some of us make them the night before the return flight, goes Jodie patting her belly.

Emma and Rhiannon crack up, Marcus I don't know because I don't want to look at him.

—He's coming over . . .

105

The word *shit* springs to mind. I'm about to do something, I mean like take a drink, light a cigarette, pretend I'm surfing in California but instead I stand up, turn to face him as he sifts through the crowd, more like shoves, and go, in a not so passive aggressive kind of way:

—What the fuck do you want?

Georgio scans round the group, one by one, then says:

—Can we talk baby?

Right cunning bastard. Right behind him, looking at me all mock shock, Jodie's mouthing *BA-BY?* Meantime, Emma and Rhiannon're looking at Georgio like he's just been imported from somewhere outside Kensington in a sealed crate labelled *this side up* because otherwise, I mean, you just wouldn't fucking know. And me, I'm like wondering which way to turn. Tell him to fuck off and then explain this, that and everything to who? To the Spirit of Ibiza. To phoney bints. Seems like people're waiting for me. But I don't know. Just want Tuesday night to come and go as easily as *tea an' a spliff*. A moment later, I choose the way of least explaining.

—Back in a sec, I go to Jodie.

She comes back with a really cheesy *I'm sure you won't be darling*. So me and Georgio make our way to his habitat, the ledge near the doors. Or more like he goes back there and I have to follow. What's worse, some *lightweight* – I mean a guy half Georgio's width – is about to perch in the same spot. Georgio gives him a look that the guy's probably only seen on TV, not in this place anyway. Guy drops his eyes, turns away, slopes off. So then we're facing each other. Georgio sparks up. After a couple of seconds, he goes:

—So, you gonna suck charlie off his dick roun' yours tonigh'?

—That's an idea.

—So wha' else was you gonna do wiv him?

—Oh I get it, so now I've got to choose between the two of you.

—Why bring him in?

—Yeah right. So what do I have to do? One blow for twenty-five grand?

—Dass an idea. Bu' one blow for twenny-five? Ah mean, iss more like y'gonna have to shag it off at five hundred a week. An' dass generous.

—If I did it for twenty-five, *that'd* be generous.

—So ... *Spi' i' ou'* ... Wha' was you gonna do wiv carrot-head?

—None of your fucking business. What d'you want from me?

—Ah can help you.

—Really? How?

—Big dick, three gees of kuf an' air-con in ma car.

—You think I need that kind of help?

—Gaggin' more like ... Y'na mean, wha' you runnin' round hairdressers all mornin' like one of them *it girls*?

—So you been following me all day?

—*Stoopid* question. Course Ah fuckin' 'ave innit. How come you visit two of 'em an' you ain't got y'hair cut?

—You think I should?

—Who's the mousey little hairdresser bitch? Ain't y'long lost *sista* innit. Go'a be y'bruvver's bint. Maybe Ah've even seen her. Maybe Ah'm finkin' he's sendin' messages. Or you are.

—I probably would if I knew where he was.

—If Ah find him maybe Ah'm gonna do him, maybe not. If *someone* find him, he's meat. Simple. Y'na mean ... Dat shut you up innit.

He glances across to where Jodie is. I look back too. Can see the top of Jodie's head a second as she throws back her hair. But in the second I turn my head, he grips my skinny arm and pulls me through the doors and into the street. I'm aware of trying to hit him in the face but he grabs my other arm and holds that too. And he holds me like that and I'm like a fucking rabbit waiting for him to hit me, wondering if he will, kind of feeling he won't as long as he's grabbing both arms, wondering then if I should knee him but scared I guess of the consequences. So he just holds me like that until some people go by, a group that's fallen silent in that second and knows but doesn't know, has seen but hasn't

107

and everyone waits and passes on, hoping something will happen to take the silence away. Then when they've gone he says:

—Ah'm gonna show you somin' 'bou' y'bruvver. Get in the car . . .

He lets go of one arm and reaches back towards the kerb, towards the door of his car. That's when Marcus and Jodie appear, hovering in the background, waiting for a sign. Catch Marcus's eye. He's gulping like the cast of *Curse of the Living Dead* are at the foot of his bed and there is only his gummy security rag to keep him from screaming. Well, whatever. Picture's clear. I mean, he isn't going to risk a kicking. Who would? Rather do some chanting. Least he makes me feel better about being scared. Georgio looks at me. Like things could go either way. But he lets go.

—Troof be tol', he goes pulling out his car keys, women ain't got no sense of danger. Till iss too late . . . Who's gonna find him first?

—He'll show at the gig, I say backing off.

—You be'er believe it.

FUCKING SUNDAY

there's a lo'a stupid bitches out there

Sunday, me and Marcus . . . Count to ten before I can swallow that phrase. Me 'n' Marcus 'n' Sabine 'n' Alv . . . No, first, I mean, I was harsh on Marcus. He stood his ground. Even if it was twenty feet away. Whatever. Georgio took off. I had to leave after that. Couldn't face telling anybody anything, explaining everything. So I had to leave and Marcus, well, he walked me back. Said it was the least he could do. And it really was the least. I didn't suck charlie off his dick. Didn't have sex. Well, we did. But it was like I wasn't there. I wasn't drunk or anything but I still can't remember it. Not much. Or don't want to. Except the bit afterwards, when he was talking, explaining his theory of orgasms. That's when I remember being there and nowhere else. Would've left there and then. But I was home. Would've told him to leave. But it was easier not to. Felt right to have someone there. Almost slept really deeply. And in the end, what was he going to do except get to the bit about his theory of orgasms. Because he'd *thought a lot about it.* On his travels. What was he saying? Something like: *With men right, it's like a line from A to B. It's straight, linear. But with women* (here he started making little circles in the pillow with his finger) *it's all . . . circular.* And at that point I remembered Sabine had had a similar thing. Different guy. Different theory. Same deal though.

Only Sabine told her one: *Richie, don't think about my orgasms, just give me one.* Right. I mean, in the end, that's why I would've slept really deeply.

But you don't think these things through on Saturday nights. More like on Fucking Sundays that couples get used to so easily and singles hate and the world divides in all our heads into no more than that. Anyway, it's not the sleeping alone, it's the waking up. But if you wake up *with* someone, there's two. And once you've got two, there's four. So that's why me 'n' Marcus 'n' Sabine 'n' Alvin (and Miles) are in Holland Park with prams and rabbits and ducks and food and drink. And spliff. I get mashed. It's really hot. Smell of grass and warm earth. Hand on my back.

Alv's great. It's not Alv's hand on my back. The hand belongs to Marcus. I'm just looking at Alv through a glass of vodka orange that he's given me, turning the glass, listening to the ice clink. He's handing out chicken legs and salad and bread and has a real way with Tupperware. I love him. Sabine treats him mean ordering him about and back-seating everything he does. But she's all mother juice and he kind of likes being pussy whupped. Not kind of, he loves it. He's all heart with a real desire to do right. Somehow my end's flawed. Sabine's like *where did you find him?* I'm like, don't ask.

Marcus is in to some script about the weather in Ibiza.

—Like people here think *this* is hot but . . .

Bla bla.

— . . . and when I get some dough together, believe me I'm gone . . .

Bla bla.

— . . . set up a business, you know, there're loads of things you could do out there.

Bla bla.

— . . . no way you can be happy in *this* climate, you know.

—Is righ', goes Alv, my Mum upped it back to JA. Montego Bay innit, palms, yam, bananas. She catches fireflies in a jar, sticks the jar on the table in the evenings for the ligh' na mean. Over the

Bay. Thass wha' I call *scenic*. Life of Riley innit. Whoever the fuck Riley was.

—Pro'ly one of Georgio's burgle buddies, goes Sabine.

—More like the alias of anyone in 4c.

—You think them kids're largin' it? Too righ' they are. Saw some kids walkin' out a shop one time an' they all had goods. Owner's tellin' 'em to come back like he don't mean it. Y'na mean. Ain't no control like there used to be.

—Listen to *you*, I go, then turn to Sabine. One chicken leg and he's all *authoritarian*.

—Yeah Alv, goes Sabine, whass all this *no control like there used to be*? Miles—

—Ain't *referrin'* to you an' Miles. Iss simple: I'm sayin' sometime you go'a *hurt* people, in the *short term*, specially kids.

—You can come round and hurt this kid Burston I've got. Like anytime.

—Burston, Riley, whoever innit. You can't let 'em take the piss. If he's a *teef* or a *bag-bwoy* or he cut someone for nu'in, he needs wha'ever he needs to straighten him out. My case my mum did all the straightenin' before she took off to catch fireflies.

—So you're saying what? Like with Burston, you'd straighten him out?

—If I knew the detail I could say but yeah . . .

—How d'you mean *yeah*? You'd do that right? You'd hurt him?

—Yeah . . . Yeah Cee I would def. In the end . . . I would. But with *love*. Y'na mean?

—Nope.

—Yeah I know what you mean, goes Marcus nodding wisely like he'd turned armies of hardcore schoolboys into gardening volunteers for OAPs.

Me an' Sabine exchange a look.

—Ice cream time, she says getting up. Gonna leave Miles with you yeah bu' don't *hurt* him righ'. Specially not with *love* innit, she goes pouting at me like *that told him*.

—Ah 'Bine wha'? You sting me . . .

111

—Ice cream anyone?

Everyone says yes so then me and Sabine're walking off to get some ice creams and behind me I catch Marcus saying *Yeah man you're saying that more control right* . . . Bla bla. I squint in the sun and put my sunglasses on and then, somewhere between a guy with a kid on his shoulder and some other guy in a bush doing t'ai chi, I start crying. I mean my whole inside sinks, just sinks, and I just go into one right there and have to take my sunglasses off again. I remember a time when it was the other way around. Sabine used to cry over anything and more or less anywhere. Especially getting off buses. Said it really depressed her, getting off, and she couldn't help *linking* it with all the other times she'd been depressed. Eventually, she stopped taking buses and only went out with someone if he had a car with minimum three months' MoT.

Anyway, after I've finished wiping my nose on Sabine's t-shirt, I tell her all the stuff that's happened. Like word for word in a Sabine kind of way. *Then this and then that and then this.* Her attitude is simple: *get the phone off Nathalie, go through all the numbers stored in it, ring them up, find out who Dennie owes money to, an' if it's Georgio then get somebody to kill that person.* Sabine's always been practical.

Back at the picnic, she retells all my stuff even though I asked her not to. She says it'll help. Only the way she retells it makes it sound like Dennie's borrowed cigarettes off Georgio and Georgio's calling them in. That's why Marcus so casually goes *oh I can lend you some dough . . . if you need it . . .* Like instant solution. Win the lottery. Yeah right. He tells me to *bear it in mind*, then goes off to find a toilet before I can say *thanks, cash only*. When he's gone, Sabine says:

—Babes you go'a be realistic. Dennie can take care of himself. He's pro'ly just lyin' low. Innit Alv.

—So's G. In a way . . .

—Wha'? Only time G ever lies low is when he's fixin' up dodgy motors.

—Nah hon, goes Alv with a mouthful of chicken, tellin' you, G's got plenty on his plate y'na mean. He bigs himself up same as usual. But he ain't causin' ructions.

—Is for me Alv.

—You don't know ructions, trust me Teach.

—*I don't know ructions?* Joking. You ever been on the receiving end of a leery class?

—I hear you, I hear you, Alv laughs, Bu' I'm talkin' *Georgio Georgianou*-style ructions innit.

—Oh yeah, superstar? Whass the difference between Georgio old style and Georgio new style?

Alv swallows his mouthful and washes it down with some water. Then shrugs. And shrugs again.

—Nu'in really honey, he mumbles. Bread anyone?

—Don't say *nu'in really honey*, goes Sabine feeding Miles a morsel of meat, eyebrow moving up her head. There's a lo'a stupid bitches out there only me an' Cee ain't two of 'em.

—Come on, ain't like tha'. You know I ain't sayin' that.

—So wha' then? We go'a *imagine* everythin'?

—Ain't tha' ...

—Well whass G got on his plate thass so fresh an' different? Thass changed him for all time?

—Ain't fresh an' it ain't changed him, not for all time anyway ...

Sabine waits for Alv to carry on but he's fixing up some more chicken for his bread.

—Alv ... We're burstin' here ...

—Oh man ...

—Alv—

—Ok ... ok, says Alv slowly wiping mouth and hands. Tell you somin'. Bu' if I tell you somin', I ain't told you. Y'na mean ...

—Yeah right.

—'Bine I'm serious yeah.

—*Serious? We're* serious. Innit Cee.

—Totally.

—Oh bwoy, goes Alv, eyes rolling like disco globes. Ok, ok ... Thing is yeah, goes Alv screwing up the serviette, thing is,

113

Nick Barlay

G, an' you ain't heard this from me righ', goes Alv pointing in turn at both of us until we have to nod, G, righ' now, like *today*, he's wha' you call a *full-on bail bandit* ... Na mean. Like *two time* bail bandit. Y'na mean. He was up for one ting yeah, bu' he duck out to Cyprus or someplace, then he come back, so they snatch him up again bu' like, *eighth wonder*, they give him bail. So guess wha? He duck out *again* innit. So thass why I'm sayin he ain't causin' major ructions. Ain't *sayin'*, I'm *tellin'* you. Cos if he gets pulled for like *droppin' litter*, it's *bye bye mummy* G ...

Alv locks a door and throws the key behind him.

— ... Go straight to jail innit, says Alv like it needs further explanation. Only it ain't no Monopoly jail. Ain't no *tunnel your way out usin' your toothbrush* shit. Like min three years. You know? They ain't playin' games. You—

—Yeah yeah ok the picture's in my head now, says Sabine. Bu' you shouldna told us all tha' no way.

—Y'na'm sayin' ...

—So how come the cops don't get him?

—Cee, they *would* have ... If they knew where he was ...

—Grass him up, goes Sabine.

—Kiddin' me? Wha' for? Would you?

—Depends, goes Sabine.

—Ain't got the heart innit.

—Got the stomach more like, goes Sabine, fingers stroking her curvy belly.

—Heart or stomach or wherever, righ' an' wrong go'a start somewhere. An' thass somin' for you two to like *tink on*. Bu' not too hard, cos like the Book say: *the Devil enter by the ear*. So thass why'm tellin' you time an' again, I ain't—

—Yeah Alv, you ain't told us. Cee?

—Yeah Alv, you ain't told us.

—Oh bwoy, goes Alv spreadeagling, hands on face. Sweet Jesus *swing* that suckin' chariot low righ' now and carry me the fuck out innit.

Me and Sabine crack up. A second later so does Alv.

114

—Like you say 'Bine, goes Alv poking Sabine's ribs, there sure is a lo'a stupid bi—

At which point Sabine dumps Miles and jumps on Alv and they start wrestling in the grass with Sabine's squealing giggle scattering the wildlife. Miles also makes a break for it with a high-speed crawl towards a rabbit. So I go after him. Funny thing about going after a baby, you start by kind of locking on to the baby's speed, walking like a stumbling B-movie yeti, arms stretched out ready to make a grab, and just as you get to them you change your mind, hold back, just to let them keep crawling on, journeying on for a little. It doesn't matter, I mean it doesn't, the fact of them, Miles, crawling far as he can without anyone interfering, his eyes fixed on the grass, on some personal mission. When do you stop them?

Then Sabine's coming up behind, grabbing Miles under the arms then half dropping him as she changes her mind too. Only her change of mind is for pulling up her shorts, not exactly a ragga dancehall queen's *batty riders* ok, but short shorts, short *killer* shorts nevertheless, that she's pulled like *right to the crack*. Then she picks Miles up, glances back at Alv who's still lying in the grass and goes:

—Thass my life right there innit: *the sex thing v. the responsibility thing*.

She waits for a smile, a nod. But it dawns on her as it dawns on me that the same is going through my mind, my life, too. Then when Marcus comes back we're all silent, hot, drowsy. Marcus kisses me on the mouth. I don't want to but don't stop him. Just because. Whatever. The sun's shining. You know. But all I think of's this thing Sabine once read out about how kissing creates *a low-pressure suction tunnel*. That's what it said. It creates a low-pressure suction tunnel that whips up this mini gale that rips all this bacteria and stuff off the inside of your partner's mouth. Your *kissee's* mouth. And it all goes straight into yours. Straight into *your* mouth. Like ready-cooked. You know?

Nick Barlay

Another vodka orange and I go into a deep snooze, kind of catching up, running after sleep then something in my sleep, neither the sex thing nor the responsibility thing. In the end I don't know what thing, just something I keep letting slip.

STANLEY AND THE KNIFE

my Mum give it me

Next to allen keys hanging on a brass hook, beside a dozen other keys on numbered pegs, above an open tool box with a torch, screwdriver and hammer, opposite a rusty three-draw filing cabinet labelled *signal generators, maintenance, miscellaneous*, below a duty roster hung from its bulldog clip, overlooking a school desk with a paint-spattered radio playing some breezy lunchtime hit, red as the red cross on a medical kit on the floor, and reflected in the fingerprinted silver side of a secret toaster, is a curled old Christmas card pinned to a cork board: *Dear Stan, merry Xmas and propseros* (crossed out) *prosporus 1987 from Naresh Patel.*

Beneath the Christmas card is a postcard, half of one, half visible, somewhere *on-Sea*, doesn't matter where, it's just the fact of there being one of each. A person. A place. One other person, one other place, outside you and yours. Pretty fucking sad. Like the rest you could almost guess from that one thing, those two things. I mean what would the postcard say? *Dear Stan, wish you were here, love Fred and Vera.* Postmark 1956. But the words make no difference. It's just the fact of someone going off on holiday, being on holiday, and thinking of Stan back here. It's just the fact of Naresh, whoever he was, or his mum, whoever she was, thinking that thing. The fact of Naresh sitting at his dinner table, five minutes before his

117

favourite TV programme, desperate to remember where the '*p*' and the '*s*' should go and if there's a '*u*' in the mix. It's just the fact of those two cards curling slowly up the cork board as summers and winters come and go and new year blessings pass their sell-by dates by years.

I mean it's like the rest just spreads out, a whole life just spreads from that thing. As if some cheesy art director guessed it all and dressed the set for a cheesy BBC drama. Dramarama. Sit-com more like, where all the jokes are not that funny, not that sad, just at that level of funny-sad that everyone can live with, just about, like *it's been real miss* but not too real. Whatever. I've never really looked in Stan's office, not like this, not enough to smell toast and tools, grease, paint and bare sun-warmed floorboards. I've never really waited by his office, door open, looking in, waiting for him to come back from some job or other, some miscellaneous couple of things or other. Like if people ask, *where's Stan?* somebody'll say, *oh he's about, busy somewhere with a couple of things or other* . . . Always the same: here but not. Out and about. Somewhere or other. Meanwhile, in his office, a whole life spreads out.

I put my hand in my pocket and touch Dennie's phone. I go to Bosco's this morning right, half hour or so after they open, looking over my shoulder the whole time, looking for Georgio, his car, just in case, and they say *Nathalie's not here, she called in sick, be here tomorrow though.* So I say who I am. I say: did she leave anything? And they say: not that they know of, no. So I say she must have. She said she would. Well eventually, after they see I'm getting wound up fast, raising my voice and the rest, they call her up, one of the girls does, the ribby Latino one, and she's glancing over at me while she's talking to Nathalie. Then finally I have the receiver in my hand and straight off I ask her about the phone. So she tells me where it is, in a Tesco bag in a white cupboard near reception. Then she goes: *Um, please don't . . . please don't call again.* Then hangs up. Hangs up on me. Not like I was going to call her anyway. Stupid bitch. Not like I'm desperate for a *phone buddy*. Or something. But she just said it. For no reason, like *please* don't call. Not *I'd rather you didn't*. Not *I'll call you when whatever* . . . Now I touch this black plastic, this thing for saying things that says nothing and that I'm not even sure how to use.

Once upon a time, as kids, we went to Somewhere-on-Sea, with Mum. We were small, and things were only half visible. We went to a fortune-teller. She had red hair. But maybe it was the candlelight. It was on the pier, some pier, and Mum gave her an object, a tiny gold pig, really old, too old to wear, too precious, that's why it was always in a hidden compartment of the labyrinth that was her handbag. So this fortune-teller, her perfume tickled my nose and I kept sneezing the whole time and Mum kept telling me to control it, but this fortune-teller told its history, the story of the pig, told it like she'd just watched it on the news. The gold pig from the man at the station in Paris, when they parted. For luck. And they had luck because a long time, a very long time, later, they met again. And were married. Mum listened to all this and when the fortune-teller asked a question – something like *does this story mean anything to you?* – Mum went: *yes, that's completely true . . . completely true . . .*

Anyway. Whatever. A black plastic phone, what does that say? Nothing. But it should, like anything. And it does. If I concentrate like a fortune-teller, it does. It says: *please don't call*, in a voice like a cartoon canary. Heart going *boom bitty boom*. Why Tweetie Pie, why shouldn't I call? *Because, um, because I tort I taw a puddy cat.* Oh yeah? Oh no! And who might that be my tiny feathered friend? *I-I-I, um, I c-cannot say.* You must! You must say! *It was* – It was *G-G-G-Georgio G-G-G-Georgianou* . . . Oh no! Oh no! *Y-Yes Y-Yes, the biggest baddest puddy cat in the land.* Is it really true little yellow canary? *Y-Yes, it's compleetely twoo . . .*

Yeah right. I go mental. Hot head. A sudden rush of anger, fizz of adrenalin. Like I'm *all set for the off.* I mean my adrenalin was rushing for days after I hit Davis. For days. Behind my eyes. I mean I walked out of Bosco's, walked down the street, all the way up Portobello, along the crowded, scuzzy pavements, over mashed vegetables, fruit skins, down Golborne, through sun, shade, past

a queue outside the Moroccan Advice Centre, along Kensal, and
so on, walked the whole way here, to school, stopped inside the
gate, looked in here, into Stan's office, a museum, figuring it all
out, did all of that, all of it, before this sudden rush. I can feel
it behind my eyes. Now footsteps behind and a *chuckle*. Hate
that word. But Stan does kind of *chuckle*. I turn, force a smile.
He's coming towards me, grey and shrunken but beaming with
big hands spread like some retired goalkeeper re-enacting one of
his favourite saves. Only Stan isn't even that old, late thirties, it's
just the way people see him that's made him old.

—Ain't nobody told you? he goes in this gentle voice, gently
piss-taking. Term's over . . .

I'm like gathering myself, trying a grin, apologising, *sorry Stan,
sorry to intrude*, like I'd been caught doing something, like I was
fourteen and caught.

—Whachoo done eh? he goes like I really was fourteen. 'Spec
you left soming behind in all that mindless violence they call
home time.

—Yep, I grin, not wanting to give him the whole spiel about
registers and addresses.

—We'll fetch it out then, won't we, he goes, shuffling past into
the office. Where's it to be?

—Staff room, I go, listening to his voice as if for the first time
and wondering why it doesn't match his things and whether all
voices are like that and don't match.

Stan picks a key off a peg without looking and we're walking
across the main yard with me asking some inane phoney question
about his holiday plans. He's saying something about his sister-
in-law having a cottage in Normandy or some place. *No phone*,
he's going, *middle of nowhere, nothing to lock*.

—What abou' you?

—Marking, I say.

Like all of us would say. Like we'd all been given the same
script. What kind of life spreads out from that word, from the
way it's said? I run through my holiday plans for him: maybe a

few of us driving to Ireland; maybe visit an American friend in New York; maybe fly down to Monte Carlo and play some cards with Omar Sharif's cousin. Lot of maybes as we go through the corridor towards the smaller yard, corridor smelling of damp wood, tables that were drenched after a pipe burst. Truth is, who knows now, about holidays? Don't even care now. Just have to seem to care. That's what marking is: seeming to care. So, because I can't think of anything else to say but feel I have to since he's doing me a favour, I tell him about needing to look at the register, and give some bullshit explanation about holiday projects, arrangements, and so on, which he doesn't really pay attention to until, unlocking the staff room, he hears the words *school play*.

—Talking of school plays, kid couple of days back, aggravating little so and so, fourth year . . . Only catch him with a knife don't I. Showing it off to his pals by the old toilets up there, you know, usual hang-out. Know what he said?

—Don't tell me, I say as I reach into the first of three cabinets for the register. He was bringing it in for the amnesty?

—Better. A real gem. I said to him I said whachoo doing with that knife son? And he goes, all smart, he says: *Mum give it me for the school play* . . .

Stan gets right into the role, leery body language, accent and everything.

—*Your mum give it you?* That's a good one I said. I said trouble is, there's only one school play a year and the last one was six months ago. He said: *Yeah, well, I'm rehearsin' for the next one.* I said how do you know the next one's gonna involve a knife? And he said, he goes: *I don't . . . but if it do I got the role covered innit . . . I mean . . . You know?*

—Yep . . .

—Took it off of him anyway. Obviously . . .

—Smart move . . .

I put on a wise smile as I'm copying out Burston's number and address, then Ridgecroft's and Witter's. Only I really am smiling, in a way, inside sort of thing. I mean, going down that list of *usual suspects*, I can't help it, I can't, and it's not even funny. It just isn't. Stan's been shuffling, leg to leg, waiting for me to finish and look up. When I do, he says:

—Never smart enough . . . Never enough.

—Nope . . . S'pose not.

I straighten up, ready to go. Stan the Man, he don't move.

—But in the end, he goes, they wake up . . .

Oh sure. Right. Bla bla. I love that kind of crap, that kind of *in the end* crap that people just come out with and call philosophy or experience or something that's easy to say because it's set in stone and there's nothing to think about. No decision to make. Because what the fuck, in the end, time will tell. Genius.

— . . . And by then it's too late . . .

—Book of Stan? I go, glancing at him, half a smile, gently taking the piss.

—Book of Life, goes Stan without a blink. Smart little bastards only get so smart before they start to get stupid again.

Well right, true enough. I mean, *my Mum give it me* is the kind of excuse that has a definite shelf-life. I mean, leave home, you're on your own. And on balance, the chances of getting smart instead of staying stupid are pretty slim. But the way Stan says it, the way the humour just kind of drains out of him, disappears, like it never existed, you just know something's got to him. All his *in the end* stuff is just his way of doing less each year, caring less and less, getting fewer and fewer cards and then none. Flatline zero. Nothing. *Can't remember the last time* . . . How much can you know of a life? Georgio wanted to show me something. So I could try to imagine the worst he could show me but what is the worst? What is the bit in the end before the zero? Then it occurs to me as Stan's locking the staff room behind me that I don't want to see this place again. Don't want to step inside that staff room again with its warm death in a tea mug, its teacher training poster (*nobody forgets a good teacher*), its on-the-blink photocopier responsible for a thousand last-second lesson plans, its safety net of paperwork, (*do the paperwork and your back's covered*), its teachers who are full of condolences before the shit's even happened. It's got RIP tagged all over it in 3-D aerosol green, all over everyone's mental landscape and that's the worst, that's the worst thing I could imagine. If I tried. Maybe this is all a bit dramatic, or a lot, and in its own way as bullshitty as Stan's Book of Life. Maybe it is. But I know I'm not coming back.

We walk back on our route, *the* route, back through the corridor, closed classrooms left and right and silence like some *ideal school* exhibition. Dennie once said he liked that silence. He meant the silence of being sent out of class and standing in the corridor while everyone was still inside, ordered silent. It's a good silence in its way but it's not this one. Then we're through the main yard, past the big silver duct and down to the gate along the only route, the eyes-closed route. The rest of life, that's just the miscellaneous bits.

Thank Stan, wish him a good one in Normandy. He says *cheer up luv it might never happen* without actually saying it. Now that has to be a special knack. Anyway. I walk off, turn to wave but the office is already deserted, its door still open, and he, Stan, Stan the Man, Stanley Knife, he's out, off on some job, some miscellaneous job or other, gone.

BULL AND GOAT

you'll have to make your tits bigger

Out in the deserted street, somewhere between the quiet trees, in among the parked cars, invisible, hidden by dark leaves reflected on his windscreen, is Georgio, sitting behind the wheel, waiting. I know he is. My hand folds around the phone. Like it was a gold pig. Like it was a weapon. Nathalie really got to me. I mean I walk down the street quickly then slowly, looking round at the cars, then pretending not to. That self-defence thing comes into my head, that thing about how you should always look back, turn round to face your attacker. Because you stand a better chance that way. Only turning round just happens to be the last thing you'd want to do. Anyway, besides, how's he going to follow me down a quiet street without looking *stoopid*? I'd see him. I'd know, wouldn't I?

Up the top of the street, where the brickwork runs out, marked by a letter box tagged with S:F4, I stop and wait, start to smoke. Then stand there like I'm looking for something in my bag, a letter. A good half-minute of pointless activity. Making sure nothing's coming. Can just see it though, can just hear the comments: *she ain't got nuffink be'er to do innit. Ain't got no boyfriend. Needs a good stuffin'. Straighten her out.* Or else: *there she is the crusty old goat, every day, standing round, always on the same corner, just staring, look, there she is now, lost in her handbag,*

125

sad loser, says she's being followed, mad bitch, keeps going on about her knickers ...

Feel better for it though, I mean when nothing happens, when nobody appears. Feel just the opposite though, I mean ten minutes later, standing in the Bull Bar on Portobello, drops of sweat running one at a time down my spine, waiting for this bar-jerk to answer my question which I've put to him twice now. He's polishing a glass extra slowly like he's a porn star paid to wank and too cool even to look at the camera. I followed Dennie here, walked his walk or think I did. The air is stuffy stale, fag ash old, too hot, and that angry heat starts to fill my head again. So I ask him a third time:

—Is Fergal around?

He holds the glass up to the light, the house light that shows up the Bull Bar for what it is, a glitz-hole, a mosh-pit, with tacky light rigs, tacky little dance floor, barely a pedestal, everything steel-grey, mirrored wherever possible, booths of black World of Leather sofas, metal spiral staircase leading to the VIP balcony. Yeah right. When bar-jerk has finished examining the glass, he puts it down, picks up a phone hooked to the wall next to rows of spirits.

—Fergal, someone down here to see you ... Eh? ... Dunno, she— ... Wants to know what you want ...

—Fergal.

—Yeah sugar but what's it— ... Yeah? ... yeah ... yeah ok, he goes hanging up. He's coming down anyway ...

Then he pulls another glass and starts polishing it like he's been snubbed. And I see Dennie walking up to the bar, up to this same creep. Dennie's in his *big-night-out* gear, silk shirt, gold chain, and maybe those mock croc Seventies shoes he said he was going to buy but that I never saw. And he's with Nats and her girlfriend. *Dennie plus two* at the door. Because sure the Bull Bar's got pretensions, you're either guest-listed or it's a long wait, *discretion of the management* type of thing, then a tenner, and no trainers or anything else the doorman doesn't take a shine to. The

Bullshit Bar. And I see Dennie: everyone's friend, *buddy buddy* with Fergal. Dennie: *so generous with coke*, a real high roller. Dennie: the Big Cheese, the ornamental McCherry with the reserved balcony spot. Dennie: *smoova den smoov*, as Burston once described himself. Yeah right, Dennie, super-smoov, impressing scores of Nathalies, envied by *geezers* and *righ' cunts*. In facts, out-cunting all cunts. *Dennie*, did you say? Did you say *Dennie*? Dennie *who*? Some guy I never even met. Never knew. Never saw. Wasn't even there cos *Ah was home wiv ma muvver watchin' Bruce Lee video innit*. I mean, who is he, my brother? Who is he, in the end?

Out of some corner door with a red-lettered sign, MANAGE-MENT – PRIVATE, swings Fergal. He's tall, like six plus, skinny, pockmarked but proud of it, like the marks spell HARD BASTARD in shades of raw red. And being so tall, Fergal's spent too much time looking down at the world to think of himself as anything but superior. He takes his time walking over to me, aware of the click of his pointed black boots in the silence of a place that's usually jiggling breasts with sub-bass. He looks me up and down, then up again. Leans in like he's going to inspect my gums and teeth. Then sits on a bar stool, feet still on the floor and still looking down at me.

—If you're looking for a job, he goes, strong Irish accent, you'll have to make your tits bigger . . .

I suppose he thinks these are *strong words softly spoken* or whatever kind of beery TV crap. Bar-jerk sniggers, picks up a broom and heads off towards the booths with the big joke repeating in his head, I can tell.

—Lucky I'm not looking for a job then.

—Well if you're looking for a *shift*, if you know what I mean, you're not my type.

—Matter of fact I'm looking for Dennie. You know him right?

—If you say so.

—I was wondering if you'd seen him . . .

—Get your top off and I'll tell you.

—Bye.

127

And I'm walking. I only take a couple of steps.

—You related to the prat?

—Take your pants down and I'll tell you.

—Yeah I thought there was a family resemblance. Hard luck. If I was him I'da chopped myself up and buried myself in my neighbour's back garden. Maybe even left my organs in a hospital wheelie bin so's I'd be of some use. Leastways save someone else doing it . . .

—Right . . . So?

—So? So fuckin' what?

Say nothing. Not a word. I can feel it coming. I can feel I don't know, something, coming. The canister of pepper spray crosses my mind but my hand's full of mobile phone. Him, he just stares at me.

—You know where he is?

—Dennie? Huh, he grunts, Try looking in a skip.

—Oh . . . Is that better than a back garden?

—You fuckin' Jews, goes Fergal quite blandly as he sparks a Marlboro and blows smoke if not exactly in my face then near enough.

Say nothing. Stare back into his watery blue eyes ringed in grey and black and blended into red pits. Nice. Say fuck all.

—Till recently . . . Till just recently, I thought Dennie was black. Funny that. Not like some jungle affie but, you know, like he had a bit of nig in him, a dose of coon, mixed race or some fuckin' thing. Mixed up, as it turns out. The blacks I can deal with. You know where you stand with all those Yardie homeboy nigger superstars. Mean they're just fuckin' wannabe popstars. And most of 'em shit 'emselves at the first sign. But the Jews are a fuckin' pain . . . Specially them that's got no tits . . .

Say fuck all. But I can feel myself looking like Nats, frozen, or pissy wet with fear, a deer, a canary, never mind goat. Fergal's having a good time though. Better and better. Say fuck all. And let the steam rise.

—So, he goes taking a deep drag, I find out Jewboy is cutting my fuckin' gear about the same time I find out Jewboy is a Jewboy. And they cut everything don't they, the Jews . . . Fact, they even cut their money . . . You know why there're no Jews in Belfast? Wouldn't fuckin' last. Belsen's a day out at the farm next to Divis Street in the old days . . . Should stick a Jew in a sniper-proof box on Divis Street. Know what I mean? Just so's everyone'd know how bad things could be. They'd soon stop complaining about them left-footed Orange cunts . . .

He flicks the butt with his thumb. Flakes of ash spiral down to the floor.

—Now run along Miss Marple . . . Oh, and do yourself a favour: save up for some silicone.

Fergal turns a second towards the bar, actually towards his reflection in it. When he makes eye-contact with himself, that's when I bring the blunt end of the mobile down on his left eyelid, hard as I fucking can. Hoping for the best, whatever that is. Fergal, well, he gargles, and the cigarette falls out of his hand, and he doesn't budge, like not an inch, and he says *Jesus* two, three times but quietly, same voice, blandly, before his hand goes up to his closed eye, his closed eyes, slowly, as if for a scratch. I feel my face all twisty-mouthed with cruelty and feel ashamed straight away, then feel like carrying on, and I try to pick up one of the bar stools. I actually try to pick it up to I don't know, don't ask, *hurl* it through the bar or something but it's so heavy, way too heavy, iron or something, massive. So, well, I don't. All twisty-mouthed and beaty-hearted like a child throwing one, a tantrum, I stand there. That's what I'm like. For a deep second. And then I think I'll run out of the place before anyone can kill me. Actually, not *think*. I know I do. I run.

THE RIDGE

my buzz

I'm sitting by the canal watching plastic bags float by. Again. Call it bag therapy. Behind me is the chimney of an old pottery. Behind that, a low-rise block like a brown bunker, and behind that, Trellick. I was too self-conscious to run very far. Like just out the door, into the street. Portobello glanced up then carried on like it was nothing, *nu'in really*. People glanced up at me a second, seeing fear in my face, unusual alertness that people automatically take to be criminal alertness, which puts them right on edge, makes them look round, ready to run, duck, dive, disappear or stand stupid, inert, staring, craning, witnessing. That look turned high tail into low profile. But it's funny, embarrassment taking over from fear, I mean like I was too self-conscious to run for my life. You know? *Women ain't got no sense of danger innit.*

One summer, another summer, this boy at school had a bee on his sleeve. This was at another school, mine, I mean when I was at school. The teacher was late and the bee was right on the edge of the boy's sleeve about to crawl on to his hand. He had his arm held out, as far away from his face as he could, because of course he was shitting himself. Couldn't move. Around him, a crowd. The whole class stared, arse-lickers, swots, tearaways, braggers, bullies, victims, all wide-eyed, fascinated, shitted too, on

131

his behalf. On their behalf. Nobody could move. Nobody could
do anything. Because they were all too busy imagining the same
terrible consequences of doing something. The sting of the bee.
Or worse, the bee loose, zubbing mad, bouncing off desk-lids,
coming after them with the words *this time it's personal*. So they
stood there holding their breaths, stopping their hearts, cancelling
all old scores, debts, payback threats as the bee crawled closer and
closer to flesh. Me, I didn't feel the danger. I wasn't scared. I know
everyone says that, said that, afterwards but, fact is, I knew what
to do. I did. Even had the ruler in my hand to do it with, to flick
the bee off. Simple. Only I didn't do anything. Didn't do a thing
because I was too self-conscious. It was a lot easier to just kind of
conform to everyone else's fear. Just be afraid like everyone else.
Like who's going to jump the queue to the gates of horror? Then
the teacher came back, figured it all out in a God-like split second,
flicked the bee off with a ruler. Bee flew right out the window and
we all had to sit down and shut up. And feel stupid. So much so
everyone paid attention for the next hour and a half. Respect the
Saviour.

Anyway. I blended in with the flow of traffic, the trails of
criss-crossing pedestrians and got more para than ever. Kept
stopping, looking round, starting off again, staring hard at anyone
who so much as glanced, stared to keep the abuse and chair legs
flying in my direction. Only thing that keeps me real is the need
to go the loo. But I can't go home just yet. Not till I calm down.
So I sit by the canal. Best thing. Watch the bags. And I almost
phone Mum. Think of her with her man. Think of her happiness.
That's why I don't phone. All that nervy energy, shivery kind of
sweat, sunlight on the water, makes me want to go to the loo
even more.

We all went back to mine last night, watched a video. Yeah
right, suddenly the TV was *my* TV. Alv just picked it up, put
it the same place the old one used to be. Covered up the space
I hadn't even cleaned since before it happened. And there it was,
my TV. I cooked. Sabine wanted Italian-style. So it was pasta and

a sauce of tomatoes, courgettes, prawns, pesto, olives, and salad and wine and stuff from Ootie's which everyone really liked. They all loved the video too. *Pulp Fiction*. Me and Alv hadn't seen it. Marcus and Sabine wanted to see it again. They all loved it. Loved the *royale with cheese* stuff and the *big kahuna burger* and the Samuel L. Jackson evangelical gangster trip and the adrenaline shot to the heart and the rednecks with the gimp and so on. A whole list of things. I hated it. All except the bit where Bruce Willis escapes from the boxing match he's supposed to throw and is sitting in the cross-town cab with the night flashing in his eyes, on the lam from the mob. The rest I hated like I hate fast food, the way it creeps into your life till it's as regular as a habit, as a list, as a diet. *Same old*. Same old regular fries and a regular Coke for the regular hit. Dose of salt 'n' sugar for the people. And the film, it was a dose a minute.

Anyway. Whatever. I go home, to the toilet, pee like a goat, and go into this *denial* phase where nothing really is happening, where there's nothing really to think about, didn't see nothing, wasn't there, how would I know? Could phone parents. B's and R's and C's and W's. But the right words haven't formed in my head, the right words to mothers generally. And eventually I know I'll run into one or other of the Flying Four anyway. Which is just a way of doing nothing in the meantime. So I mark their projects instead, their stories, to take my mind off my own.

Write a story entitled My Buzz. The first one, an Anson brother football-hero story, I only get a paragraph into. Same old. Like he'd written the whole thing on ten tins of Tango. Like his mum sticks him in a room with a crate of fizzy sugar and doesn't let him out till he's done: *Then I got the ball again and scored another one* . . . Six pages.

So I go through the rest looking for any signs of the Stanky Massive. Not long before I find Ridgecroft's story book decorated in heavy biro with two-dozen Stanky logos. I flip through and find his two pages of crossing out. Ridgecroft is one of those people who always covers himself with loads of artistic crossing out just so he

133

can deny almost anything. *Tha' ain't wha' I wrote miss no way. I been framed* ... Anyway, these stories are meant to reveal stuff:

I am with the crew and we are looking for the baddest buzz. We already have done so many mad things but there is always one more activity to beat the one we done before. We call it performing. But when we cant think of nothing new we go back to the one special thing that is called surfing. It is the lick. Surfing is when you get on a train and go somewhere but it is not like paying the man for it because we never do. What it is is getting on a train without paying. We cant pay even if we wanted because of the money. Nobody is supposed to see us getting on the train so you have to ambush it at a special place that only we know that is down by Elkstone Road signal box. We have tagged the place which means writing our crew logo on it by a tool box next to the line. This is because everyone will know that they cannot mess with our place. It is our lifestyle. Surfing is a dangerous thing because you get electrified by the line if you step on the electric one. It can kill you. So far I have never stepped on it. I am extra careful. We sneak down by the line because the train stops there. There is a red light, that is why it stops. When it stops we bush the train which is called ambushing. Then we all come out from behind the tool box. It is a mega tool box not like an ordinary one so we cant be seen. So we get on between the carriages and the people in the train dont see us because we are out of sight under them. Then the light turns to green. When I am waiting for it to turn green that is when my guts get going and I start to sweat even when it is freezing. The train starts with a big shove and you got to be ready otherwise you fall off. Then we climb up on the roof but you need real guts to climb up and half the crew dont do it because they are chicken. But I can handle it. You have to hold on as strongly as you can because the wind comes right at you and can get into your gear which blows up like a balloon and makes you lose control. The wind is the most powerful thing. It is full on so you cant stand up, you lie down flat like paper. The train gets faster and faster and faster. When I am on top it is the wickedest buzz and if someone says it isnt the wickedest buzz it is because they have not surfed the roof. Stealing things is a buzz as well but not the same as surfing because you dont die even if they catch you. You get more respect if you surf than when you steal but if Dad finds out about the stealing which I dont do no more he gets more mental than with surfing. But he cant stop us from doing it. Nobody can. It is my buzz. It is the ...

There's another line or two but they're impossible to read. So it ends in the middle of a sentence like that's the point Ridgecroft fell off the train. Anyway. Whatever. Stuff like this kills me. Sit there in a daze listening to a distant toilet fill. Stare at the answering machine, messages blinking. Think again about phoning Mum. But Mum has a tendency to scream *watch out*, no matter what, even if I am just sitting watching TV.

So I press playback instead. Marcus tells me how much he enjoyed last night. Then three messages from Sabine. They range from *check me back soon as you get in ...* to *babes you be'er come round Alv's righ' now ...*

ROUND ALV'S

the silent majority

Sabine leaves Alv's address, ground floor on Ridley Road just up by Willesden Junction, ten minutes, so I go round. And Sabine opens the door with a look on her face, all eyebrow to say the least, like I'd mislaid Miles somewhere while babysitting. So I ask her, nothing else I can do though I feel straight away that I don't want the answer, I ask her what's happened. She folds her arms, turns round and walks down the corridor, turns in to the front room. For a second I'm alone in Alv's corridor with rows of deformed cactus plants down both sides against dark walls like the Kew Gardens of hell. Then I follow Sabine's steps. Crashed out in a black leather armchair by the bay window is Alv. The whole room's dark and light. Like only Alv's silhouette's visible with the late-afternoon sun streaming in through Venetian-type blinds from behind him. Say *hi Alv* as I squint to try to see his face. He says nothing. Sabine says nothing. She's still got that look and her whole body language is telling me to go closer. So I step closer to Alv, still squinting, until I can see him properly. *Shit*, I mutter, *Alv . . . what happened?* Or words to that effect. I mean his bottom lip is split down the middle, swollen like a purple bladder. And his face is all puffed up below both eyes. Still he says nothing which makes the whole thing

137

really heavy and knots my throat. I suppose I ask the same thing again only audibly because, next thing, Sabine's laying into me:

—Wha' d'you *think* happened? *Look* at him. Thass cos o' *you* babes. Thass cos you're *interferin'* in stuff—

—'Bine—

—No Alv it's true. You've been goin' on for months pissin' everyone off. This ain't just abou' this it's everythin', your whole attitude. This is just wha' happens when you go round doin' stuff you shouldn't be doin'.

—What've I done? What happened?

—Cee, wha' d'you *think* happened?

—Fuck *I* don't know. Tell me.

—*You* goin' round the Bull Bar makin' trouble with Fergal thass wha'.

—'Bine, goes Alv wincing and slightly slurred, leave it hon.

—No way Alv. This has go'a stop. Cee—

—Wha' has? Wha' happened? Alv—

—You wanna know wha' happened? I'll tell you: Fergal gets smacked in the face by some stupid bitch and straigh' off's bellin' up Georgio who's s'posed to be sortin' out this same stupid bitch's brother. Georgio ain't too hot when it comes to figurin' things. Georgio, he'll just—

—What's Alv got to do—

—Thass wha'm tellin' you girl. Georgio's s'posed to be sortin' out all the dollars Dennie's run up left an' righ' innit. Righ'? Thass wha' you said. Righ'? Trouble is, wha'ever Georgio likes to make out he ain't the one with the biggest shoe size on the street y'na mean babes an'—

—But wha'—

—*Wha' wha'*? Cee, you go'a stop all this *now*. Today. Righ'?

—'Bine's righ' na mean. Ain't nobody gonna give you life insurance you carry on like this.

—They know you now. They *know* you. An' it's righ' on your doorstep. Didn't tha' click with you? Georgio already thinks you're all cushty with Alv an' he don't like it. I mean he don't even like it on a *personal level*.

—Is righ'. Issa personal ting.

—Never mind business. It's go'a stop . . .

—Fuck's sake . . . I just still don't get what I'm supposed to've done. So I hit that fuckin' racist pig but you should've heard—

—It ain't abou' nothin' he said wha'ever he said. Iss abou' you bein' there first place. *Messin'.* Iss abou' Alv who used to work the door there way back. Before any of this. Him an' Fergal ain't exactly sisters. An' him an' Georgio ain't for def.

—Na mean . . .

—An' there you go bustin' in all over an' doin' stuff thass way dafter than Dennie. Pro'ly just as well he ain't—

There Sabine stops dead and there's this dreadful silence. Maybe like the silence after falling off a train and hearing the train trail off like the conversation, disappear like a life. I take in Alv's place just to look at something, think about something else. Everything's in black. Black metal. Black wood. Stereo rack, speakers, TV, lights, furniture, blinds, everything like a kit, like equipment, male.

—Alv . . . look . . . I'm sorry if—

—If? *If?* Cee it ain't abou'—

—'Bine shush . . . Cee, it ain't your fault. Geor—

—Alv I'm—

—'*Bine shush* . . . Ain't down to you Cee, really it ain't. Georgio . . . guy's a one-punch merchant. Been scopin' round for an excuse since time innit. Should know him by now. Thass him. Like if someone tell him to unload a gun he's gonna unload it by *firin'* it. Na mean. Thass his brain. The Fergal ting go way back tellin' you. You go'a be careful. Serious . . . Georgio's ge'in pressure an' if he's ge'in it he's gonna be givin' it. Sooner la'er na'm sayin'. His case iss *monkey get monkey give.* Me, wha' can I say? My placin' an' timin' was all wrong. Bu'm bouncin' back trust me. Long as you ain't—

—Alv, Alv I still don't—

—Cee I can't believe it. You go'a—

—'Bine *shush* . . . Fix me an ice-pack hon . . . please . . .

Sabine goes off to the kitchen giving me a long dirty look though I keep my eyes down and don't even try to return it. Alv waits till she's out of earshot.

— . . . Iss abou' me an' G much as any other ting. We used to work the door same time way back. An' the Bull Bar is just one them places nobody trust nobody. You know? Yuppie bar staff don't know nu'in. Issall down to the door. You get a loada titty girls come down . . . sorry yeah bu' y'na'm sayin'? Like bra, panty, mobi, wraps an' disco powder innit.

—Yeah yeah . . .

—They get straigh' in, rubbin' up all the door staff an' all. Then you get a blackhead crew, five six *Tommy soldiers*, an' you *know* they ain't ge'in in. Policy innit. Fergal reckons they's all *niggers with attitude*, out to cause ructions innit. So thass where the needle start. Plus Georgio's skinnin' all the featherweights with the pat-downs. Innit. They leave a dollar in their pocket, he skank it. I ain't *functionin'* on tha' level. I mean like I didn't mind bein' *approached* or nu'in. Goes with the turf na mean. Nice honies all over, my eyes on springs, my wood achin', thass the game. Bu' the rest . . . I mean any *ting* could go off yeah? Bound to go off. Tenner, Friday nigh' an' two free drinks . . . gimmick like tha' an' soon firms is showin' up, checkin' down the people an' iss all glass in there. Should be servin' up in placky cos glass is askin' for it. One merchant green-eyein' some other merchant's titty girl. Is all it takes an' the glass is flyin'. Add to it we all got shit radios. *Never* workin' bwoy. So if somin' go down you can't call in backup. Innit. So . . . one nigh' somin' went down. Some ragga star firin' lick shots into the ceilin' na mean. An' some guy caught one. Fifty people like *righ' there* an' nobody saw nu'in. Ain't into tha' *silent majori'y nonsense*. Ain't righ'. Guy bleedin' up the floor, dyin' all over. Titty girls screamin'. Georgio, he's usin' the ruction to cover hisself. Skankin' the people. Bags, everyting. So he's smart. So he's fast. *Big-timer* innit. *Bloodclat* Fergal he don't care, he just want the take an' no closedown. Only it ain't the way it happen tha' nigh'. 'Pon hearin' the gunshot the place drain like a bath. Then Fergal he's orderin' me to shift the guy outside, na mean shift the body *before* the bulls show, make like it all happened on the *outside*. Me I ain't shiftin' *nu'in*. Fergal's cussin' me righ' off. Everyone is gettin' vex up, arguin' in the office 'bou' wha' to do. So in the end G done it. Squeezed a wedge ou'a Fergal *for* doin' it. Things settle a while. Start the clear-up. Then, *lo an' behold*, come the anonymous phone call to the cops. Na'm sayin'. Half hour la'er ... Man, tellin' you, vanloads come down. They screw the place down like a coffin for three month. All laid off. And guess who gets fingered yeah for the call? *Yours truly*. Thass where the needle *continue*. Rest is history.

Not yet it ain't, I'm thinking. I mean, it's a Friday night story, you'd have to say, I mean, it's Friday night and it's just a story. I mean what does all this make sense of? For me? What's this all say? To me? I look down at my hands a second not to look at Alv's lip. Then I go:
—Was it you then? The call I mean ...

Alv looks down at the coffee table where smoking stuff is scattered as well as a CD with finger-lickin' coke streaks on it. He pulls a king size blue Rizla and crumbles some sticky skunk into it, starts to roll it into a long, thin cone.
—So ... Was it?
—Nah, as it goes ... It wasn't ... Bu' same difference na mean. All I'm sayin' is you cannot mess no more with them people. You tink Georgio's the boss, meet Fergal. Tink iss Fergal, meet Mister X ... You get me?

Sabine's come back by now and she's been standing at the door, juggling an ice-pack, listening in silence, giving me the silent treatment. So I say kind of to both of them and hoping it's the last word:
—You know why I've been—
—Cee you wouldn't be doin' none of it if you just *waited*—
—'Bine, leave the girl be.
—She's go'a understand.

141

—I do.

—You don't. No way do you. You're way off track babes ...

Then silence again and I'm thinking it's time to be going but can't think of an excuse straight off or anything for that matter.

—Cee, says Sabine staring at me.

—What?

—Cee ... Wha' d'you do with tha' phone? Dennie's phone tha' you were goin' on abou', wha' d'you do with it?

—The phone? I say taking a deep breath and knowing something in that second, something new, entirely new, a taste like the taste of a lie before you've told it. Didn't do anything with it ...

—You've still got it?

—Yeah I've got it. But it's ... not working. Was busted anyway. Even more busted after Fergal's head. That's what I cracked him with.

—I'da shelled out to be there y'na mean, goes Alv with a pained grin.

Even Sabine lets her arse down a bit.

—Good, she says. I'm glad it's busted.

She sparks up Alv's spliff that he's left lying in a black metal ashtray. Alv gets to his feet slowly and goes:

—Want a drink, smoke, somin'?

—Nah it's ok man I've ... I—

—Sure?

—Yeah ... Gimme a hug or something ...

So we embrace with the low sun still coming through between chimneys but the room settled in grey where the light and dark have merged, and he pats me on the back, pats me and tells me it's all ok.

—Ain't lost my smile or nu'in ...

—That would've been some loss, I say which is cheesy I know but anyway I can't think of anything else. See you later maybe. You coming tomorrow?

—Yeah babes ... Course ...

—Why don't you come round for a bite on Wednesday. I—

142

—I'll check you tomorrow, goes Sabine giving me a quick kiss and avoiding my eyes ... Cee wait ... Alv, should she be goin' on her own? I mean—

—Yeah iss ok. Ain't Fergal's style ...

—It is Georgio's though innit. Beat up his ex-wife an' everythin'.

—Tha' was in his drinkin' days.

—Serious, you think—

—Sabine ... It's alright. I'll be ok ... Seriously. *La'ers babes* ...

—Easy Cee, goes Alv.

Easy. Whatever. I walk back the very long short walk to nowhere.

LIFT SHAFT

three hundred and eighty-three steps

Trellick's lobby, a kind of stained-glass psychedelic church, is warm in winter, cool in summer. That's one of the two reasons the old guy always sits there. The other is he waits for the lift. He's the kind of old guy you only recognise by his hat. It's the kind of hat you only recognise if it's got the old guy underneath. Bob doesn't actually wait for the lift. He waits for the people coming out of it. Every time the doors open, it's like flipping a channel. But Bob says it's better than the tele because with the tele you know exactly what you're going to get whatever time you switch on. Whereas with the lift you don't. Could be sitcom, slapstick, fly-on-the-wall, sex. Could be anything. Lucky dip. Laugh or cry. So Bob's often there. He sits there mostly when he's not having something replaced. Trouble is he has stuff replaced as often as he sits there. Recently it was a hip. Before that, can't remember, lung or leg or something. First thing he says to me, deadpan as a sage at a crossroad:

—Three hundred an' eighty-three steps. Maybe more cos I never counted 'em.

So I know there's fuck-all point in pressing buttons. The first forty fifty stairs are easy. It's when you start coming across bones, human remains, empty plastic bottles of water and *may God forgive*

145

fingernailed on the wall in blood that you realise you should've stocked up at Ootie's before setting out. Well whatever. I'm saying it's a long climb that's only bearable in silence. But there's always voices above, below. Up above, way up, a couple of guys are laughing. Before them, between seven and eight, I catch up with a mother, Mrs Ferenc, Hungarian, and her girl, both wide as corridors, one behind the other, with a speed limit of one step a minute, one every two minutes for the girl who's getting left behind. If they get close enough together I could tunnel through their arses.

—Zis vill kill me, she goes, letting me squeeze through.

I carry some of their shopping up to twelve and leave it by the door. Should've done my shopping. The down trip is always worse. Really. Kills the knees, turns them to jelly after a few flights.

The two guys are closer now, practically close enough to hear what they're saying if it wasn't for the echo. Split second later the stairwell is hit with a flute solo. Below me the mother's shouting, her girl's screaming. Me I've got my fingers in my ears. Fluteboy Gaj: the world's his stage, any stairwell's his rehearsal studio, and any sad loser in earshot's his tough shit audience. Still, it's jazz right. He's almost the whole way through the solo, whatever solo, Greensleeves, Coltrane, with a few other bits thrown in, when he appears a flight above with some guy behind.

He stops right there, still playing, looking me in the eye like some serenading fiddler in a Benidorm paella joint. Yeah I've been there. Nas even bought the red rose off the fiddler's sidekick. He'd won a free trip in a competition. Anyway. I have to obey, put my life on pause and let Gaj finish. Only there's never an end to a solo. The guy taps him eventually and Gaj depuckers his suckers.

—Fanfuckintastic acoustics. Should get some of the guys up here for a jam.

—Really? Could turn in to a *dead musicians on the staircase* mystery.

—Yeah ok, he laughs as he, they, come down. Like a parallel universe up here innit.

—With you as the Pied Piper.

—Fried Piper more like. Tryina get my head straight for tomorrow . . . This is Carl. Carl Cee . . . You're neighbours. Almost . . .

Carl seems to wince.

—Yeah, I'm on twenty-one, he says like it was some kind of designer-drug habit.

—Right, I smile back, thinking how you could live forever, I mean here, and never see certain people, never know a thing about them, see others all the time, know too much. And looking at Carl, ponytailed with a tuft of beard sticking out of his chin, I'm thinking this must be the guy from the parallel universe. So Carl, I go, you know Dennie . . .

—Know him? goes Gaj. People say they share DNA.

—Wha' people? goes Carl.

—No serious, goes Gaj putting his paw round Carl, Carl's drummin' tomorrow . . .

—At the Slice?

—Yeah, says Carl looking down at all the interesting bits of the stairs.

—Yeah he's taking over from Rodger the Bodger whose counting only goes up to *one and* . . . Innit Carl . . .

—Yeah.

—But since we're on the subject, I go'a tell you Cee, we got a new bass as well. I mean sorry but Dennie, he ain't been in touch so . . . Wha' can you do? You know? We had to sort out another—

—Yeah, well, I thought—

—But if he shows, no prob yeah. *Why I'll drag the udder guy outside and break his chord fingers wid a ratchet.* Mean the other guy can't even *walk* the bass. Innit Carl.

—Don't swing, goes Carl.

—Don't swing the guy. *Useless.* Dennie he swing like a jungle vip. Any case, knowing D he'll make a last-minute guest appearance. *Laydees and gents, tonight for your exclusive listening pleasure we have* . . . You know, just like on his own birthday that time. Remember? Keep the audience in suspenders innit.

—Well I'll be there to see it.

—Nice. I'll stick you on the door otherwise it's three squids.

—Thanks.

—An' a plus one.

—Yeah thanks.

—An' a free drink.

—Oh sure.

—Hey listen . . . Cee, got this sax right, I mean it *was* D's, goes Gaj taking off an army-style kitbag and pulling out the same old dented sax he was trying to palm off at Slack. So, you know, he should really be the one to, you know, *take charge* of the thing. An' I mean, since he ain't been . . . I mean, I *could* sell it . . .

—You mean you tried and couldn't. So what is this, a *sale or return* scheme?

—Nice. But no, ain't that . . . I mean it's just about *balancing* things out, returning gear to *rightful* owners an' all that.

—Nah look, seriously, I've already had enough hooky gear flying my way this week.

—Oh yeah? Cee *Superfence*. Jesus I didn't know you were in business. Everyone needs a good fence innit. They should provide one if you're on Social. Invite me round and we'll talk turkey.

—Fix the lift, I say putting my foot on the next step, and I'll think about it.

—No wait, Cee, you don't get it, goes Gaj lowering his voice, The beauty of this sax is: *it ain't hooky*. It's D's. It's bona fide goods. It's pure *property* with a capped up P. An' if it's D's it's Cee's, no catches, no small print, it's in holy braille for the blindest sinner. Let there be peace in the Middle East.

—Your flute solo was better. I mean come on, wasn't it—

—Nah, no, course not. That was all just gab an' chirp . . . Telling you, teefs are the *vainest* people on the planet. Always biggin' themselves up an' dissin' other people's modus. Almost as bad as musicians.

He nudges Carl who nods, grins, goes *yeah right*.

—You know? There you go. It's the gospel. As Allah is my witness. As Mohammed hitch-hiked to the mountain. My parachute failed to open one time but here I am. Trust me. Peace in the East. Here, take it. It's D's. 'Sides, worst comes you can always pawn it.

—For two ninety-nine.

—Least a fiver ... Or you could hand it in.

—Right an' ask for thirty other offences to be taken into consideration.

—You're a kidder but it's yours anyway. Here ... Go on ...

Gaj holds out the sax and I take it. He knew I would. Carl standing there's making me nervous, making me think the whole time about where my computer ended up, where it all ended up. And fucking *knowing*, like you do, when you know. But I don't know how to deal with it. It's the Nat factor. The deer factor. The *what to do* thing. The not wanting to look too closely at Carl to see the truth whatever it is. The truth, for instance, that if Dennie took my things, if he *stole* them, *if* he stole them, then it was the least of his stealings, the least of his takings and his doings, whatever they were, are. So I take the sax, not because Gaj is so funny or because I can't handle looking. Not because of these things. Not because I believe. God forbid. I take it because it's the next thing, the thing that takes me, like any object with a history, somehow closer. Me to Dennie. Cee to D.

MARCUS

your nose is so cute

First thing, I put the sax in the cupboard where Dennie's bass was. There's another message from Marcus asking me if I got the first message. He says he'll come by. He says it's on his route back from the stereo shop where he works via his flat which is *just round the corner* and that he's in the car anyway so it's no problem. I dial 1471 to get the number of the shop to tell him not to come but they say he's already left. A while later, he does come by. He says he had to stop on the twelfth for a smoke just to get his wind back and got shouted at in some language or other by some huge woman. I want to say actually I'm busy and that I need to be on my own or whatever but he puts a bottle of wine on the table and says: *I'll get some food together.* He knows this is a tough offer to refuse. To make it more difficult to say no, he says things like: *baby your nose is so cute.* And he touches the stud in my nose with his finger.

Then when he's pouring the wine he says things like: *I'm a terrible driver*, as if to let me know how sensitive he is. He'll be the *first to admit it*, he says as he's cutting vegetables, that he's a *really bad* driver. He says he's had more than one crash that was clearly his fault. Marcus says most guys think they're good drivers, even that they're the *best* drivers. Marcus says a lot of guys have

Nick Barlay

false confidence in their abilities. Marcus says that when you've been taken down a peg or two, like he has with his driving, especially after the time when he put it into reverse by accident, you come to understand that, after all, as a guy, *you ain't all that.*

After dinner, Marcus reads from his diary. He reads me a dream he says he had about me. He says he doesn't usually read from his diary. He says it's very personal and that's why he doesn't. He almost says *but baby you're the only one.* Almost. Then he reads me this dream about how his semen flew to me one night, across the city, how it just found its way to me but not on public transport or anything. What Marcus reads out doesn't make me feel better even though he asks me if it does. Marcus asks me if I can figure out the meaning of the dream. I say no. I mean I'm not exactly desperate to interpret it. I mean, if it all boils down to sex and death then flying semen is pretty much in the ball park, right? Marcus says he *thinks* he understands it. He reckons it has to do with *an unconscious desire to, like, transmit his genes.* He asks me if I've ever thought about babies. I say it's tough juggling babies and a career. And he goes: *yeah I understand, you're really committed.* And I go: yeah, I am. So I ask him if he's thought about babies. And he says he's *not like ready at the moment* but he's *really good with kids and always loves other people's and would probably make a really good dad.* He says something along these lines only longer.

After sex, Marcus says things like: *I really meant it when I said your nose is cute.* Marcus says that if all women obsess about one particular bit of themselves then with me it isn't going to be my nose. This sounds like the beginning of a long guessing game to discover the bit I do obsess about. So I tell him no, in fact it is my nose that I obsess about.

Smoking a spliff, Marcus says things like: *I've still got the video receipt from the other night.* I ask him if he always keeps stuff like that. He says he does. He says he keeps all that kind of stuff in a box because *it's always funny to kind of look back.* He says a relationship is like a *rolling programme of events* and that if you collected all the tickets, cinema tickets, theatre tickets,

152

airline tickets, laundry tickets, restaurant bills, postcards, beer mats, tokens from machines, stubs from museums that you go to in foreign countries, if you collected all these as well as like matchbooks from bars, hotel brochures, maybe napkins of the sort that have names on them, if you got all these together, in a box, it would be better than having someone's CV in front of you. It would *really show what someone was really like*.

I ask Marcus if he knows anything about mobile phones and if he does could he see what numbers have been stored in the one I have. Marcus says he may be an unreliable driver but he's good with technology. I wash up while he takes the numbers off the phone. *Should charge it up*, he says. And a few other technical *shoulds*. I wash up and try to show no interest in the phone.

After I've washed up, we smoke another spliff looking out of the window. Marcus says stuff like: *the view is amazing but you're too high to actually see anything. You can't see the people, who they really are. You can only kind of trace the routes of cars at night when they've got their lights on.* Then he touches my nose again. *Everything gets hidden by the view*, he says. We watch this old black and white film, *The Samurai*, with Alain Delon playing an assassin. Marcus says the best bit is at the end when this girl walks along the Metro platform chewing gum. Marcus says she's the coolest thing in the film, even though she's just a walk-on. But she appears in the credits, kind of immortalised as *La jeune fille au chewing gum*. Marcus says she's me.

I put the sax in the cupboard exactly where Dennie's bass was. I put it there hoping, in a way, that if they, whoever, come back, they'll know where to look, nothing hidden, they'll just know where to look to steal the fucking thing. Because it'll be on the thief's route. Just like Marcus is on my route. *La jeune fille au chewing gum* walking down along the platform. Somehow unavoidable. But looking at these numbers, I know I'm about to step off my route to who knows where. What more can I say about Marcus? He falls asleep before me.

NIGHT BEFORE

still dark

From the moment the lights are out I know I won't sleep even though all I want is to sleep. Right through tomorrow. Wake up when things are all back to how they were before. Whenever that was. But I'm wide awake. Too wide awake with lists of names going through my head: Albigheri, Anson James and Jonathan, Bolam, Brightman, Burston, Clarke, Felton, Fredericks, Hammond, Karmesh, Lazaros, Leighton, and so on down to Witter. Then other names: Nathalie, Cee, Gaj, Carl, Rocko, Georgio, Amanda, Chantelle, Fergal, Collette, Roger, Soper, Sabine, Nicole and Eugene, JJ, Oz, Marv, Joe and so on like a magical mystery tour of Dennie's head, like his life was spilled out in front of me, like it was open like a box with all the tickets you ever got from anywhere. Better than a CV.

Or worse. In an interview when they ask you about stuff on your CV you go *oh yes that's right*, you grin, you nod, you confirm every fact, you deny nothing. Go down Dennie's list there'd be nothing but denials. Wasn't me, wasn't there, don't know him. *There was too much smoke coming out of the gun to see a fucking thing, officer.* Maybe the list of names is exactly like a CV in that it really says fuck all. All those facts, things, dates, tickets: they say fuck all. They'd say fuck

155

all about anyone. They're just facts and there's no life to them, in them.

But there's one thing. There is one thing, a name, that, since Marcus wrote out the list and gave it to me, since I read it, saw it, that name, it sticks. Something that Nathalie said. Something she said about somebody some night somewhere, course she doesn't know anything because it was too dark, far too dark, it all happened, whatever happened, too fast, and the noise, too much noise to hear, and they were all so off their faces, but a name, there was a name that was like, what did she say, something like, *sounded um like, um, soap?*

It sounded like soap. That's what she said she thought she heard, maybe, through the noise, through everything, in the fast, noisy, faceless dark. Soper, that's what it sounded like. Soper: looking at it written down; hearing it. I mean, that name is not like a friend's name, not like your sister's name, not like a nickname. More like a last name. And last names, they kind of exist in some world apart from first names. They exist in the world of registers, and football teams. Institutions. Prisons. Soper is not a name like Joe. It is not a name like Collette. Soper could be a woman, sure, but you just know Soper is not a woman. Without first names, last names are like bricks. They're one thing, only one, robbed of whatever it is, personality. You just know Soper is male. Soper is a man known as Soper. Soper is Soper. Carved into a brick. Not into a tree with a heart round it. And if you asked someone about Soper's first name they'd say what? *Dunno, he's just Soper innit. Wha' you askin' for?*

Sure, Soper is someone who lost his first name one way or another. But not by accident. He came to be known as one thing. Even *for* one thing, like a reputation for a thing. Or more than one thing. Little by little big Soper, adult Soper, Soper with the rep, *Soper* Soper took over from the other one, the little one, the grinning one, the one with the first name. I mean, face it, if you had to choose, in the pitch dark of ignorance, in the noise, off your face, under whatever screwed up conditions, if you had to choose whether Dennie was down twenty-five grand to Collete or to Oz or to JJ or to Joe or to Soper, I mean, which one would you choose? And then what?

Hi ... Soper? Hi it's Cee, Cee Harper, Dennie's sister, how you doing? I was just wondering ... Oh sure. But I do it anyway, dialling one four one up front. There are three musical bleeps, then a woman's voice, crisp, English, perfectly spoken: *The number you have dialled has not been recognised. Please check and try again.* On the wall by the door right where he wrote it up is Georgio's number. How come I never cleaned it off? It's like down by the railway on the toolbox near the Elkstone Road signal box is Stanky's tag. Maybe I never cleaned it off because like a tag it would just reappear.

Then I'm thinking about this thing I once read about John Travolta. It was one of those *supposedly* kind of stories. Supposedly, after his big comeback, he got some crazy money like fifteen million dollars for a movie. Then, supposedly, he found out that some other star had got twenty million for *their* next movie. So, supposedly, he asked for the fifteen million to be changed to twenty million *and one dollar*. Like I guess you could say he had a rush of Saturday night fever. But really he couldn't help himself: he just had to put his tag back on the wall. And if there was one already there, well Big John, the Comeback Kid, he'd just tag right on over it.

Then I'm thinking about Ridge who keeps crossing railway lines to get to the place, to tag the special place, ready to *bush* the train, to *bomb* it. Then beyond, right up on to the train. Then beyond, right up on to the roof. Then beyond, right up to who knows where just so's he can be the one, the one with the extra dollar, just so's he can be The Ridge, the Guy Who Surfed The Roof. Everyone has to leave something behind, even if it's just their tag on a toolbox down by Elkstone Road.

Down by the signal box the light is green. They could be down there right now, spray cans working overtime. That's one of the great mysteries of life, like when do taggers do their thing? They just appear, disappear. Nobody outside them and their heads

Nick Barlay

ever knows where and when they'll appear, but you know they will, you know somewhere there's a patch of wall to tag, some wall along some railway line, some bridge, some shuttered shop. There's always that extra dollar to go for.

At four a.m. I try to phone Georgio to tell him what a fucking bastard he is. Again I dial one four one up front just in case I change my mind at the last second. Not that I know exactly what I'm going to say to him. But his phone's off which, I mean, is a big relief. I hang up wondering if Georgio's asleep, *snuggled down* somewhere, teddy bear lying on its back next to him, wide-eyed with legs sticking up towards the ceiling, while G dreams sweet dreams, uncomplicated dreams about scoring goals and getting off, dreams of flying but not dreams of flying semen. Then again, maybe he's out in the low night, street lights flicking across his windscreen. Maybe Dennie is too, about to appear.

THE FLYING FOUR

hold on to your balls boys

Marcus wakes me up with croissants. Really. He's obviously just discovered the café with the croissants. Says things like *they're the best breakfast* and that he's *always wanted to live in Paris* and that *we should go sometime.* These kinds of plans, holiday plans, always seem to make some sense of the future. But right now he says he's got to take off to work and that we'll hook up later. At the Slice he means. Says he'll see me down there about half eight nine because he's got stuff to do and do I mind *about not going together.* I say no and he says: *any case you'll be going with Alv an' Sabine or Jodie an' all them lot or someone.*

When he's gone I look out the window. The day's too bright. Doesn't the sun stop shining? I mean, it's hardly gone ten and I'm *perspiring all over* just thinking. And the traffic out there on the Westway is humming, churning, coming in through the window like blue haze. I feel sick. I don't want to go to school. I feel sick. I sit and stare and do nothing.

About eleven, the phone goes. I don't pick it up. It's Sabine. *Babes . . . Don't be mad at me yeah. I'm sorry I got mad I really am . . . I mean, still sisters righ'? We'll talk . . . Check me abou' tonigh'. An' I mean wha' I said abou' bein' sorry . . . La'ers hon.*

Sabine. Sabine's more, well, *mature,* she really is, than I'll ever

159

be. Because I can't let it go, all that stuff, I can't let it go so easily, what she said, or about Dennie, or anything. She says sorry and I forget. Just like that. A deal is struck between friends. She says sorry. I forget. What could be simpler, more natural? In the end maybe she's less, whatever, *mature*. Hate that word. Because she just wants to pretend nothing's happening, that it's all ok. And sure, like Gaj said, there was that time when Dennie nearly didn't make it to his own birthday. Turned up when everyone'd given up. Almost too late even to be late. Turned up with the words: *I'm the star. I've got a right.* And everyone laughed and knew he was right. But what's the opposite? The rest, those who aren't stars, they've got no rights.

Anyway. Whatever. Then about twelve the phone goss. Marcus. *Hi baby you're probably out soaking up the rays. I just wanted to hear your voice even if it is your answerphone ... It's gonna be one helluva scorcher out there in the big apple ... See ya ...* Hate messages in corny American accents. I hate this one for about a whole hour. Then about one the phone goes. *Darling, Jodie, how're things going with you-know-who? The two of you look really good together, really, I mean it. Anyway, you want some goss, here it comes ... my boss, Fergal, the one I was telling you about, he got beaten up by gangsters. Really. Woo it's all go isn't it. Anyway give me a tinkle later cos Jake's really into coming tonight too. Bye.*

Beaten up by gangsters. Makes me smile. Can't help it. Love the plural *gangsters*. That's one to stick on my next job application under *special interests*: I like being gangsters and beating people up. Then I feel proud of it, that I did something that's become an instant lie, a myth already, a grapevine myth involving *gangsters*. Shit, now I can look myselves in the eyes and go: hey, I acted like men. There must be big enjoyment in creating fear, being responsible for it. Or with people like Jodie, getting them to tell stories in lowered voices. Life's just pulp fiction to her anyway, a late-night movie set in the big apple. Or *big stinking onion*, as Dennie called it. But whatever, me and Fergal is fact. Like there's a wall somewhere, some street corner, with writing, with the words: *C H woʒ ere.*

Then the phone doesn't ring. By about two I'm going mental. I mean I feel sick, right in the pit of my stomach, loose bowels and everything like I'm about to audition for something, like it was *my* gig, *first* gig. I've been smoking spliffs to chill out, pass the time, whatever. But it just makes my mood worse. Then, sick or not, just to be out, to get out, I'm outside the door of Trellick in *sunglasses and a baseball cap*, you know, looking round for people I don't want to see or talk to. No sign of Georgio. He knows where I'll be tonight anyway. On the other hand there're plenty of signs of the Stanky Massive. They've been busy. There's a tag, a fresh tag, on the bus stop opposite, and I'm looking at it in baseball cap and sunglasses and a black singlet thing, like some phoney disguise. Which I guess it is.

On this side of the street's another tag, leading round towards the underground car park. Like a trail, the same *cartoon cat* trail. Like the boys they're just wheeling along, just stopping here and there to leave a mark, working the walls in blue, yellow and black: Fly; Stanky Fly (with a lightning flash); F4 (in psychedelic circles); Bunboys; Killer Bud; STANKY: HOOJ.

I wonder which of them is the real artiste. The Flying Four go *bombin'* down by the tracks but they go *bunnin'* up by the canal, maybe cycle out along the tow path to some special place, their bench, their tree, their wall. Thing is though, the tags continue down the ramp to the car park which splits off into an access road. Big metal wheelie bins cluster there among gritty oil patches, walled by cold stone that's always damp, petrol smells, water dripping on plastic bags. Crushed cans. Couple of cars that haven't seen a high street in years, that nobody would fess up to owning. *No naked lights. No smoking. No dead bodies.* I never go down here, never need to. Just the fact of it now gets me thinking, imagining things about what goes on down in the damp underground inside wheelie bins on quiet nights, about the stuff that Fergal said about Dennie ending up in a bin or a skip or someone's organs ending up in one or something. Still, what does he know, he was beaten up by gangsters.

161

On the other side of the access road, the tags continue up a narrow walkway, one of a few long narrow walkways that go off past chicken-wired waste ground to another low block, like routes burrowed out of stone. Up this walkway there's a point you can turn off and link up with the tow path just beyond a scummy patch of thick-skinned water that I suppose is someone's idea of urban landscaping. Sign that says *dog toilet*. But no, it ain't that bad really. I mean along this route there's a kind of comforting feeling that I'm nowhere in particular, that nobody knows where I am, that you couldn't even name the exact place if you tried.

There's a spray can thrown into a bush that separates dog toilet world from tow path land. Cycle tread, empty Ribena cartons, smoked-down roach trodden into the dry ground. Then voices. And further up, around a bench, somewhere near where the canal bends alongside Harrow Road and just before the footbridge that curls over the canal like a pube, there's a big argument going on. Not big, HOOJ. Ridgecroft's voice, high-pitched, well pissed off:

—*But they's makin' ou' I can't take a pina colada.*

—You can't.

—Wha' you sayin' B? *I can take a pina colada.* I had three in a row round Vin's the other nigh'. Din do *nu'in* for me.

—Liar. You was lick up so bad I had to put your hands on the handlebars innit.

Big laughter of the *Big Fold* variety.

—Still got home din I.

—*Backwards.* At *five* in the a.m. Followed by Mrs Ridge slappin' you silly for *t'rowin' up* innit.

—Ain't never threw up *nothin'*. Held it down *easy*. Three pinas: I can take *three bottles*. I can take – Oh ma God . . . Hold on to your balls boys iss Harpic.

—Wha'? goes Burston as he turns to see me walking up. Oh ma God . . . She look *criss* innit.

—*Psycho* more like, goes Witter, spray can in hand.

—Yeah man *bad*, goes Big Clarke as I reach them. Like dat Linda Hamilton in *Terminator II* when she—

—When she combats evil, destroys it and saves the world. That Linda?

—You seen it miss? goes Big C, astride his bike, rocking it back and forth, an unlit spliff in his fingers that disappears into his palm.

—I'm living it, I smile, nice and sweet in the mouth. So, crew, you all satisfied with your day's work?

They look at each other to confirm the ancient law of silence. Witter's spray-can hand drops down by his side, rolls behind his arse and plays dead. Ridgecroft glances down at his bike which is lying next to two others on the grass by the side of the path.

—Wha' work? he says. We ain't done no work.

—*Artwork* I'm talking about.

—Tha' ain't—

—Don't say nu'in. She ain't got no authority ou'a school innit.

—Ain't got none *in it* neeva.

—Is righ', grins Burston. Bet she can't wait for next term innit, plottin' the whole time how she's gonna get me.

—You don't have to worry about that ... Won't be there next term.

—Wha'? goes Witter. Wha' d'you mean miss?

—I mean I won't be there next term.

—Sama'er? goes Burston. Dey given you the P innit.

—Yeah man, the B an' the E. For Davis.

I say nothing. Nothing to be said about Davis. Not now. Witter's got a more or less horrified, at least seriously thrown, look on his face like it was his mum who'd just announced she was quitting on him.

—How come you ain't goin' back miss? he goes.

—Don't feel like it.

And W's face is like all their faces. I mean, teachers don't tell the class they're *quitting*. And they aren't supposed to do things because they *feel like it*.

—You go'a go back.

—Yeah, why?

163

W looks to the crew but they ain't got no answer to that one. Then Ridge goes:

—Only teacher I ever liked died on the job.

—Cue the violins innit, goes Burston.

—Mr Garrett, goes Witter. Couldn't take it. Had himself a heart attack.

—Yeah, in the staffroom, in his chair, three weeks before the end of term, goes Ridge.

—Man was dead long before the end of term only nobody told him, goes Burston.

—Man was pro'ly markin' *your* homework when it happened innit B.

—I like to think so y'na mean.

—So have you had a heart attack miss? goes W.

—She'd be pushing up daisies dummy.

—No she wouldn't, goes Ridge. My gran had about ten of them and she never died. Fell over in the end and nutted herself on the washbasin.

—Wha' you runnin' off at the mouth for? Ain't no heart attack. She's just sad ... Sad quitter innit ... Can't take the *pressure*.

They're all looking at me for a reaction, trying to figure out if I'm really not going back, which I'm not, and whether I care, which I don't, and whether they should really be having this conversation.

—See ... I'm righ', goes Burston all big in the chest.

So I say, casually, *out of the blue* casually:

—I talked to your mum earlier.

Now that's a statement not to mess with. Even so, Burston tries. In front of his crew he has no option.

—No you never ... She don't care anyway.

—I did and she do.

No answer. They're all shifting about now, probably wondering if the canal's the best place for all the evidence. Clarke's itchy on his bike, ready to split, wondering if he could make the footbridge but probably aware that there's nowhere to run, nowhere to hide, once MUMS are involved. Burston goes:

—Wha' my Mum say?

—About what?

—Wha'ever you talked to her abou' I dunno.

—Well I had to tell her didn't I. It was either that or the police.

—Wha' d'you mean? Tell her wha'? Why pick on me? Teachers're always puttin' me in the frame. I step in the class——

——Half hour late.

——I step in the class an' dey start in righ'——

—You think it's just you?

—It is. Ridge, give your version.

—I'm with you B. They's victimisin' you big time. It's brutali'y.

—Wha'? Ain't no *brutali'y* goin' down dummy. Iss *treatment*. I'm talkin' 'bou' the *treatment* innit.

—You think this is treatment? You ain't seen nothing. Especially after what you've done. Because you know what this is about . . . Right? You do know don't you . . . Anyone else want me to phone up their mum? Or dad?

—We never did——

—Shu' it cakpants, says Burston staring Ridge down.

Ridge keeps stumm. Big C and little W have made themselves invisible. So I go:

—I read your story Ridgecroft . . .

Ridge's baggy pants really do look like they're filling up with ten kgs of cak.

— . . . Really enjoyed it . . . Must be a great buzz, the trains I mean . . .

Ridgecroft's fixed on his trainers like they were about to give birth to a new pair. Probably shitting himself at what'll happen if I *talk to his dad*.

—I mean, it takes a lot of guts going up there, surfing the roof . . .

Ridge glances at Burston, split second, no more, and Burston suddenly goes:

—Wha'? Is dat wha' he wrote? He wrote 'bou' him *surfin' the roof*? Ridge, is dat wha'——

—Issa story innit ... Iss just homework innit.

—Issa *lie*.

—Iss just a story B.

—Issa *gross lie*. S'posed to be a *truelife story* but you never surfed no roof. Did you?

—Issa story is all. I—

—You never surfed no roof an' you know it. Cos you bottle it every time. Every time, gets to the crucial time, an' you bottle it. Cos it was me an' *only me* wha' surfed the roof. You s'posed to be my homie an' you teefed my story ... Innit ...

Burston's about to grab Ridge's T-shirt but I step in the way.

—Why didn't *you* write it then? I didn't see your story among—

—I don't write *nu'in*, goes Burston stepping back. I live it. Just like you.

—Oh sure, like you were really living it when you broke into my place, going through all my stuff, taking—

—Ain't got nu'in to say.

—No? What about going through my stuff, taking out—

—The *bra an' panty* was all Ridge's idea. I don't do dem fings. I got a honey name of Adele y'na mean.

—You fuckin' grass B. You're s'posed to be the don an' you grass me up.

—Cos you're always runnin' off at the mouth. *And* you teefed my story.

—Cos you're always screwin' me down.

—Was still your sick idea innit. *Panty bwoy*.

—Wha' you—

—SHUT THE FUCK UP ... *Both* of you, I go, shout actually, pretty loud in fact.

And they do. They shut up. Not because I shout, which I have to say is unusual. But because of the *f-word*. That word takes us all into a whole new scenario. A whole new relationship. Now they *believe* I'm not coming back. Now, even I do. Big Clarke and little Witter have been still as squirrels on fence posts hoping the whole thing will pass them like a plastic bag down the canal. But they look up when they hear that word from *teacher*. What did I ever teach them?

—Wha' you gonna do miss? goes Witter.

After a second, I go, really quietly:

—I want to know, now, the whole thing. Or you're all in serious shit. Guaranteed . . . Mums, dads, heads, police, exclusions . . . I want to know what happened to my things . . .

Well, that's the first thing I say. I mean after the shock of those words, they serve up four huge salads seasoned with denials, versions and counter-versions. Origins of the universe? They've got their alibi. They could probably even rustle up a note from their mums to prove it. But what it boils down to is this: my things really didn't leave the building. They ended up in Ridge's cousin's flat a few floors down. No prizes for guessing who Ridge's cousin is. The Flying Four, they just helped to do it, had some fun in the process, and got *wedged up* with a little *spliff money*. They say they were given a list of things to take, to do, to *work on*. Like the door. I tell them next time they want to make something look like a real burglary they should make sure all the marks are in the right places. They say they couldn't make it look like a real burglary *cos we ain't real burglars miss*. Ha ha. In any case, they say, Carl had a key, so they weren't really doing anything wrong. *Carl said we were just helping out a friend of his*. Really.

And the goods? Only took one trip down, they say, each of them loaded with some item or other. Carl went up and checked afterwards. Carl was the one who got the bass, they say. *He was givin' the orders miss*. Carl this . . . Carl that . . . So Carl could have been the dickhead who closed the cupboard afterwards. Another big thinker. And the hole in the kitchen? Who did that? Who cut the hole in the floor? *Hole? Wha' hole miss?* Yeah right. And no mention of Dennie. I mean I say to Burston, I ask him, how come he knows my brother, how come he makes comments about him in the middle of the street. Burston says *it was never in the middle of no street*. So? So they know Dennie from *bein' round Ridge's cuz one time . . . He sorted us innit*. Then Ridge starts blabbing that in fact it was all to do with Dennie, *everything*, and that *Carl had nothing to do with it*, with *anything*, that they only ever saw Dennie *one or two times round Carl's* and that anything they know about Dennie comes from him. So then they start arguing, B saying it was Carl (to get back at Ridge for teefing his story) and Ridge saying it was Dennie (to get back at me for grassing up his story). And things start to get really confusing. Then Ridge practically shrieks at B:

—*You're dissin my blood*.

But the way he says, like *you're dissin ma blood man*, it makes everyone else laugh, me too, inside, before the confusion as to who knows what about whom or who did what to whom really sinks in.

—Wha' you gonna do miss?

Witter's been driving me mental asking this same question about ten times. But I just don't know how to answer it. I mean I want them all buried alive to their necks in an ants nest in Holland Park, heads smeared with honey. I want a deckchair opposite, and a cool drink. That's my idea of fun. A real good time. *Wha' you gonna do miss?* Marry a gangster, rob post offices. Or make a *deal* with them. For instance: *if you do whatever for me then I'll say nothing about what happened*. Bullshit. Total, unrealistic bullshit. Anyway what could they do for me? They're too hopeless to trust. And me, I've been hopeless too, letting everything slip, letting my brother slip from view. My blood. I tell them what they've told me is *nowhere near enough* and that until I get my things back they're on my hit list. That's what I say, *hit list*. And stuff like: *did you really think you were going to get away with it?* Which keeps them para. And silent. But the whole thing gets me where? Nowhere except Carl. I mean, their answers in the end leave more questions than I had questions in the first place.

Wha' you gonna do miss? I say I'll think about it. But in the meantime, I tell them, don't say *anything*. Understand? Otherwise it's *Parents' Evening II* ... Na mean? Or worse. Much worse. Like *Naming and Shaming*. Like that boy in New Zealand who set fire to the local church. They made him apologise to the whole congregation *and* do sixty hours digging ditches for the community *and* go on a fire prevention course *and* see a psychologist. After that the poor boy must have been begging for a quiet cell in Sheep Dip Jail, Last Rock in the Pacific. Probably would've been glad to swallow the key as well. But God knows I don't have to tell them this because The Flying Four, pretty canny when it comes to self-preservation, have made the necessary connections. And it shuts them the fuck up.

And Harpic, she walks off into the late afternoon. She walks off. She goes home. She phones Jodie and tells her she's going to the Slice with Sabine. Then she phones Sabine and tells her she's going to the Slice with Marcus. Then she starts to wonder whether Alv will stay home on account of not wanting to see Georgio. And whether Sabine will stay home on account of Alv. And whether Georgio will stay away on account of not wanting to see Alv or any of Dennie's friends. And whether Carl with the brains would even think about risking going under the circumstances. And whether somebody like Fergal might just be shitty enough to turn up with the words *kill a Jew bitch* written on the sole of his boot. He might.

Or it could be that nobody'll turn up. Just in case somebody else does turn up. It could be that only one person will be there, Dennie, supping a quiet beer, smoking, bass lines going through his head, waiting for his sister to show, to explain things, to level with her, to put things back on track. And that's why she has to go. Just in case he turns up.

THE SLICE

transfixed in my rear-view

Upstairs at the Slice there's a crowd. Like a tribe that gathers, the people travelling whole landscapes to hook up with their brethren, their family. Daytime, the people all belong to other tribes. Night-time, a gig brings them together. Ten-way mobi conversations bring them together. The man coming down to sort the people, that brings them together. Money, gear, stories, gags bring them together. There's always a friend of a friend, a DJ, warming up the room, *vibin' the people up* with some *bangin' drum 'n' bass*, like *phatter than phat*. Then other DJs who've always got a record bag with them just in case. Then wannabe DJs and friends of wannabe DJs talking music, talking drugs. Or else comparing hi-energy drinks, Red Bull, V8 vegetable juice, ginseng, guarana, taurine, and the latest natural highs that help you get over the unnatural ones.

Then there's always some desperate muso looking for his Moog, his DX7, his Fender, the effects pedal he borrowed out last week and that so-and-so was supposed to bring down for the gig. There's always some wise crusty has-been guitar hero who now runs some shite recording studio holding forth about the PR end of the business, how he would've had better *flyers, stickers, laminations, logos* but how in his day *it was just about the music*. Then there's

171

always some guy in red trainers and a woolly hat or green trainers and a baseball cap, or whatever, whose mobile is chirping every other minute. He's the one with the plastic bags down his pants. He's the one with the runnings to do. He's the one who seems to go through a pair of trainers a week. And there's usually ten other guys dotted around who're trying to look just like him, as secretly obvious, like they were playing out some computer game: *Fantasy Drug Dealer*.

And then the women. There's always three girls in a group who've *staked out* the three-foot-square patch in front of the low stage like an hour before even the DJ turns up. They're all girlfriends, *the* girlfriends, you know, of the drummer, the keyboard player, the singer, whatever. They're the ones who scream and whistle and clap the loudest and longest and shake their booty to stuff that even Michael Jackson couldn't work out a routine to. In a low-key place, they're the ones who *dare to bare*, who under-dress the extra yard, whose lips seem to take centre-stage on their faces. They're the ones who check out other women, who make other women's claws appear, who make you wish the three-foot-square patch they were standing on was a trap-door. Then there are the good-time girls, the *sweet young thangs* all flushed in the face from the excitement of being with people who know people, who know the Next Big Things. Usually one of them's someone's younger sister who brings all her friends. And they'll all be gorgeous, Miss Selfridge smooth, with this season's eye-shadow *applied in three easy steps, we show you how*. And they'll all be giving guys the eye over the rims of their Hooch bottles. And the guys they'll be giving the eye to always seem to be the ones with the mobile phones and hats and record bags.

Then there's the has-been guitar hero's woman looking like Keith Richards before a twelve-step programme, always with a cigarette held an inch from her mouth, skin-tight snake-skin trousers, stilettoes, black-leather jacket with tassles. And she'll be having a conversation with her best friend, another crusty rock chick but single, and a bit blousy, carrying more weight, and they'll both be saying stuff about how *aromatherapy's really great*.

Then every band member has their own little posse of *normal people*, waifs and strays who work in real jobs and have to get up tomorrow, even relos, who turn up, stand around for the first half of the set, wince, tap their palms together, make their excuses or just slink out. You get all the band members flitting about before the gig, cutting short their *number one spars* with the words: *just say hello to my invites*. And those are the invites, people nobody actually ever gets introduced to because they're from some other life.

And then there's us. We're over by the bar, in our group, with our regular people, Gaj, Sabine and so on, Nas, Norm the guitarist and his friend Linda, and her friend Carla, trumpet player Max, Ginnie, an actress, some friends of hers, and so on, and in the middle, in this perfect, cool-red, fine cotton shirt I got him for his birthday, shot of Jack in his hand and still sniffing from his last trip to the toilet, is Dennie. He always looks right. Like some musicians spend a whole gig looking uncomfortable, like they can't wait to come off. And when they do come off stage they just disappear, vanish in the crowd, there's none of that larger-than-life stuff going on. Dennie, he walks on stage like it's his living room. And everybody else just happens to be there and that's fine. And when he walks off eyes follow him. And even when he's just loping at the bar, into some story, some story or other that may not even have a point, people'll listen. I mean, he's laughing, saying something above the noise, something you just know is leading somewhere daft, something like:

—Yeah man yeah I understand. But you ever seen a fifteen-stone woman rollerblading up the Westway?

—A wha'? Sabine's going.

—Yeah I swear, Dennie's going. And you won't *believe* who she turned out to be.

—Who?

—I'm getting to it, Dennie's saying. But see the picture first: she must've been *at least* fifteen, packed into one of them all-in-one

173

Lycra jobs, you know, *knee pads* that were like *squeezing* out her calves an' thighs.

—Aagh shut up, goes Gaj.

—No man telling you it was so bizarre I couldn't help slowing down as I passed her. Then I got in front and I was *transfixed* in the rear-view. She was all sweated up, must've been doing *thirty*, puffing like a steam train, with like *loads* of radioactive make-up—

—Yeah for *safety reasons* on the highway, goes Nas.

—Exactly cos the whole traffic was going mental, bippin' away, swerving, vannies going past, windows down, wolfin' at her, shouting *go on luv, give it some*. You know?

—Yeah righ', goes Sabine with full eyebrow. So all this be'er be leadin' somewhere . . .

—It is. I mean, she was. Up the Westway. I mean the whole time I just kept thinking any human who looks like that, who's got the bottle to do that, has *got* to be in my address book.

—In your what?

—Sabine, it was a just a *platonic* thing.

—A wha' thing?

—No listen listen, we're coming down the ramp round White City and by now she can see me, like I say, transfixed in my rear-view. And get this, she's *smiling* at me—

—I've heard enough.

—No wait Sab. I pull over, *she* pulls over—

—On blades?

—Well you know what I mean, skids to a halt and piles into a dustbin then blades it round to the passenger-side window. And *that* . . . that's when I realise, like a bolt from the blue, who she is . . .

—Oh really? So? Who was she?

—*Shirley Bassey*.

—Jesus H, goes Gaj, I don't believe I got suckered into one of your stories. Again.

And Gaj speaks for most of us even though people're laughing.

—So tell us star, goes Sabine, wha' was Shirley B doin' bladin' up the flyover in the middle of the afternoon? In Lycra ...

—She's on tour Sabine. Bit swelled up, getting in shape. You know ...

—Yeah yeah. So who the fuck was she really? goes Gaj. And this better be worth it.

—Ok ok ... Remember Nenah? From that rap crew in Harlesden?

—The ones that got the music award thing?

—Yeah them.

—Ain't seen that Nenah in years ...

—Yeah, well, they're coming down tonight and guess what? I'm gonna be managing them.

—Oh yeah? goes Gaj.

—Yeah but prestige gigs only. You know? Showcase. Strictly guest list and A'n'R.

—Oh yeah? Well don't forget your people when you're doin' lengths in your heart-shaped pool. Meantime we're on in five. For a *prestige* tenner.

—I'm there ... Just gonna greet up my invites ...

And Dennie moves off into the crowd, everything grey, dark around him, him in red, kind of unbelievable, and yet you believe in him, believe that he's ok, that he'll be ok, that if he talks big for long enough then suddenly one day he'll just *be* big, that *he's a guy* and he'll work it all out. I mean he has conversations with everyone. He gets about, makes moves, says stuff, tells stories. He'll always have some story for anyone. Like the story of the time he got busted on Moss Side, armed officers against a weed-smoker with a water pistol. Or like the story of how Nazis chased him along the Paddington basin, the canal, the fight, the scar, the legend. Or like the story, his inside story, of how he shared a cell with the son of a bigtime gangster whose dad's now *looking after him*. He gets respect, he makes people laugh, he shines. And you kind of forget your disbelief. Especially when they're all on stage, checking the audience, waiting for the count with people shifting forward, the crowd kind of swelling towards the stage, the talk dying off. Then the lights fade, and for a second it's all dark. And in the dark you can almost believe anything.

Thing is though, this whole second was long ago. All this was Dennie's first gig after he came out. And it was long ago. I mean I never actually made it into the Slice. I mean I went. I got there. Hot, sticky evening. Stood at the door, the swing doors with yellow frosted glass, warm perfume, smoke coming through the crack. Laughter and music beyond. Stood there and couldn't go in. Or maybe was about to. I was about to go in. Then Georgio was standing there. Told me I was *livin' in fuckin' dreamland*. Told me it was time to *wake up and smell the roses*. And other stuff probably even more clichéd. Then he said, like he said before, that he had something to show me, about Dennie. And that maybe it would jog my memory. I told him like I told him before that I don't know where Dennie is. But as I said it I knew for sure it was pointless going in because wherever Dennie was it wasn't going to be in there.

And I looked at Georgio and there was a whole load of stupid things I couldn't answer. Like the feeling of wanting to phone Mum, the police, some missing persons helpline. But I started to wonder how long someone had to be missing before they were missing. I mean, *dear big sis, I'll be dropping out of site for a while* ... The police would just be polite about it. And then what? I'd give them theories. And then what? Sure, a spontaneous national manhunt. And Mum, if I didn't tell her, she'd ask, and if I told her, even half, she'd worry sick. And then what? And then I looked at Georgio and thought this is the creep who hit Alv but I'm not scared of him, not at all, for the stupid reason, I mean, because *he fancies me*. Anyway, whatever. I mean, I thought: I'm not going into the Slice and I can't face going home and nobody else is really going to help me except Georgio, even if he's *only obeying orders* from Fergal. And then another thing. I remembered reading somewhere that people born on a Tuesday were more likely to go missing than anyone else, which made me feel ok because Dennie was born on a Saturday. I mean all this stuff went through my head really quickly. In the end I don't know why I did what I did. I mean what else would I have done? I mean, where am I? I'm in Georgio's car heading west up the A40, the Westway, towards the M25, the motorway that marks the end of the concrete.

MOTORWAYS

snatchin' an' zuppin'

Georgio says nothing through Northolt, Ruislip and Uxbridge. I don't blame him. I say nothing too, trying not to breathe in the car air, aftershave, deodorant, hair gel, stuff with added aroma of testosterone. Then when we get a certain way out of town, everything's just street furniture. Signposts, roundabouts, street lights, verges, bus shelters, painted lines and maybe the odd empty site with a Sainsbury's sign in the middle with its scheduled opening date. It's only when we pass a blackboard outside some trashy theme pub that Georgio grunts to himself. Written on the board in multicoloured chalk: *Tonite – table dancing, Sat – The Drifters Tribute Band, Sun – Full Monty Strippers.*

—Reminds me of Purfleet, he says, which I have to say takes me kind of by surprise.

—What, as in *country roads take me home to Purfleet* type of thing?

—Nah, iss where Fergal started out, wipin' the bar in some pisshole fulla geezers, robbers mainly. An' of course strippers, housewives mainly. Everyone'd be up Esher or Chorleywood robbin' gaffs an' be drinkin' in Purfleet in time for the Monty. Dass the great thing 'bou' the M25. Snatchin' an' zuppin' innit. Robber's Highway.

—Full on life you must've led.

—Nothin' on you. You got a magic touch. Left Fergie lookin' like a panda in love. *Double shiner.* An' concussed all over like he had a head-on collision wiv his dream date innit.

—Yeah right. And after that he told you to go out and beat Alv up?

—Nobody tells me to do nothin'. Specially not Fergal.

—Don't tell me, you wouldn't piss on Fergal right?

—Wrong. Ah fuckin' would. Ah'd store it up for him. He had it comin'. So did Jesus Christ Superstar, from way back. 'Sides, Alv din get no beatin', just a thick lip. Call it a souvenir jus' like the one you give the Duchess Fergie. Troof be tol', Fergie's a cunt an' Ah laughed in his panda mug when Ah laid eyes on him. Tell you, Ah folded up like a chonga wrap seein' him proper wound up. So Ah had to tell him jus' to stop him weepin' dat Ah'd sort you out, you an' y'bruvver . . .

—But . . .

—But you's an outlaw now an' Ah like outlaws. We's two consentin' outlaws on a driveabou' innit.

—Sounds like my dream date come true.

—Lighten up. Ah ain't dat ugly.

—You're not on postcards either.

—Yeah but look who is. Ah mean, some dem Mohican nonces get on postcards an' dey's all *seriously ugly*. Y'na mean. 'Sides, Ah don't need looks, Ah got a plan innit.

—A plan, ok sure. So the driveabout's all part of your *plan* is it? Bonnie and Clyde? *Snatch an' ʒup.* What d'you expect me to say, *Baby, I love the way you rob?*

Georgio laughs or more like his lungs go into a convulsion until he gets a lit cigarette in his mouth.

—Ah can see the way your mind is finkin' bu' no.

—So what then?

—Simple. Ah reckon D's got some shells stashed. Or some gear. Or bofe. An' dat he ain't gonna be payin' nobody back. Cos he thinks he's gonna live for ever. Dass the diff between me an' him. Ah just became a robber the day Ah started eyein' up ma Mum's alarm clock radio. Dennie, he's all rock 'n' roll innit. Finks he's gonna get away wiv one big one. So him an' the goods is all somewhere. Bu' question is where. Dass where you come in. An' when Ah show you wha'm gonna show you, maybe y'gonna remember all sorts. Maybe the troof is gonna dawn 'bou' how smelly it could end up for you an' him.

—You mean for *you*. If it isn't already that way.

—Wha' you sayin'?

—Well it sounds like you're in a big hurry to get on with the rest of your life.

—Wha' you sayin'? Who you been talkin' to? Wha' dey say 'bou' me?

—Not para are you? Just that I seem to keep hearing a lot of things about Georgio Georgianou.

—Dass cos Ah dare fings uvver bruvvers don't. Ah'm the real deal innit.

—What like Robin Hoodianou? People's hero.

—Ah'd be a proper hero if der was a war on y'na mean.

We approach the junction of the M25. More street furniture. Only signposts change to let you know you're travelling. Georgio corners tightly round the roundabout, takes the exit going north, then floors it down the ramp and accelerates to eighty just to impress me. Am I insane doing this, being here? Bit late to be asking myself but I feel, I know, that it's the only thing that's made any sense in days, weeks, and I can't even guess the sense. We're in the fast lane, right behind some big white car that Georgio has to flash several times before it sluggishly moves over to let us pass. Georgio comes alongside, calls him a *cunt* but the driver, overweight business type with his jacket hanging from a side hook, stares fixedly ahead even though he's well aware by now, like he had *road rage victim* written backwards on his bonnet. When Georgio's finished his personal struggle between good and evil, he accelerates again to maybe ninety.

—Feel that. Williams three conversion. Limited edition. Lo'a geezers after dis.

181

—Mostly in uniform.

Georgio smiles at me like I understand his whole vibe, like I'm
playing his game, like that's all it is, a game, like we're somehow,
what's the word, *complicit*. If he really is a bail bandit, on the run,
hiding out, whatever, what's that make me?

A few more miles of silent motorway and Georgio switches
suddenly across four lanes, down a slip road and then left towards
Chorleywood.

—So what's the plan? Are we *robbin' gaffs up Chorleywood*? Or
just visiting your auntie?

—Jus' visitin' as it goes. You fink Ah'm gonna take you wiv
me on a bender? We wouldn't be friends no more. Turn out all
wrong like wiv ma cuz Panos. He work wiv us one time. *Only*
one time after wha' he done. Told him to sort some balaclavas for
the off. Simple job jus' to test up his abili'y innit. Turns up on the
nigh' with *baclavas*. In a fuckin' box wiv a pink ribbon round it.
Easy mistake, he said. Said he was good at takin' orders. *Usually*.
Stoopid malakas. Rarver go to work wiv a toddler an' a sheep den
family and friends y'na mean.

We're on some dark A road then B road, no street lighting, only
headlamps skipping across hedgerows, the odd late-night rabbit
projected like some disfigured hand-puppet along the tarmac.
Georgio's slowing down as we pass houses set back behind
hedges, walls, driveways, sweet protected suburbia glowing with
warm lights. You can imagine the sliding doors and patios, the
fruit baskets on squeaky clean surfaces, the twenty-piece kitchen
knife sets, the stereos, TV, jewellery. Houses like secret orchards
waiting to be plundered by Georgio and his Purfleet crew. Then
again maybe he's seeking his *bruvver's pile*, some mock-Tudor job
built on the sweat of a thousand break-ins.

He stops on the road beside the entrance to a gravel driveway,
glances at me with a quiet kind of relief, like we were a
couple just back from a long weekend, home sweet home to
his Volvo and my easy-to-park hatchback sitting outside the
front door.

—We're here, goes G, reaching behind his seat for something. Best leave your bag in the car . . .

As I get out I notice he has a briefcase, attaché type thing that's like the sort TV coke dealers normally take out of the boot in secluded car parks just before they get shot by Miami Vice. So straight away I'm thinking he's on some business or other, that he's just using me because maybe there's less chance of getting pulled with a woman in the car. Anyway, as we're walking up to the door, floodlights come on and I'm a rabbit again but with six shadows. Georgio clunks the brass knocker. It's got a horse's head on it with a coiffed mane. The house, kind of mysteriously, is called *Cliff View*. Then we hear footsteps. Georgio clicks open his case, pulls out, of all things, a *clipboard*, and clicks the case shut. That's when I know for sure that whoever's in there is a complete stranger to him. By that time the footsteps have stopped long enough behind the door to peephole us. The door opens, woman, middle-aged, glasses, cardie, slippers. Not Georgio's aunt. No door chain. She purses a smile. Automatically I try to do the same. But her smile's more practised. Like the words *no thank you not today* might as well be on a cue card behind her. I can't help looking at the ground and smoothing my hair back just to avoid doing or saying anything.

—Yes?

—Hello, sorry to intrude like dis. Ah'm Bob Marriott, area co-ordinator, an' dis is Susan, my assistant. We're from the Victim Support Liaison Group an' we're monitorin' the Victims' Charter in the area to help reduce crime. Ah understand you's burgled recently, goes Georgio looking down a sheet on his clipboard. Missis er . . .

—Stanwell.

—Stanwell, goes Georgio ticking something on the sheet.

—Well yes, yes we were just—

—Who is it dear? comes a man's voice from somewhere inside.

—Oh, er, they're from the Victim Support Liaison Group and . . .

And bla bla bla bla bla. I mean she repeats, word for word,

the whole bullshit to him indoors. Then she looks back at us embarrassed for being so silly as not to open the door. I smile at her sympathetically. I mean the smile must just be there on my face because she opens the door further. Hubby's standing there by this time. He's more or less her exact computer-matched double: glasses, cardie, slippers, only with some large, square dressing plastered on his temple.

—We'd just like to ask you a few questions, see how you're gettin' along. If iss convenient . . . Only take ten minutes . . .

—Well don't keep them standing dear, goes hubby.

—Yes . . . Come in . . .

Georgio doesn't move. She looks at him, still a bit embarrassed, confused.

—Aren't we forgettin' summin? goes Georgio flashing a big grin, prolonging her confusion for a second before holding out some sort of plastic ID card.

Mrs Stanwell's actually too embarrassed to look at it for more than a split second.

—Of course, well, yes, I'm sure you're all bona fide, she laughs, coughs, steps aside.

Amazing.

—Can't be too careful, says Georgio loving that line probably more than any he's ever uttered.

He makes a big show of wiping his feet on the doormat. And we walk in. Amazing. I'm just trying to work out which of us is more stupid, me or Mrs Stanwell. We follow them, Georgio in front of me, through a thickly carpeted hall into a thickly carpeted living room where every item of furniture has its place and nothing gets moved without written consent. Especially the display cabinets. They do like their display cabinets, the Stanwells, all four of them. One's got trophies in it, horses on pedestals, lots of coiffed manes. Another's full of souvenir mugs, Valley of the Kings with a pyramid on it, J'♥NY, St Lucia with a rasta under a palm tree. Another's full of photos in special, silvery frames, family pictures, family occasion pictures, family holiday pictures. And the fourth is empty with even the glass missing.

Georgio's blabbing:

— ... burglary's up four point six per cent in the current period which is to say over *four an' a half million's* worfa stolen property's goin' walkies.

—That's awful, goes Mrs Stanwell gesturing to us to sit down.

—Ah was tryina make you feel better actually.

—Oh, goes Mrs Stanwell laughing, still embarrassed.

—Least you ain't on your own ... Susan here got burgled recently. Now she does volunteer work.

—Yes, Susan can't help saying.

—Well things are a lot worse these days I'm afraid, goes Mr S. Is violence up as well?

—Depends on the area. Overall abou' two per cent. Dass a lo'a individual incidents Ah know, bu' generally the Squad's got their caseload under control an' the figures are dippin' ... Shall we er ...

—Why don't you start and I'll make some tea shall I? goes Mrs S.

—Oh please. Ah could murder a cup, goes Georgio glancing at me.

I nod, smile at Mrs Stanwell who goes off.

—So, goes Georgio noting something on the clipboard, Mr Stanwell—

—Peter. And my wife's Maureen.

—So, Peter, er, if you don't mind me askin', how're you copin'? Alrigh'?

—Well I suppose so, under the circumstances. One tends to be a bit more wary of course.

—Had extra security?

—Heavier chain on the door, one or two more window locks and of course the lighting, back and front. But, frankly, we were already pretty secure, burglar alarm and so on.

—Not much use when you're at home.

Nick Barlay

—Unfortunately not as we found out. Last thing one expects, quite honestly, to have someone burst in like that.
—Specially round here. Normally dey's gonna be after antiques, then iss round the M25, down the A23 to some lock-up before iss Brighton, dodgy antique capital of the UK.
—Quite. I suppose that, at least, is a consolation, that nothing of particular value was taken.
—So wha' happened? If you don't mind me askin' ... Ah mean Ah know the police pro'ly asked you—
—They didn't really. That was perhaps even more surprising than confronting a stranger in one's own front room. They seemed quite bored, astonishingly. Said it was highly unlikely they'd catch him. When I pointed out that it was by no means a straightforward burglary, more like hit and run—
—Well wha' it is, Peter, is *aggravated burglary*, an' Ah can assure you dey take it very seriously. Dey've even stepped up patrols in the area ... An' you can go for the compensation scheme even if dey don't catch 'em. So, er, least you musta got a good description ...

Mrs S comes back with a tray – pot, cups, biscuits – and sets it down carefully on the table between us on the sofa and Mr S in one of two armchairs opposite.
—Still find it a bit spooky at the back, Mrs S murmurs as she pours the tea.
—He came in froo the kitchen?
—No not at all. From the garden yes, but he actually simply walked through the doors.
—You see we've got sliding doors that we'd left open hadn't we?
—Well we'd been sitting outside ...
—Such a lovely warm evening.
— ... And then we'd come in to watch television.
—*Antiques Roadshow* actually.
—Yes, quite ironic. In a way ...
—So den he just ... ?

186

—Burst in . . . All of a sudden. He had a mask. Just appeared inside, goes Mrs S, her voice trailing off. Well . . . Help yourselves to milk and sugar . . .

Mr Stanwell puts his hand on Mrs Stanwell's. And Georgio leans forward for the milk, pours, stirs, takes his cup and turns slightly towards me before he sips.

—Wha' happened next? he goes quietly. Ah mean only if you feel like carryin' on. Sometimes it helps . . .

My hands feel cool and damp. Mrs Stanwell's hands seem dry, steady and warm by comparison. I can't help avoiding their eyes. I lean forward, put some milk in a cup, stir it slowly and take the cup, lean back just looking into it, wondering if there'll be leaves at the bottom and what they would say if I could read them.

—Well it all seemed so unnecessary, Mr Stanwell's saying. We would've given him the money, jewellery or whatever anyway.

—He was shouting throughout, obscenities mainly, as he put everything, rings, cash, whatever else, in his pockets . . . And he smashed the cabinet over there with all my great-grandmother's china in it . . . With a baseball bat.

—I think it was too short for a baseball bat dear. More like a rounders bat.

—And then he just hit Peter. It was just so pointless. We were terrified anyway. You would be wouldn't you . . .

—Quite inexcusable really. When one's in a situation like that there really is little point in resisting and—

—Course, don't make no sense to risk it over valuables.

—That's why I can't understand it. He just looked at me—

—He had a mask on didn't he dear.

—Balaclava?

—Or a ski mask, you know, the sort through which only eyes and mouth are visible . . . Odd thing, he just seemed to . . . seemed to *think* about it, and then just swung the weapon. I actually remember having what seemed like an eternity to look at it. It had the letter V on it with subsequent letters apparently scratched off . . . The whole thing seemed quite cold and calculated. Quite ruthless in fact.

—Lo'a dem're high, dass the trouble. Crack cocaine is spreadin' in the criminal class . . . You been checked . . .

—Er yes yes, it's nothing really, goes Mr Stanwell touching the dressing.

—But he still gets rather bad headaches and dizzy spells. And it's been over two weeks.

—They did say that that was fairly normal dear.

—Nothing damaged though?

—They say not.

—Haven't been able to drive though have you Peter.

—As Maureen says, it has affected my vision but I'm sure that's just temporary. The blow came from the side and struck me just above my eye. Knocked me right off my feet.

—Bein' as he was so close, you musta got a good look at him . . .

—Oh yes. Peter was a little dazed on the night—

—But nevertheless I remembered him – we both did – very clearly.

—Had very dark staring eyes. That's the first thing I saw. And a sort of mark on one eye.

—*On it* dear?

—Well, above. I'm sure there was something. That's what I told the police. A mark above his eye, his left, I think.

—I'm not quite sure about that dear. But certainly he did have an unmistakeable stare.

—Was he a black man?

—Wouldn't say *black*. Not exactly . . . But his arms were quite dark weren't they.

—Yes, as Maureen says, it was a warm evening and the intruder was in a t-shirt, a black t-shirt—

—His arms were bare you see.

—Yes, we actually told the police he was sort of *mixed race* or possibly of Mediterranean origin. Certainly a shade darker than your colleague whose name I'm sorry—

—Susan, I go, so quietly that Georgio has to repeat it. So, um, you think he was on—

—Oh he was definitely on something, like your, er . . .

—Bob . . .

— . . . Like Bob said. I'm sure he was.

—Well be that as it may dear, he certainly was *psyched up*, so to speak. He knew what he wanted, got it, struck me, then walked straight out the front door, brazen as you like.

—That was after he'd threatened us.

—Before he left? Wha' d'he say exactly?

—Just that if we called the police he'd be back one night and he'd put petrol through the letterbox. That's what's most worrying really, the thought that someone can just walk in, rob you like that and there's nothing you can do. And if he wants to come back . . .

—Well I wouldn't exaggerate the danger dear. It's highly unlikely—

—Peter's righ'. Iss highly unlikely. Dass just summin dey say.

—Just the way he said it I suppose. Can't get it out of my mind . . .

Everyone falls silent. Somewhere on another planet Georgio's sipping his tea. But all I can hear in my head is ringing like I was the one who'd been struck with a rounders bat.

—Yes, well, goes Georgio arranging the clipboard and replacing it in his attaché case. Ah'd like to reassure you, Peter an' Maureen, dat the police do all dey can. Meantime, fank you bofe. You been most brave abou' your ordeal. Susan?

—Um, well . . . Yes, I mean—

—We've got *you* all upset now, goes Maureen.

I get sympathetic looks from all of them and everybody smiles at everybody.

—Luckily I was out, I go. I mean when I was burgled. So I didn't have to go through . . . all that . . .

We all stand and start moving. At the front door Georgio pulls out a card and hands it to Mr Stanwell.

—Call any time . . .

Everybody thanks everybody like we were all in the good fight together, standing firm in tough times.

Then me and Georgio are at a roundabout. I don't know where. On the way back I suppose. I just told him to stop.

—Just don't ask me if it was really Dennie.

—Well—

—Come on . . . Wha' d'you need? A video frame innit, wiv time an' date.

—You could've just told me.

—You'da never believed me an' you know it. An' den we'da been back at square one innit.

—I still don't believe it. I mean how did you know it was—

—Cos it was me wha' marked the gaff for him. Y'na mean. Ah told him how the crimes is all out dere already. Waitin' to happen. Just needs someone to commit 'em is all. Ah showed him the ropes innit.

—You showed him how to do that?

—Nah . . . Kiddin'. No way. Not wha' *he* done. Dere's a typea violence dat go wiv *every* situation. Every situation's got its own typea violence. But Dennie, he come over all wrong. A lo'a times, if you do it righ', dey don't even triple nine innit. One word answer why: fear. If you put the fear inside 'em dey ain't gonna say *nish*. Dey ain't gonna be heroes. Dey ain't gonna screw wiv you. Dass when you give 'em the *proper* fear. An' you don't even need to whack nobody. But old Peter an' Maureen, dey got *anger* in 'em. Ain't obvious. Dey keep it quiet. Bu' iss in 'em Ah know. Ah seen it. An' if you get 'em angry iss all pear-shaped. Wha'm sayin' is, Dennie din need to *use* no bat on 'em. Just wave it abou'. Smash some glass for special effect. Call 'em wha'ever names you want. Dass the fun bit. An' den, like the geezer said, he'da just handed it over an' wrapped it up wiv a pink ribbon an' all. But Dennie, he's *double d*: dumb an' desperate . . . Y'na mean.

—So—

—So now iss your turn, goes Georgio driving off. We go'a move. Don't wanna get a pull . . .

—My turn for what?

—All Ah know yeah, is you know summin. So if you wanna

find Dennie ... Na mean, you got a bi'a pressure. Cos now he got one two *free* lotsa geezers after his arse innit: the bad, the badder an' the baddest. He could be holed up some place ... He *is* holed up. Some B an' B somewhere. You ever heard him mention anywhere? Round London? Round the motorways? Some duckhole? Even as a joke?

—No ...

No, I never heard him mention anywhere. But Sabine did. Sabine I remember reeling off all the stuff Dennie did and didn't say, all the reasons and reasoning about what he was doing, where he was going, why he never went to Spain. How he joked about going round the M25 instead. Because *Carshalton was beautiful this time of year*. What was that all about? Even if it means something, I mean, where's Carshalton? And where in Carshalton?

—Must be summin no? Out of area. Some place or uvver. Ah just know it. Fink ...

There's no way I can tell him that. But I have to tell him something. I mean, he could still help me. Clear my throat.

—There's Carl ...

—Who?

—Guy called Carl ... Lives in Trellick.

—Friend of Dennie's?

—Mm.

—So whass he go'a do—

—I think he had – He *did* have ... something to do with breaking into mine ...

—So Ah was righ'. Your gear din go down no firty floors. Still up inside innit. Ah knew it. Maybe your slippy bruvver was involved yeah?

—Maybe.

—Maybe *for def* innit. Less go see Carl.

—Now?

—Sooner den now.

—He won't be back till late. He's playing tonight at the Slice. Any case, no way I'm going down there ... I need some time.

—Wha' time? You ain't got none. Dass your whole trouble: you go'a decide fings an' just do 'em. Ah get an idea Ah just go innit. 'Sides, longer you leave it the more chance Dennie's gonna get rumbled.

—How d'you mean *rumbled*?

—Well, maybe you's the sor'a citizen who's gonna get all wound up playin' mental tug of war abou' whevva to grass everythin' up to the pigs ... Like you just grassed Carl up to me ... But you ain't gonna grass up your bruvver. Cos he'll get more den a coupla months y'na mean. 'Sides, he ain't like dat crackhead who bust in someone's gaff last year, someone like dem Stanwells, an' tortured 'em for a buzz. Don't get me wrong, burglary is a buzz. Sneakin' round while they're out or asleep an' all dat. Better'n bonin' believe me ... But puttin' out some geezer's eye for laughs is *lawless*. Y'na mean. D din do *nothin'*. Remember dat. Whass done is done. Fing is now to find him.

—Find the money you mean.

—Yeah well, can't live wivout ... But troof be tol' ... Ah'm up against it ...

Right. There's a fine line between helping Georgio to help himself and finding Dennie. And finding Dennie to do what? To save him? The traffic's thicker coming back in, like I'd been to the outermost twig of a big tree, looked out into the Big Nothing beyond. Back here it's all confused branches. But how am I going to *grass up* Dennie? How could I ever? There's no way I could. He hasn't killed anyone, I repeat to myself like a Buddhist chant. And what he did was in Chorleywood, far away, another place altogether as they say. It's just that there's no telling what Georgio will do once he gets close to the money he can't live without. And maybe there's something else, the fact that Georgio's afraid Dennie might say something about him if the police get him. I have to find him only I don't know how.

—Who's Soper?

—Where you hear the name of Soper?

—Was on Dennie's phone.

—Yeah? *Malakas*. Should mem up dem names for security . . .
Trust a teacher to do her homework innit.

—So you going to tell me?

—Soaps is who Dennie owes. An' you don't screw wiv him.

—I thought nobody screwed with you.

—Is righ' . . . Nobody 'cept Soaps . . . Now you know enough to
get Norf London banged up. Just set you off on the Yellow Brick
Road you'd do it all by yourself. Regular Judy Garland innit.

—Yeah well Judy's having a bad hair day. I can't think straight
right now . . . I just need some time . . .

—Fuck for?

—To think. Give it a go one weekend. You might even take to
it.

—Now you're blabbin' like a bint again. Wha' you need time
to fink for? To do a disappearin' act? Ah'm gonna want to see
dis Carl. *Tonight*. Sort out your gear as well. Maybe he knows
summin dass gonna save D. An' don't tell me you ain't got the
anger in you . . . You got it. Uvverwise you'da *shat* yourself by
now. Yeah righ'. So hold tight Judy, we're off to see the
Wizard . . . Meantime, you can do all the finkin' you want, keep
finkin' if you ever heard a place, a name, any place D ever mentioned,
out of area. *Anywhere*. Somewhere round the twenny five. Yeah,
specially somewhere round the twenny five . . .

ON TWENTY-ONE

the naked troof

It's just past midnight when Carl steps out of a car. He kisses the woman driving for about three solid minutes through the window during which there's an uncomfortable silence between me and Georgio, like his manhood was being disrespected or something and he had every right to hate Carl. If you can't beat up your wife, ex-wife or girlfriend, there's always someone else's boyfriend. He keeps tapping his ringed finger on the steering wheel until Carl waves goodbye and goes in.

—Give him a couple.

—That's if they've fixed the lift.

—Ah meant a coupla shiners like you give Fergie.

—Don't even think about it.

Minute later, we're in the lift. I almost hope Carl disappears because I suddenly feel totally guilty for, like Georgio said, grassing him up. Fear or anger, I don't know. I mean, fear keeps people from grassing someone up. Then the same fear makes people grass everyone up. Where does anger come into it? Except towards Dennie. And Carl. And Fergal. And Georgio. And even Alv who I feel I've known a long time. And even Sabine. What the fuck did they do for me? *Forget it; leave it*: those are their answers. And if the lift wasn't working I'd have

Nick Barlay

a hit list like a phone book by the time I got to twenty-one. So maybe Georgio's right.

When Carl opens the door in a towel, vulnerable, flicking his lank hair out of his face every second like a nervous tic, pale skinny body glowing white in the light of the corridor, bloodshot eyes from drumming in a thick fog of smoke, I give him a look, my killer look, of slow death. I mean he shrinks from me because he knows straight off what it's about. Then he sees I'm on my own because Georgio's out of sight right next to the door. So he chooses the bullshit route, starts mumbling about how late it is and how whacked he is, and can't whatever it is I want just wait. It's only a half-second later, when Georgio appears, that Carl actually sees his life flash before his eyes. Georgio kicks the door, which stubs Carl's toe, then saunters through to the front room. Nothing Carl can do except wince in silence and make sure his towel's on tight.

—Carl, says Georgio without turning, Ah can see you're all cushty an' Ah'm aimin' to leave you the way Ah found you. So come in an' shut the fuckin' door.

So Carl lets me in and shuts the door. He gives Georgio's back a nasty but pointless look, blanks me altogether, and hobbles the few steps into the living room with me behind him. Then he tries another approach, chirpy, friendly, as if Georgio was a regular little amusement in his life:

—So, what can I do for you? How can I help?

—Listen to Carl. Paint your nails Carl you'd be a receptionist. Y'na mean. In a fuckin' *health spa*. Look at you . . .

Carl picks up some cigarettes off a low coffee table, kind of nervously trying to reclaim his territory, lights one and tosses the disposable lighter back on the table. Trouble is, once the cigarette's lit he doesn't know what to do with his free hand. So he picks up the lighter again, examines it for damage.

—It's pretty obvious what it's—

—Like she says Carl, iss obvious. But in case you got trouble finkin' so high up off of the ground, let me draw the picture.

196

Numma one: where's her gear? Numma two: where's her bruvver?
Full disclosure gets you a mystery gift.

Carl takes a long drag, blows the smoke out into the stale air
then flicks ash in the direction of the table. I mean the front
room's a tip. Same size and shape as mine but cluttered with
all manner of stuff, none of which is familiar. Drum stands,
drum cases, an acoustic guitar with stickers on the body and a
broken neck. Floor-level furniture, cushions, bean bag, ashtrays
like buckets, a neat row of sixteenths in clingfilm, wraps cut out
of a magazine, scales, all the signs of comings and goings, long
sessions in the dust under the bare bulb surrounded by tie-dye
hangings on walls and windows. I imagine the Flying Four up
here, seeing Carl's world as a doorway to some other world, a
world they can't stay away from. Because in *Buzz World* there's
always the promise of a new buzz. There's late-night drum 'n'
bass on the radio, turned right down, DJs *reachin' out to the
'burbs*, sending coded messages to the people. Only they're saying
nothing to any of us. Carl hovers. He potters. As Georgio would
say, he's *finkin'*.

—Time's up.

Carl looks at Georgio, winces a grin.

—You're er, you're a friend of Gaj ... Aren't you? he goes
to Georgio, still blanking me, trying, I guess, to feel his way
out of this.

—Yeah dass righ', goes Georgio. An' also, Ah like eatin' out,
The Archers, long walks in the country, an' cats. We could catch
a movie sometime.

—Wha' you on abou'? goes Carl forcing a laugh.

—*What am I on about? Good Lord I'm stumped if I know* ...

—Listen Carl—

—You're a drummer innit?

—Well, yeah ... You guessed it ...

Georgio reaches in his back pocket.

—Carl, as a drummer, you're gonna look pretty fuckin' stoopid
drummin' wiv stumps. Cos see dis, goes Georgio pulling out his

mini-blowtorch, Ah'm gonna torch your fuckin' palms down to the bone . . .

Then he lights it. The flame sounds like a jet engine even with the music on. I open my mouth, nothing comes out, like a silent witness.

—No man . . . This isn't happening. You go'a be joking . . .

—Yeah Carl? You fink Ah'm funny?

—Look man . . . There's no need for any of this.

—No? Try tellin' dat to my mate Terry Torch.

—I'm telling you man . . . Look . . . There's no need. What d'you want? Her gear's all here, goes Carl like *she* wasn't even in the room. It's all here. In the cupboard. Look, it's all here. See? There's her computer, everything . . . Look, look over there, under the cover, I swear, look . . . Serious man, nothing's been nicked. It's all here. Nobody nicked her stuff. Nothing. I had fuck all to do with it anyway. Wasn't like that. Ask Dennie. He'll tell you.

—Do you know where he is, my brother?

—No, not right now, no. But your gear is here. You can have it. It's yours. Give you a hand taking it back up . . .

—*Jolly sporting of you old chap.*

—Come on man, you asked about her gear, it's all here. You asked about her brother, I don't know. Can you turn that thing off now? Come on man, goes Carl drawing on his cigarette.

—Wha' you keep callin' me *man* for?

Carl's so stumped by the question he swallows the smoke.

—Um, I . . . Cos . . . Why? . . . Cos you are one?

—Fuckin' joker is old Carl. If it wasn't for her Ah'd fuckin'—

—Listen m – I'm telling you the truth.

—*Bollock naked troof*, goes Georgio tearing off Carl's towel and pushing him into the bean bag, Dass wha' Ah want. Talk to me Carl.

—Look, goes Carl with his cigarette hand over his crotch until he feels the heat and changes hands. Her gear's all here I swear.

—You fuckin' told me dat. But my mate Terry, he's hungry for knowledge . . .

—Dennie, goes Carl after a moment, he left a thing for me that's all. It's in that sleeve, the record sleeve on the shelf. You can have it. Take it . . .

Georgio pulls down the record that's leaning against a bone-dry pot plant, reaches inside the sleeve and pulls out a small coin bag with several wraps inside.

—Six gees of chonga in there, says Carl.

—Cheers Carl, goes Georgio pocketing the bag.

—That's it. That's what I know. You've got it all. It was Dennie's thing right. Ok? . . . He did it. I helped him. That's all. Ok? That's it. I mean—

—You say *he did it*? Wha' Dennie do? An' stop shakin'.

—Well, *this*. It was his idea to take her gear. Said he had to. That's what he said. That's all I know. If you wanna know more, ask Dennie.

—I would but I haven't seen him. D'you know where he is?

—Me? No. That's what I'm saying. Told me he was gonna be *incommunicado*. Said he'd be in touch. That's what he said last time I—

—When was that?

—Dunno . . . I don't know. Week ago. Can't remember exactly . . . I'd tell you. It was a week. Or more. Can you turn that thing off now? Is he gonna turn that thing off?

—What d'you mean *he had to*? You said he *had* to? Take my stuff you mean?

—All I know is he had some gear stashed at your place, says Carl flicking ash then drawing his knee up to cover himself while he rubs his eyes. Fuck . . . It was totally mental the whole idea. I mean I told him . . .

—You ain't makin' no sense . . . Is he makin' sense? Oi smeg, Ah'm talkin' . . .

—I'm listening . . . I am . . .

—Good cos uvverwise Ah migh' as well pick up a phone an' talk down it wivout diallin' . . . You're sayin' wha'? He had gear stashed at hers an' then he burgled hers to get the gear out yeah?

—Yeah right ... Whatever ...

—*Whatever?* goes Georgio leaning over Carl. Whassa' mean? *Wha'ever. Wha'ever* don't answer *nuffink. Wha'ever* is a noncey cop-out word. Y'understand? It don't mean shit. The answer to the question is *yes he fuckin' did Terry* or *no he fuckin' never Terry.*

—Yes ... He did.

—An' the answer to the question *where the fuck is Dennie* is the name of a fuckin' place. A *real* place. Not fuckin' *la la wha'ever land.* Innit you cunt. So, where—

—I told you ten times I don't know I swear. I swear I don't fuckin' know ... I don't. I *do not fuckin' know* ... What can I say? Are you gonna turn that thing off now?

Georgio straightens up, takes a step back, and puts his mate Terry away. Then he shakes his head in disgust, picks up one of Carl's cigarettes and lights it. Walks a few steps, looks at stuff on a shelf, cards on a pinboard. I look at Georgio, cotton-wool mouth, feeling like I must have missed something.

—I, um, don't understand ... Why would Dennie—?

—Cos Dennie, goes Georgio, He's like Ah said innit, *double fuckin' d.* All he done your bruvver, he just cooked up some plan innit. Make it look like all the peas he owed was burgled. *Gor blimey Soaps, Soapy me old china, would you adam 'n' eve it ... just as I was about to sort you ... you'll never guess wha' happened, it's predesti-fuckin'-nation Soaps ... Oh what a shame,* says Soaps, *Never mind, live an' learn, sunny side up, it'll all turn out all right in the end.* Dass it. Dass the big fuckin' idea. Innit. Innit Carl ...

—Well—

—Innit Carl ... An' don't say *wha'ever* ...

—Yeah. I s'pose, more or less. Yeah ...

—Stoopid cunt finks he can walk away from payback ...

Carl sneaks a look up at Georgio, clears the fear from his throat.

—Can I have my towel back please?

—Carl, goes Georgio throwing the towel back, first fing, you're gonna take all her gear back. Righ'?

—Righ'. For sure. I'll do it. No worries.

—Yes der is worries. And now Ah'm gonna tell you wha' to worry abou' an' wha' not to worry abou'. Righ'?

—Yeah ... Sure. All right ...

I look at Carl. He's somehow sleazier than anyone I've ever met, like someone who isn't shitty enough to be Fergal, who hasn't got enough bottle to be Georgio, who wouldn't *dare fings wha' uvver bruvvers don't*, whose fear keeps him where he is in his scummy comfort zone with his sixteenths of weed for schoolkids. And yet looking round his place, with its clutter of objects, strewn books, old records, unwashed cornflakes bowls and mugs, cork pinboard with a photo of a blonde on some beach pouting at the camera, red gas bill, lurid tickets to some rave last year, I mean, looking at these things, it's like Marcus said. Carl, like the rest of us, like the Stanwells, is just a collection of objects. Nothing more. And for a second I don't even hate him. Then I hate him all the more for being nothing but objects, for going along with everything, like he was sleepwalking in *Buzz World*, which is no place at all, a *la la whatever* world between right and wrong. But fuck help me, if *troof be told*, my world. Whatever. When Georgio's finished with his ten commandments, I go:

—What did your cousin, David Ridgecroft—

—Nothing. Nothing, really.

—You know I'm their—

—Yeah I know.

—Who? Wha'? Where? goes Georgio. Wha' you ain't been tellin' me?

—It's nothing, I go. They, some kids, from school, just helped carry my stuff, didn't they?

—Yeah that's all they did. I mean they got off on it a bit, being in ... Well, you know ... Kids. Talk to your brother. I'm ... wha' can I say. Sorry. It wasn't personal, you know what I mean. They're not gonna get in trouble right. Are they? I mean, they're

201

just kids. They come up for a smoke. B's just getting into jazz. Tapes all my Coltrane. Ridge, he just tapes all my ragga. You know? They're just kids. They shouldna done it but ... They'll learn. They're kids.

—Der ain't no such fuckin' fing. Any case, you shoulda told me dis before. Tellin' you now Carl, if Ah find you been—

—Yeah, you told me: *Terry Torch gets busy* ...

Georgio takes a deep breath. Just when the clench in my stomach is unclenching, he punches the pinboard hard enough to shake loose most of the pins, then rips a chunk of cork off. Carl watches the photos, postcards, scraps of paper spiral to the floor.

—*Fuck, fuck, fuck* ... Righ' ... Carl: tomorrow: her gear: upstairs.

Carl nods, mumbles *yeah right*. Georgio smooths his hair back with both hands, turns and walks away towards the door. Me and Carl exchange the briefest of glances. As I turn, he bends down, picks one of the scraps off the floor and pushes it into my hand. Then the briefest of shrugs with his eyebrows. I don't dare to look at the paper. Jam it in my pocket. Georgio's already outside. I step out after him and Carl closes the door before Georgio can think of any other parting lines. I feel so alone. Georgio stands still for a second suddenly looking too bushed to press the lift button.

—What do you think?

—Wha'? Wha' d'you mean wha' do Ah fink? Fuck all, na mean. The gimp don't know *nish*.

—So what now?

—Ah don't fuckin' know. Ah'm runnin' out of places an' people. But now you got the time you was after. So use it. Like Ah said, you keep finkin'. An' Ah'm tellin' you like Ah told him—

—Save your breath.

The lift doors scrape apart and Georgio steps inside, finger on the button.

—You comin' in or wha'?

—It's ok I'll walk up.

Georgio takes the coin bag out of his pocket and pushes one of the wraps into the top pocket of my denim jacket.

—Seein' as how iss your bruvver's . . . The rest is downpayment. Ah'll be in touch.

LINE-DANCING IN FREEZYWATER

take your partners

The stairs are cool, breezy almost, compared to the suffocation of Carl's place. Far below I can hear the lift stopping, the main door opening then swinging shut. I wait a few seconds, just to make sure he's gone, before reaching into my pocket for the scrap of paper. On it, in capitals, like a title or address, are the words:

LINE-DANCING,
FREEZYWATER

At first I think Carl's taking the piss. Or, more likely, he took a big risk for me, for Dennie, but in the heat of it just picked up the wrong scrap. Which basically means I'd have to go back down only to have him tell me it's the right scrap and that he doesn't know what it means and that that's all he knows. The words are handwritten but the capitals don't tell me for sure if it's Dennie's handwriting. It could be. It could just be his sense of humour rollerblading out of control down the Westway. But it's too silly to make sense of. Like some clue. Like Dennie's run off with a bunch of line-dancers. From some place called Freezywater. What a rebel. What a joke. Carl held out, fooled me, fooled Georgio, understood what Georgio was about. And this is what he held out for, almost martyred himself for, I guess, if I hadn't been standing there, treading the air somewhere between grassing him up and having him torched. So it's back up the stairs.

And upstairs, caught in the letterbox, is a note. Life seems to be big on notes right now. *What happened baby? Let me know whatever time you get in. Big X. Marcus. It's about 11.30 now.* Could only have missed him by minutes which is kind of just as well with Georgio and his under-sexed mate Terry on the march. I go in, flop, then suddenly decide to call him, avoiding messages blinking at me on the phone.

—Where d'you get to? he says kind of hurt. Your friends were going mental. You said – I mean you should call up Sab—

—Yeah, I know. I know. I'm um, really sorry and everything. Um . . . It's a long story . . . Marcus . . . Did – . . . Dennie didn't show up . . . Did he?

—No. No he didn't, apparently. I mean Sabine said he hadn't. I hung around, like a while . . . For you I mean. You know, the gig was . . . ok. It was ok. Look, I'll come round . . . If you want . . .

—It's pretty late but—

—You ok?

—Yeah yeah. Um, look, I've got to go, I mean, the thing is I need to find . . .

—You sure you're ok? You don't sound it.

—Yeah yeah. No. I'm not. Not really.

—Do you want me to come round?

—Yeah. Yes. I do, really. No, that'd be great . . .

—But . . . ?

—But . . . It's just that – You ever heard of a place called *Freezywater*?

—Wha'? *Freezy*-water? Nope. What's happening there? All-night rave or something?

—Not exactly no . . . But I need to find it.

—Tonight?

—Mm . . . It's um, complicated . . . Look, I know it's late

and I don't even know where it is and you've got to work
tom—
—It's not that . . . I'm just a bit blittered . . .
—Well, there's a gram of crazy here. If that's—
—Yeah? laughs Marcus. *Woo darling*, I'm on my way. I mean,
I don't mean it like that, like I'm on my way only
because . . . But, anyway, I'm on my way. I mean, I'm on my way
anyway. Yeah?

Yeah. I laugh. It sends heat to my face, a happy heat that I feel
I haven't felt for days. But Freezywater isn't in the *A–Z*. It isn't
in the phone book. It doesn't even make an appearance on this
other map that's a few years out of date, but still. Places don't
just appear overnight. Not in London. They get announced. They
get built. You get to hear about them long before the handshakes
and the ribbon-cutting. So it's probably one of those places that's
more a feeling than a reality, a bad smell that people get used to
and call home.
—Try directory and see if there's a Freezywater post office. Or
Freezywater tandoori. Or Freezywater kebabs. Something that
everywhere's got, goes Marcus when he arrives a blinding ten
fifteen minutes later.

Just the thought of coke makes some people go faster, with
their bowels working overtime before they've even had any. So,
after he's been to the loo, and while he's credit-carding some lines
on an upturned plate, I try directory. They've got nothing listed
for post offices but the nice man finds a *Freezywater* with EN for a
postcode. EN for Enfield. Or Ponders End. St Albans. Somewhere
round there. On the map Enfield's a long way from Carshalton,
which is right on the other side of town. But then Carshalton is in
the middle of nowhere, between the arcs of the South Circular and
M25, a bit of a wild goose and difficult either to get in to or out of,
at least by Georgio's standards of snatch an' zup. Enfield, Enfield
Wash, on the other hand, is right next to the *Robber's Highway*.
It's where the M25 squashes down above London. And it's a much
more realistic zup from the Stanwells in Chorleywood.

—It's the closest London gets to its own orbital route, observes Marcus. But surely, I mean, can you orbit yourself? Like *actually?*

—Actually? Dunno. Maybe they've got a plaque up there in Freezywater explaining everything. Otherwise you'll have to write to someone.

—Yeah, to that guy in the wheelchair, the one with the electronic voice, goes Marcus pinching his nostrils. *Time and space. Freezywater. In orbit. Around itself . . .*

Then we do the coke and the gladness gets pretty general. Marcus says he loves adventures. I'm just glad to be with anyone but Georgio. As he gives me back the wrap, I can't help wondering what to tell him, and when, about what exactly we're doing, why we're doing it. Thing is, I don't know either. Anyway, what can I say? Past one I'm in Marcus's car like Georgio's before it and Alv's before that. Only Marcus and his car aren't exactly like Georgio and Alvin and their cars. For one thing, he has a Metro. For another, the seats are buckets leaving my knees at eye-level. As if to draw attention to the seats, the safety belts are red. And then there's Marcus's driving.

—Told you I was shit, he reminds me as we pogo into the road. That's how I failed my test the first time, *not finding the meeting point quickly enough* . . . And I couldn't remember whether it was manoeuvre, signal, mirror. Or the other one.

This time of night the A406 takes us north without the traffic that would make Marcus's driving really stand out. Occasionally a truck blasts us when Marcus drifts absent-mindedly across a lane. Eventually he builds up enough speed to get flashed by one of those cameras that never records anything anyway. I look at him driving, kind of in a world of his own, strangely innocent with me somehow a lot less innocent and I can't help really liking him and hoping I don't mess him up. I touch his face. But that just makes him look the wrong way for the crucial turn on to the A10. A couple of minutes later we're in the car park of Tanner's End Jehovah's Witnesses. How, I don't know. *We are all sojourners in Egypt*, it says on the front of the building. *What the fuck's that mean?* goes Marcus. The other sign outside the place is a bit more obvious: *Banish the Devil*. Although I doubt if any of the Satan Massive would bother turning up here. Then we get lost again among the grey high-rise slabs and shopping centres of Edmonton Green. Then we get wrong directions in a petrol station, drive by a canal, the River Lea in fact, and some kind of reservoir. After all, it's all too easy to get lost on a straight road, the straight and narrow parallel roads of the A10 and A1010 that lead to the junction of the M25, which is where the last night-bus to Waltham Cross just gives up and dies.

And it's all too easy to miss Freezywater. I mean, Freezywater turns out to be a half-mile stretch of nothing, with a sign at either end: *Welcome to Enfield Wash and Freezywater shopping precinct.*
—So this is a precinct, goes Marcus. I always wondered . . .

At one end is the Texan Cantina, which looks like it was bought at Homebase and thrown together one night to surprise Mr and Mrs Jones. According to Marcus. More or less at the other end is a branch of Victoria Wine like a last outpost supplying the final frontier. Between them, as we turn round and cruise back down, there's a spatter of hoardings, businesses, spare parts merchants, plumber, electrical goods trader, an Italian holiday specialist, G. Farley and Sons – scientific glassblowers. They all seem to have washed up in scummy Freezywater like they'd tried, but failed to get out of town. Or maybe they couldn't get any further in. But it's the place that catches Marcus's eye that gives this whole outing some sense.
—*Yeeha. Buckin' Bronco's: Western Wear . . . I do declare . . .* Cee, check out the Stetsons . . . This is one weird burb I'm telling you.
—Wait . . . Stop the car a sec . . .
—You dragged me up here to window-shop Western outfits? Either there's a new club thing I don't know about or you're just a cowgirl at heart, goes Marcus scraping the tyres along the kerb as he reverses.

I get out and go over to the shuttered front. Inside there are fancy studded shirts and belt buckles, in fact everything you'd need to make it as Sheriff of the Precinct. Flyers and notes about forthcoming attractions are taped on the window. At the top of one is a drawing of a grinning cowgirl, hands on hips, one leg cocked, clicking her boots in a pool of spit an' sawdust. Over her head are the words: *Take your partners*. Below her: *Line-dancing* . . . Beginners, advanced, all welcome. Details of times, dates, prices. What the fuck was Dennie on about? Feel like I'm being tortured for no reason. And the coke's wearing off. *Then I woke up. It was all a bad dream*. Marcus is next to me, grinning.

—Jesus, line-dancing. Shall we do it some time? Be wicked . . .

Standing opposite, he hooks his arm in mine and starts walking me round. *Yeeha*, he goes. We do a full a circle before I stop him. Can't look at him. Just rest my head on his shoulder, wondering if I'm going to cry.

—Wha'? What is it baby? he goes stroking my hair, my ear. Look, you're not ok are you? I mean . . . Do you wanna talk about it? Tell me what this is all about an' everything? Maybe I . . .

As he's talking, I become aware of a yellow light in my eyes, just over his shoulder, a yellow light in the window of Buckin' Bronco's. The light is a reflection of a sign above a glass front door on the other side of the street. The sign itself is a small plastic box with a hole in it. From between the letters, the neon inside shines brightly: *Bed & Bre—ast*. Obviously the work of local talent. Looking round, there's a light on in an upstairs window. *Vacancies*, it says on the ground floor. I hear Marcus say *it's about your brother isn't it?* but I'm already crossing the street. Marcus crosses with me.

—You're gonna call in there *now*? You think your—

I press the bell, which rings far away. Marcus has gone all tense, probably wondering what he might be called upon to do if and when the door opens. But this is it. This must be the place. What else could it be? *He's holed up some place, some duckhole*. And this is it, the only one it could be. I press again. A door inside, a hall door, opens, then the front door is unlocked, twice, the chain clanks against the glass before it's slotted in place, then finally the door opens and there's a low, doggy growl from inside. Profile of an old skanky dog with his poor balls to the floor in the dim light of an energy-saving bulb.

—Shut it, says the back of the woman's head but straight away there's another low growl. Bobbo: shut it. Now.

Marcus nudges me. I can feel him smirking. She turns her head towards us then back again really quickly like she's trying to surprise Bobbo.

—Face like the dog's bollocks, Marcus breathes at me.

Which is just about right. Apart from specks of foundation still clinging to the rolls of wrinkles, and the blue nylon nightie.

—Yes?

I don't have a clue what to say. I mean, the truth or some story? Bobbo's padding round giving out a mixture of miserable low noises, growls, slurs, pants, whines. Marcus glances at me.

—We're looking for someone, he says.

—Who's that then? Bobbo: sit and shut it.

Her voice is steady enough but it's when she tries to fix her eyes on Marcus that I realise she's pretty pissed. In which case the truth is the only thing that's going to keep her confusion to a minimum.

—Dennie Harper.

—Who? No dear, nobody – Bobbo: sit ... Nobody here by that name.

—He's quite tall, short black hair, dark eyes—

—Grrrr.

—Bobbo: sit and shut it now. Tall, dark and handsome did you say? she grins.

—No but yes he—

—Young is he?

—Yes, twenty-five ...

—Drives a flash car does he? Bobbo: *sit and shut it now*.

—Um, yes, maybe ...

211

—What d'you say his name was?

—Is he here?

—No. Right Bobbo: you know you're asking for it making a nuisance this time of night. Right? Right? Sit. Bobbo: sit. Sit Bobbo. And shut it.

—When was he here?

—Well he still is here dear, in a way. He's paid up to noon tomorrow but I tell you I haven't seen him. Paid in advance so I don't mind but as I say—

—When did you see him?

—Oh, she says puffing her cheeks out. Well, he paid two weeks dear. Paid and went. S'pose he'll be back by tomorrow to pick up his things. Tonight even. They get keys you know. Was there anything—

—I'd like to see his room.

—What? I'm telling you – Bobbo: *sit or beg, that's your choice* . . . Now why couldn't you sit in the first place? No answer to that have you? Right, as I was telling you dear there's nobody there. I do know who comes and goes in my house.

—Well he's *care in the community*, goes Marcus out of the blue. We need to trace him as soon as possible. Needs his medication. He's um . . . an epileptic—

—Look dears, I may be one over—

—I'm his sister . . . He's been missing . . .

My voice is all over the place. Can't help it. At least it gets to her because she looks straight at me, suddenly almost stone-cold sober. It affects Bobbo too who starts howling.

—Bobbo: SHUT IT, she goes giving Bobbo another *sit or beg, it's your choice* look. Why didn't you say so in the first place? I am a human being. Unlike some. You think I can't tell the resemblance? I'm good with faces. But as far as coming in—

—It's really important that – I mean I need to make sure it's definitely him . . . It is really important . . .

She looks at me and begins to focus.

—It is really important . . .

—Yes dear, I heard. I'm sozzled not deaf . . . Well you don't look like muggers, she laughs. And there's always Bobbo . . . Bobbo: you can growl now . . . Bobbo?

Bobbo skanks back into the shadows as she opens the door properly. Me and Marcus smile at her. The hallway smells of bacon, then toilet freshener, then bacon again.

—This way, she goes, heaving herself on to the stairs.

The bacon smell gets heavier the further up we go, like all the breakfasts she's ever cooked have their own rooms. The house itself is deceptive. Off the first-floor landing, smelling of a different freshener, *wild heather* or something, is a long corridor with two doors on one side, three on the other. She unlocks the second on the left, pushes it open. Yet more smells, furniture polish. I step inside, wishing I was on my own. *No smoking in bed*, it says above the bed which doesn't look slept in. *Breakfast: 7am–9.30am*, it says on the closed cupboard. Chair, table on the smooth untrodden carpet. Basin. Nothing looks like it's been touched. No clothes anywhere. No sign of anything. All of us are a little surprised to find so much nothing. She puffs out her cheeks then says:

—Well I did say he just paid and went . . .

Then something occurs to me.

—Do you think we could stay? Till noon I mean.

—Oh I couldn't allow that. And he might be back mightn't he.

—Well if he is I . . .

I notice that she's got her eye on Marcus's hand in which there's a twenty pound note. As she takes it, she smiles at Marcus who's smiling at her with his pretty white teeth.

—Well dears, she says puffing out her cheeks. It's late and under the circumstances . . . I am a human being . . . He'll turn up by noon. They do . . . If they've left anything. Will you be wanting breakfast?

We mumble something, a mixture of yes, no, I don't know.

—See how you feel . . .

Then we all pretend to yawn, say goodnight, and she's gone and the door is closed.

213

—Marcus, I go putting my arms round him. Thanks . . .
—It's alright. I've always wanted to elope. Just that Freezywater Bed an' Breast never occurred to me before. Know what I mean?

We both know we're not going to sleep. So I take out the coke and we do some more, quite a bit more. Pretty soon Marcus is trying to remember which pocket he put the condom in. And then we have our first, unbelievable shag. Really. We lie there smoking in bed, on it more like because it's too hot and the sheets are nylon and you could practically run the national grid off the sparks.
—Don't you mind being without your toiletries? says Marcus.
—Wha'? I go, sensing one of Marcus's theories lurking.
—Well you don't seem to mind. A lot of women can't stand being without their toiletries. Like even for one night.
—I guess there's other stuff on my mind. Otherwise I'd be going crazy trying to find a twenty-four-hour organic facial-scrub dispenser. You know?
—I didn't mean it like that, laughs Marcus. I just meant a lot of women . . .
—Yes . . . ?
—Not you. But, well, they have like a toiletry for everything.
—Like blokes have theories for everything.

Dennie and me and Dennie's washbag, on the beach, Freedom-on-Sea. I look over at the basin, gleaming, no toiletries, no hair-conditioners, no washbag. Then I get up and start to put my clothes back on. Marcus is like: *I didn't upset you did I?* I tell him I want to search the whole place, all ten feet by ten feet of it. But there's nothing to look in except the cupboard. Metal hangers knock against each other. Trying to be helpful, Marcus looks under the bed, under the mattress. There are no loose floorboards. There are no buckets hiding holes. Even on the street there's nothing. It's four in the fucking morning. What did I expect?

Marcus is crouching over something on the carpet. He seems like a boy fascinated by some legless beetle. I tell him it's ok and to forget the whole thing. I say sorry. Again. And in the same breath I burble on about how mean I think I've been to him and how I've been under it and so on.

—Look ... This is weird ... Cupboard's been moved, he says, his finger following a curve where the carpet fibres have been scraped up.

—So? I've looked in there.

—Yeah but if you're thinking he stashed something, could be *under* the cupboard. Base is most likely hollow.

—Let's move it.

But it's so light I practically pull it over on my own, hangers tumbling inside. First thing I see as Marcus drags the cupboard away is the grip, the wooden thickly taped handle. Once the cupboard's out of the way, the rest of the bat appears. The letter *V* that Stanwell saw. Followed by scratch marks. Marcus reaches down, picks it up. He feels the weight of it then slaps the fat end into his palm. Our eyes meet. Marcus grins.

—Wha', is Dennie a rounders star?

—He was always into sport, I mumble.

There's a plastic bag down there on the floor too, thin, red, stripey, with something dark inside. Marcus follows my eyes to it. I want to pick it up, hide it, make it disappear. He can see I'm not going to pick it up myself. So he does instead, drawing out the contents between index finger and thumb like a true professional.

—Fuck me look at this ...

He holds out a balaclava. Puts his hand into it. His pink skin shows through the eye-holes, the mouth-hole. Pink dead skin. Feel sick. Sad too. So sad. Too sick and sad to cry even. Marcus can see I'm not exactly buzzing.

—Cee ... What's he done?

I'm about to ask him what *he* thinks Dennie's done, whether the inspector's got a theory upon noticing balaclava and bat upon the aforementioned floor at precisely 4.54 a.m.

—Do you think he's used this, the bat? I mean did ... Cee ... Come on, I mean, he's not a nutter is he?

Great. Fucking great. I want to say yes he is and I hate him. But

Marcus is grinning, wincing. No, he's not a nutter. No, of course not. He's the *nicest guy you'd ever meet*. Full of life. Soul of the party. *Everyone* loves him. Ask anyone. He's a musician. He's an artist. You know what they're like. Bit mad. Bit crazy. Goes on a bender. Goes with territory. But he *cares*. He cares about people. Wouldn't hurt anyone. Wouldn't hurt a fly. Drop everything for you. No he's not a nutter. He's worse, far worse. Fucking great. But Marcus doesn't even mean it like that, in a general way. He means, pretty specifically, will Dennie go mental when he turns up at 11.59 and sees Marcus, bat in hand, with his sister next to him looking seriously sorry for herself?

—No, I go. He's not. He's just ... got himself involved with some people.

Fucking great. What a line. And the lies begin. Or began already, some time or other, and already I can't remember when.

—These people, *they're* the nutters. That's what you're saying right?

—Yep ...

Marcus looks around the room, unnerved, chewing it over.

—So what we gonna do now?

—We'll just wait. I suppose ... Maybe you should call work or something ...

—Fuck 'em, I don't mind. Sort this out. I mean, I guess he's gonna be back for his things ...

But Marcus is wrong. Because dawn and noon just come and go and there's nothing we can do. Except slip out when the time comes, while she's on the phone and Bobbo's snoozing, Marcus with the bat under his shirt, me with the bala in my pocket, the bed left as we found it, only a few fibres of pale blue carpet sticking up to suggest anything happened in an empty room on a street that's nowhere in particular.

THE VILLAGE

out levelling with friends

—It's like everyone remembers where they were the day that musical toilet turned up on Portobello, says Sabine laughing and putting pastry in Miles's mouth. It's like you and Marcus in Bobbo's B and B: you'll always remember it.

—That's probably true but is it a good thing?

—Couple of lines an' a bit of aerobics is always a good thing.

Me and Sabine are sitting outside the Lisboa in the mid-afternoon, me eating breakfast, loads of people about or squatting in any patch of shade with drinks. I've told her everything. Before that Sabine kept saying sorry for all the things she'd said. I did too. Even then, I wasn't going to tell her everything. But once I got started, it just all came out. I was too wrecked, still am, to choose between what to tell and what not to. Sabine says that's all a good thing too, to just *level with friends*. To not miss anything out. So I just went through it. I didn't miss anything out, from standing at the door of the Slice, Georgio, the Stanwells, Carl, my things, the bat, the fact that Dennie *might have done something bad* – that's how I put it – to the coke, the line-dancing, Bobbo, and the shag on the nylon bed. And that's the first thing she says, about the toilet, to cheer me up, how *love is like the toilet appearing on Portobello*, about how we'll *always have Freezywater*.

217

Chrissie and Lana, two of Sabine's friends from a crèche off Ladbroke Grove, *Muvvers United* as Sabine calls it, pass by. They all say *alrigh' babes* at the same time and make funny faces at the contents of each other's prams. When they've moved on, Sabine puts her arm round me. She smells so nice, the heat bringing out her floaty, lavendery perfume thing.

—It'll be ok hon, she says.

When she says that, I know it will be ok because Sabine always gets her world to carry on just the way it is. It's like I could tell anyone I know about everything and they'd all say *it'll be ok hon* or *don't worry babes*. They'd all lie for me to keep things as they are. Marcus walked out with the bat under his shirt and never even thought about doing anything else. In fact, it was him who suggested making sure there was nothing left in the room. Because then one day we might have to explain those things. And it made sense. It was obvious. We were never going back there, not even for an anniversary celebration. He lied for me and for himself. And for Dennie somewhere in the middle. And so would Sabine, for all of us. And so would Alv. And the more I share it with people, or the more they get dragged in, the more ok everyone's going to say it is. All I can think of saying is: *It's not over* . . .

—I know, she goes. Look hon, you said it yourself: you don't know if Dennie's missin' for sure. Not *really* missin'. He could be somewhere or other an' if you report it you might get him in more trouble than he would've been in if you hadn't. Same with callin' up your mum. Especially *your* mum. I mean you've said it yourself: *big Jewish mamma vibe*. Still cries over *Fiddler on the Roof* an' whass the other one?

—*Victory at Entebbe*.

—Yeah. Wha' you gonna tell her? Supposin' D's just . . . whatever. Your mum's gonna be silly with worry innit. It's like there's things you *cannot* tell mums. Like I never told my mum how I induced Miles.

—How did you?

—Drivin' over speed bumps.

—No.

—Well it was the three-point turn that did it in the end, Sabine laughs. Well, five-point actually. You know wha' I'm sayin' though . . . I'm just sayin', you know, Dennie turns up an' you've been gettin' people involved an' takin' all these risks for nothing. That's the thing babes. You can't just keep trottin' abou' like you're lookin' for the right dance class down the gym. You know? Poppin' your head in everywhere. Don't wanna lose you hon, she says turning my face towards her. I don't . . .

Then Jodie's walking past with a puppy in her arms and a big flick of her sun-kissed hair for anyone watching, then another flick when she spots me.

—Woo, god, Cee, I'm sooo sorry we didn't make the gig. We had *a last-minute sitter blow-out trauma thing* and then there was this fire – Oh, this is Samsara. her name means *transmigration of life* which is like this spiritual *Hindu* thing. Jake got her for Joliette. She's gorgeous isn't she, aren't you, yes, she goes kissing the puppy on the nose. Joliette loves Samsara doesn't she, yes, yes she does . . . So, go on, tell me I missed a really great night out . . .

I introduce her to Miles and Sabine, and Sabine tells her *yeah it was really really great.* Then before Jodie can figure out whether she's taking the piss or not, Sabine asks to hold the dog. Which jumps into my lap instead. It's all warm and furry and enthusiastic about the world with its whole little body like one big heart beating. Sabine shows the puppy to Miles who reacts by taking his baseball cap off and dribbling into it.

—Ah, he's a doll isn't he . . . How old—

—Did you say you had a fire? I go.

—Oh God no, not us, though you can always make some rent money out of a little *controlled conflagration* darling. If you've filled in the right forms I mean. No but it was *wild*, thought you'd've seen it from the top floor. It was just over the road in Brondesbury Park. Some *youths* set fire to a stolen car. *People Power, yeah*, goes Jodie raising a clenched fist. I thought *wicked*, a riot, summer's definitely here. You know what I mean? Just

219

like the old days. It was great. We were just coming back from Jake's mate, Steve, lives on Tiverton, just by the park, when *woo*, fire brigade, police, sirens, lights, car blazing, people hanging out and watching. We just thought, *yeah*, *wicked*, and Jake skinned up and we watched the whole thing till they put it out. The flames were unbelievable, like *thirty feet high* with like really *fierce* bits in the middle that Jake reckoned looked like the dancing lights of Shiva. Well ok whatever it was, Joliette was *really* into it. It really was like *totally trippy*. Reminded me of beach parties in Goa. You know? No but listen, Cee, goes Jodie grabbing the dog back, I'm actually rushing darling. Come over for some pasta at the weekend and tell me about you-know-who. Give me a ring ok. Say *bye bye* Samsara. And sorry about the gig. I'll make it to the next one. Love to Dennie. *Bye bye* Miles. Bye. Ciao . . .

As Jodie disappears, Sabine's eyebrow moves up her forehead.
—*Well trance me out babes* . . . Who the fuck was that?
—Jodie: *people power, yeah* . . .
—Solar power more like. Straight to her head.

Sabine's mobile goes as Ootie and his cousin Amil go past in a big hurry carrying boxes of Persil and Daz, both of them grinning and jutting their chins to whoever they recognise. Ootie just reminds me of Dennie, of the sixty quid Dennie owes him, the sixty quid I'm going to give him one day. And I wonder if I'm going to cover all Dennie's tracks, clear up his whole life so that it'll be just right for when he returns. Like it was completely natural.

Sabine says Alv's on his way cos she's got to take Miles in for a check-up. Then she launches into this thing about what a great guy Marcus is and how he's really good-hearted and everything and how she thought he was iffy at first but that the *ifs have turned to defs* and that even she could fancy him now. I tell her I've been through the same feelings, more or less, and that I almost said things to him out there on the A10 that I might be regretting if I'd said them. I tell her I almost feel I owe him for what he did. She says: *you only owe him what you feel*, and that in any case *men like the coke an' aerobics thing as much as women*.

Few minutes later, Alv turns up, triple-parking and looking round for uniforms although certain parts of the borough are kind of exempt from most things, like triple-parking on Golborne. Alv, eyes beneath wraparounds, his lip looking not much better, is between meetings, and between calls too, a phone ringing in either hand. Of course, between all of his doings he wants to know what happened last night. I go through it again. The Slice, Georgio, the drive to Chorleywood, what Dennie did, Carl, Dennie's big idea with the burglary, the bat with the letter *V*. I leave out the aerobics thing. Sabine's contributing the whole time with stuff like: *he was wearin' a bala ... Georgio had a blow torch ... Cee ain't even slept ... Dennie needs a good talkin' to ...* By the end Alv's looking round nervously, shaking his sweaty head, trying to smile.

—Can't believe this stuff ... You sound like a couple of them Mafia wives whose hubbies come in for dinner with someone else's brains all over 'em and they just think: *That'll be a fast wash with extra rinsing and fabric conditioner.*

—Yeah they call 'em *pentitties*, goes Sabine.

—No 'Bine, the *pentitti* are the *grasses*. They grass up all the dons innit. The Mafia wives are the ones who run it all when the dons get blown away. One of them wives on her own's tougher than all the Yardies in Kilburn put together, *so help me* innit.

—Cee's just tryin'—

—Cee, you wanna know wha' *I an' I tink* ... Get rid of whatever needs gettin' rid of. If you ain't already.

—Course she's done tha' Alv. Haven't you?

—Well—

—Look, Cee, do it ASA double P. You get me? Serious. Does Marcus know all this?

—Marcus is alrigh', goes Sabine.

—So where's he now?

—He's out saving his job. But the um, the things aren't with him anyway. They're at home.

—Yeah well, Cee, wherever *dem tings* are *now*, they'd better be *somewhere else later* innit.

—Alv, is that a logical thing to say?

—'Bine, you know what I mean. I mean to *rid yourself* innit. If your brother's gone low-pro or if he's still out there, *line-dancing with his cowboy bruvvers* or who, then Georgio an' whoever's still gonna be out lookin' for him. You get me? You don't wanna — I can't *believe* this stuff. This is all — hate to say it ladies — *boys' stuff*. You know it is. Don't be dealin' with it . . . You started summin'. Ok maybe you didn't start it . . . bus the same. Now you have to walk away . . . Trust me . . . *They that meddle: none of them can by any means redeem his brother*. Psalms forty-nine. 'Bine, wha' time's the appointment? Cos I've got runnings . . .

—'Bout twenny minutes . . . Can you still drop us?

—Yeah yeah, bus go'a be now girl . . .

We leave together, a regular rounders team. I walk them to the car.

—Cee, goes Sabine hugging me and getting in the back with Miles. Come round la'er yeah?

—Can't. Carl's supposed to be returning my things. I'll call after . . .

After what? I shut the car door behind them, wave to Alv and they're already arguing about something as he pulls away, weaving in and out of parked cars, lost in themselves. And I almost wish I was with them.

CARL'S BIG IDEA

going past Go again

Carl's obviously between floors because there's a pile of stuff outside my door. His far-too-cheery-to-know-the-truth girlfriend is standing guard, her navel-ring twinkling below a kind of *babe soldier* camouflage t-shirt.

—Hi, I'm Michelle, *Miche*, says Miche, small, mascara'd eyes checking me out from head to toe like I was opposition. You must be Cee ...

—Mm, I go, opening the door. I really appreciate you helping out.

—Oh it's no problem really, she grins. I know what it's like when you're moving in. Just like going past Go again.

So I pick up my speakers and, well, move back in. Miche is behind me with my computer screen. Put it anywhere, I tell her. She just starts asking friendly questions about the flat, how I got it and so on, and makes friendly comments, about the view and so on, then asks how long I've known Carl and whether I see him often, and tells me she hasn't known him long, *still early days*, she says, wanting my understanding, sympathy, friendly advice and so on. I try not to look pissed off. I say as little as possible. I try to stay as cheery as possible. Then Carl's there, flicking his hair out of his face, avoiding my eyes, and Miche is off downstairs, self-consciously touching her bottom as she turns to go. Between me and Carl there's a weird embarrassment, silence. It's like one of us should be apologising to the other. But I can't think of what to say to him. Or how to say it. There's something too kind of intimate about having seen someone scared. I've seen him; he's seen me. Instead, we're just picking stuff up, setting it down, keeping busy in silence, waiting for the other to start.

—Um, he goes eventually, biting on his lip, That thing, you know, the piece of paper Dennie left ... I mean, it was an address or something no?

—Turned out to be. More or less. Dennie wasn't there though. Hadn't been there in a while. But thanks for—

—No. Don't thank me. Thing is I want that guy off my back.

—And what am I supposed to do? Click my fingers? I mean seriously, if you want the support group number I'll give it to you.

—You don't get it ... You just don't get it do you? *You*, you're ok. *You're* fine, goes Carl, moving towards me and raising his voice. You've got your stuff back and that's that. But he was gonna do it. Right? He'd do it. He'da done it. If you hadn't been there, he'da done it ... It's *me* that's gonna end up somewhere. That's what it's all about innit, *blokes doing blokes*. You know? You understand that? Thing is, Georgio, he's a Rottweiler. *Jaws on legs*. You know? Takes a bite and won't let go. *Period*. Why should I be dealing with this? You're ok. It's me that's got to worry about visits. He won't just go *boof*, into thin air. Will he? I'm telling you, he won't ... Not unless you've got a bone to throw.

—How d'you mean *a bone to throw*? What bone?

Carl goes silent, now aware of the open door, and listens for Miche. His eyes skim across the place, highly nervously to say the least, trying to find somewhere to rest: across furniture, windows, stuff piled on the floor, the monster TV, books, computer, everything. It's as if he's going through a whole story, a whole chronology of events linked only by my things, linked by his knowledge of them, from a door with a new lock all the way round to a hole in a kitchen floor. Then he looks back at me, and says, whispers more like:

—Thing is, Dennie left some sheks with me ... I mean he left 'em here ... But, like, when I came up I ... I mean, you know, I got 'em out. You know?

—No. What're you talking about?

—I'm talking about *sheks*, quite a lot of 'em as it goes. You know? And I mean, I know it's Dennie's an' everything but, like, you know, where the fuck is he? You know? I mean, this is what you'd call a *situation* he's left me in. I mean with Georgio. And you. And the sheks. So ... I mean, I don't wanna be involved. I'm not involved any more ... Me, I sell weed to kids. Ok? You know? That's what I do. I'm a musician.

Yeah Carl. Sing us a song. *A one, a two, a one two three four* ... I turn away, I have to turn away from him, for a second, turn away from everything, face to the board, so that nobody can see me. Because I can feel it coming. Carl, hero, held out against the forces of darkness. He held on to the money and gear too. But Carl, hero, what did he hold out for?

—I mean, what I'm saying is, I was thinking, you could, you have to just, like, sort this out with him. *Get the dog off me.* You know? Cos that's what he's after innit, all the sheks Dennie owed. I mean, you know, what happened, before, whatever, it's water under the bridge, no hard feelings ...

—Isn't that supposed to be my line?

—Whatever. Whatever. But this is down to you. Me, I'm not General Custer. You know?

—Yeah right. You're a musician. So these ... *sheks*, they were in the kitchen, weren't they? Stashed in the hole ...

—Yeah.

—How much is there?

—Right, well, thing is, goes Carl stepping closer and lowering his voice again, It is an' it ain't *liquid* sheks. You know? It's money *and* gear. About five grand cash. And some kuf. About two ounces. Fifty-six gees. Which is a lot at sixty a gee. That's

225

what? Three thousand three hundred and sixty right? So you're talking a wedge all totalled up.

—You've worked it out ...

—Yeah right, I've worked it out ... I took a tenner off for a new pinboard. That's all. The rest, just get it to him, to Georgio. You know? He's not interested in me. Or you, come to that.

—Isn't he? Carl, he's just never gonna believe it, me turning up with that when—

—He'll believe whatever's in his hand that's not his plonker.

—No, no way, listen—

—Keep your voice down cos—

—Yeah yeah ok. Point is, A, that's not enough to cover what Dennie's supposed to owe and B, it's just gonna come out of the blue after I've told him a hundred times there's sweet nothing. Anywhere. Like you say, he won't let it go. And like he keeps saying, he'll *go the distance*. Especially if he thinks either of us haven't been straight with him. And *especially* if he gets his hands on something. Georgio, he'll just come back for more. He'll never believe that's all there is, no matter how much you get him. You see what I'm saying?

—Yeah yeah I understand all that. But get real. People settle. They do. You know? They settle. Everyone wants to step on, right? He'll say: I've got this now, in my hand, or I can ponce about forever looking in refund flaps. You know? In the end there's only him. He gets enough, he'll settle too. Like everyone. He's got his *own* situation. You know? Like everyone.

—But he's still not gonna believe, like, *out of nowhere*, there's this—

—No wait, I've thought about—

—Where shall I put this? goes Miche coming in with a stack of records, one of Dennie's rare Charlie Mingus albums on top.

It's just one of those things. As she says that, we all look at each other somewhat surprised, one way or another, us in particular because neither of us heard her coming. Miche sees straight away there's something going on with this *other woman*,

something secret on Carl's face, an expression she's not supposed to see, me automatically looking away, and so on and
so on and so forth and, in a split second, well, Miche's decided:

—Oh right, she goes. I'll just put them here then shall I?

By the time I say yeah yeah great thanks, Miche has turned tail,
touched her bottom in the same place, and walked out.

—Oh fuck, Carl mumbles as he flicks his hair. You really bring
it all into my life don't you.

—Oh sure, keep talking. You think—

—No. I'm gonna say this: I've restashed it all inside one of
the speakers. There's a white dot on the back, you'll see it.
Just take the panel off. So that's my end. That's me gone. I
could've kept mum couldn't I. But I didn't. I just wanna be
out of the whole thing, goes Carl backing away, palms up like
he was innocent of all charges. So, you know, do what you
want . . .

—Carl—

—No, sorry, I'm gone. Don't get me wrong. We can be neighbours
an' everything. I mean, as long as you haven't messed up my
relationship.

Oh boy. I shrug. He turns and is almost at the door when
something occurs to me.

—One thing . . .

—What? he says turning back.

—What happened to Dennie's bass?

—His bass? Well, he took it didn't he.

—But when? It was at my place right?

—Day after. Came to mine for it. Course he was gonna take it.
That's his baby innit. I guess if his bass turns up, he turns up.
You know?

No. I still don't know. So as Carl leaves, I go past Go.
Again. Or more like just find myself past it. Wake up on
the other side, in a new place altogether, wondering what I've
got, checking through the balance sheet. Credit: money, coke,

a TV, a phone, a bat and a sax. Debit: one brother; one guitar. But Dennie, if he's actually missing, has been missing for what? Four days. And a bit. And what's that? It's no time at all.

RETAIL THERAPY

shoppin' ain't all it's cracked up to be

I'm standing by the chess sets in John Lewis from where I have a good view of the candelabras. When I called Georgio I told him Brent Cross instead of him coming to mine. He knew what it was about, knew straight off. *You got summin innit*, he said. He said it'd be safer for me to stay put, safer for him to come round. He kept saying there were too many people at Brent Cross. I said it was Brent Cross or nothing. Then, to try and put me off the idea, he said: *shoppin' ain't all it's cracked up to be*. Which is the sort of thing Sabine would say after hunting for the perfect A-line skirt then getting home and realising she hated the one she'd bought. Anyway, I told him to be by the candles in an hour. For some reason he found that funny. The idea actually came to me on the spur of the moment, kind of half-conscious on a sleep threshold. I knew he'd be totally para in a public place, that he'd want to get out of there fast, no messing, no questions, no big farewells. That's why it's good. I mean I thought if he had anything to tell me, about Dennie I mean, he'd tell me right there. He'd be smelling the money, tasting the coke just thinking about it. At least that's what came to me when I heard his voice. And I knew he wasn't going to get into discussing it on his mobile. Guys like him get mobis to conduct their *ting*, their *binniss innit*, and then they're

229

too para to talk except in pseudo-code that everyone knows and understands anyway. *Whole tings* and *half tings* and *usual tings* and *double tings*. So when I told him I'd be there with the *ting ting* I could feel his heart-rate increase. So then I carried on, asked him if he wanted me *to clarify the position*. Sure he said no. Said ok he'd be there. But I knew I'd be para too, with a plastic bag inside my bag, looking and feeling like I'd been jumping over counters armed with pepper spray and a foul mouth. Or worse, imagining some daft telemovie where a screaming model-turned-actress gets stalked by a heavy-breathing model-turned-actor with plenty of adult-oriented muzak to maintain the tension.

The bus was practically waiting for me. I put the bat in a separate bag, dumped it in one of the wheelie bins down below, crossed the street and got on the bus. Simple. Feel terrible somehow. Anyway. So I arrived early, earlier than early. Because I knew that's exactly what he'd want to do. Check the yard. Case the joint. Whatever. So I wandered, took the long route round to John Lewis, through the North car park, along the bright, white, synthy mall with a big dark pair of shades to hide my face like some cabbaged Liz Taylor gripping her handbag, fresh out of Fucked Up Anonymous. But people didn't look at me or anything. Too busy with their retail therapy. Or even more general therapy, *mall therapy*, everyone vacantly hunting and gathering, thinking *there must be something we can buy*.

Security guards in one-size-fits-all green stare into the blurry domed brightness, jolted now and then by a crackle from their radios. A group of Asian girls all with Kookai shoulder bags and platforms search for accessories and groups of boys. Spouses waiting for spouses, eating burgers, dragging kids by an arm, costing up their dream lifestyle. I take up my position, chewing gum by the Samurai chess set that even if anyone bought would just stand in a corner, get dusted once a week, commented on at Chrimbo when the guests run out of conversation. Whatever. All I know is, nobody's bowels are looser than mine and shopping centre toilets are always too far away, maybe deliberately, to keep people shopping under pressure.

Any case, I'm too hidden now to move, tall houseplants behind me, curtain fabrics and stuff to one side, cutlery and saucepan racks to the other. Beyond the chess displays, more saucepans from overhead hooks. Beyond that, candlesticks, wrought-iron candelabras, ceramic candle-holders and so on. I'm costing up my dream lifestyle. Can't help thinking about it. With all my extra pocket money, I could have pretty much everything in this place boxed up and delivered. Georgio doesn't know how much there is. I could give him as much or as little as I want and he'd take it. In the middle of Brent Cross he'd take it. But he'd know. He'd look at me and he'd just know.

I start to feel self-conscious, standing there, not browsing, not moving, not checking prices, not playing the consumer. Maybe he'll be late, just to make sure there's no ambush, no grinning cops waiting to do an *a cappella* style round of *you're nicked*. One of the shop assistants has noticed me. She smiles into the dark bits of my sunglasses in case I'm looking her way. I don't get suckered by that but can't help picking up the Samurai king, big, metal, heavily armed. The assistant's just dying to assist, weight on the front of her feet, ready to move at a moment's notice. Not before time, coming in the opposite entrance, I spot Georgio, shades perched on his head, sifting, idling, glancing this way and that as if shopping. I say *as if*. I mean, Georgio doesn't exactly fit the John Lewis customer profile. And the Body Shop bag he's got in his hand just makes him look worse.

The assistant's started moving in my direction. So there's nothing for it. I give Georgio a big wave. *Hi Georgio*, I go. Panic on his face, eyes flitting about till he sees me. The assistant stalls, trying to reread the customer situation. Georgio comes over quickly, totally oblivious to her, manoeuvres round the displays till he's on the opposite side of the chess sets.

—Keep it nice an' discreet why don't you, he's rasping. Dey got fuckin' video all over na mean.

—You're getting the picture.

—No but dey fuckin' will be innit.

231

The assistant, bright, stupid, *no sense of danger innit*, keeps on coming, beams at us:

—Can I help you at all? Would you like to see some other sets? We've got Egyptian Mythology. We've got Richard the Lionheart. We've——

—Oh, Richard the Lionheart, goes Georgio. The kids'll love dat innit . . .

She's about to do the full display routine with Rockin' Richard and his Dodgy Crusaders but Georgio stops her.

—Iss ok darlin' we're sorted.

I put the Samurai king back, say *thanks*. Her disappointment is our cue to move out of the shop, out on to the main concourse. Georgio looks at my bag and I realise it was a good idea, the bag inside the bag. Whatever Georgio is, he isn't a bag boy, and I can't see him snatchin' an' zuppin' through the crowd, especially not with his crack-pipe lungs.

—Come on, gis wha' you got an' less chip.

—Let's just take a walk.

—A *walk*? Wha' is dis? Lonely hearts go shoppin'?

—Looks like you've already been shopping.

—Dis? Had to get summin innit. Look daft uvverwise.

—So what is it? Avocado conditioner? Rose-petal foot rub?

—Shut up . . . Kin 'ell . . . Well less fuckin' walk den . . .

So we drift out of John Lewis, along the walkway, with Georgio muttering about how the *whole gaff is fulla bints an' nonces*.

—Where you wanna go?

—Just stroll.

—*Stroll*, she says. Iss in your bag innit, he goes putting his hand round my shoulder and touching the bag strap.

—Don't touch me, I go jerking away.

—Wha' you gonna do?

My hand's been on the pepper spray so now I pull it out, waist height so that he can see it. Georgio blows through his nose, then laughs.

—Dat fuckin' joker. Ah give the man wha' give the man

wha' give your malakas bruvver dat. You'd be better off wiv hairspray.

He reaches out again.

—I'll fuckin' scream, I go kind of sneering in his face.

—No you won't.

—I will. I'm an actress. I scream good.

Georgio considers this for a second then backs off.

—Ah knew you was trouble. Clued-up chicks always is.

But flattery gets him nowhere. I take him up the escalator to the first floor, in the middle of the middle where it's busiest, looking down at shoppers' heads milling, sitting, around the fountain. *Please keep children away from the water feature*, it says below. Beside it, people are going up and down in the *glass lift feature*. And spectating, beady-eyed, from inside a glass box is a bunch of durable, washable, flame-resistant £9.95 Brent Cross teddy bear features.

—So wha' you after? An' don't say an even split.

—I don't want the money. Or the coke.

—The wha'?

—Yeah right, there's a big bar of it.

—In the bag?

—Where else?

—Jesus fuckpants. Can't believe dis shit. Who give it you?

—My business.

—*Your* business? Your bruvver's business more like. Someone been givin' him pressure, givin' him more to sell more innit.

—How should I know?

—Ain't askin', Ah'm tellin'. Way it is. So wha' you want if it ain't—

—A few things Georgio. A few things . . . General peace of mind for one. You know?

—Long as you got dat gear you ain't never gonna have peace of mind.

—As long as you haven't got it, neither will you.

—Yeah ok ok cut to the chase innit. Wha' Ah go'a do?

—I believe you've got things to tell me.

—Believin' ain't knowin'.

—Believing's enough right now. First off, I believe you went and saw Nathalie . . . And she told you something . . . Didn't she?

—Like wha'?

—There's other things too, like about Soper.

—Ah'll business wiv him ok. Dass my end.

—You're gonna have to tell me more than that.

—Bollocks.

—Whatever genitals take your fancy but you're gonna tell me anyway.

—Ah am? Ah can visit anyone anytime anywhere. Remember dat.

—Maybe but you won't get a fucking penny out of it.

—Oh yeah? How you figure dat?

How I figure dat? Ok. I put my hand in my bag, into the plastic bag, pull out some notes, give them a little wave under his nose and, before he figure dat or anything else, the notes are over the rail. Well, the water feature isn't the mother of fountains but it does a great job of vacuuming the notes into a downdraught, holding them an instant in the spray, before sucking them in and drowning them.

—Oh ma God you stoopid fuckin' bitch, Georgio's muttering.

But the faces in the lift tell Georgio's story better than his own face. Mothers open-mouthed, children, *look Mummy look*, hands pressed instinctively against the glass, reaching in vain. As for me, it's probably the highlight of the week. But I can't stick around to enjoy it. I start walking off. Strolling off, neither fast nor slow, past clothes shops, shoe shops, with Georgio following. What else is he going to do?

—Ok so Ah saw the bint.

—And?

—She said Dennie chipped to Spain.

—Bollocks.

—Bu' Ah found his motor.

—How d'you mean?

—How do Ah mean wha'? Ah mean Ah found his fuckin' motor innit. He told her he was off to sunny Spain anyway, wivout her. Malakas left his bint to face the music din he. *And* his sister.

—Only he didn't go, did he?

—Only he din go . . .

Behind Georgio, from the other end of the walkway, a security guard is coming towards us, blabbing on his radio.

— . . . Ah know cos like Ah say, Ah found his motor. Hooky motor, ringed an' clocked an' all dat offa some merchant in Carshalton, some merchant dass known to people. People like me y'na mean?

—So where is he now?

—Gis the fuckin' bag.

—You know—

—No Ah don't.

Georgio sees me looking behind him, turns, clocks the boy from security, looks back at me, fight or flight, for once he can't decide, can't even move.

—They'll believe anything I tell them.

—Will dey?

—Where is he?

—Ah don't know, goes Georgio scratching his neck. Bu' . . .

—But what?

—Ah know he ain't go'a worry 'bou' Soaps no more . . .

—Excuse me sir, is there a problem? says Gary Fryer, a security boy whose shaving rash is like a permanent alarm on his cheeks. Only you dropped some money back there . . .

—Yeah, goes Georgio, we was on our way to fish it out.

—So it's all—

—Yeah iss under control, goes Georgio firmly then adds in a confidential tone: Just me an' the handbag havin' a domestic over ma hard-earned wedge.

Georgio smirks, maybe even winks because all of a sudden they're blokes together and Gary's nodded, walked on like a well-trained dog, blabbing on his radio. Fine. I still have the bag.

—What did you say about Soper?

—Look Ah ain't got a clue where y'bruvver is righ'. Wherever he is iss down to him.

Sly, slippery, evasive. And totally para, shifting around like a truant attending his first counselling session.

—But Soper you said was—

—Wha' you worried 'bou' Soaps for. He's just a geezer innit. An' one day he's gonna drop dead just like a geezer.

—And you're gonna live for ever.

—Pro'ly will.

—It's not the way you talked about him before.

—Ah told you all sorts. In the end Soaps is a pussycat, just like me wivout the jokes. Now—

—That's not what you said before though.

—Iss wha' Ah meant innit. Uvver words, Ah'm *dealin'* wiv him righ'. Na mean. Dass as long as Ah got summin to give him . . . So gis the fuckin' bag an' get it over wiv.

What do I do? What do I believe? What do I do? I start walking back towards the middle, towards the rail.

—Oh ma God don't fuckin' start, goes Georgio grabbing my arm.

We're looking at each other and I don't care any more and he knows it. His eyes search around, squint up from dark-ringed sockets at the bright dome above, then go to the shiny floor.

—Soaps . . . He slipped up din he, he says under his breath.

—What's that, slapstick? Or some prison joke, some insider's joke. *He just slipped on a bar of soap officer, fell off the toilet* . . .

—Ah'm tryina fuckin' tell you summin. He slipped up righ'. All the fuckin' way up. An' yeah it was on soap. Y'na mean. Full fuckin' stop. An' he ain't slippin' no more.

—What—

—You know wha'm talkin' abou'. You understand. You understand innit.

—So why don't you just say it then?

—Ah am fuckin' sayin' it but fing is, wha' you don't know, wha' you don't understand is summin else. Wha' you don't understand is dis: it could just be y'bruvver wha' done it.

Georgio waits for this to sink in, which it doesn't, it can't. Then he reaches into my bag, slowly, very slowly, looking at me the whole time for a reaction. His fingers find the plastic handles.

—Time you got back to your life innit, he goes very quietly, pulling the bag out.

And I let him.

BURN OUT

bruvvers an' geezers die different defs

He's telling me stuff. He's telling me there was a body inside. *Torso* is the word he uses. He asks: *when was the last time you saw him?* I'm trying to pin it down for him. Try to play back the days, the weeks even, to the particular hour. But I don't remember, don't remember the particular time. He asks me to try to remember. So I try. He was here two three weeks ago, spent a night or two, was at his friend's place, his girlfriend, after I don't know. *His girlfriend, you say?* Then he asks for her name. *Nathalie, you say? Nathalie . . . ?* I don't know, I tell him.

Have you talked to your brother since? he asks. I tell him about the note, not the exact words, just the fact of it, the note about going away. *A note you say?* It's a thing of his, to turn things round as questions. Nothing strange in it, I tell him. He says he didn't say there was anything strange in it.

All along I tell him things, and all along I could say more and I could say less but I say just what I say. I say the things that tread a line, the line that everyone treads, Nathalie and everyone, Sabine, Carl and everyone, Alv, Georgio and everyone. I can't say more how can I? And it's not possible to say less. I say I've been worried, tell him about the gig he never showed at. I tell him I think he might be missing. *Missing you say?* When

239

I say nothing, he goes: *a quarter of a million persons go missing every year but this is different.* He says missing persons *usually turn up quickly,* within days. *Or they don't.* But in any case, *this isn't a missing person inquiry.* So I ask him what it is about. That's when he mentions the car.

He says it was burnt out. He says there were a lot of calls, a lot of emergency calls, that night. *But unfortunately there were no actual witnesses.* There were people there, watching as the car went up. So they're still hopeful, about the witnesses he means. But nobody, he says, has so far come forward. Nobody saw the car driven on to the playing field in Brondesbury Park. Nobody saw it being torched. Jodie, Jake and Joliette are who I think of, watching their trippy fire, just like a beach party, just like Goa.

He's telling me the emergency services were delayed. Took twenty-five minutes to get there. Whoever called first got the name of the park wrong. And so on. Then youths, a group of them, obstructed the fire brigade. *So it was pretty fierce all in all, the fire.* And so on. But the thing, he's telling me, the thing is, there was a body inside. *Torso* is the word he uses. It was inside the boot. He says he's calling it a torso because, even though it was burnt beyond recognition, it was still obvious, even at a glance, that the head and hands were missing. He says *this is because, very likely, it was the intention of the killer or killers to prevent identification of the victim's body.* He looks out of the window into the sky, for what I don't know. Me, my head's clouded over, started clouding when I opened the door to the two of them. Just went cloudy, whole body weakened, began to float, light as nothing the moment I saw them. And since then I've been looking at the floor mostly.

Then he says: *torsos, you see, don't have dental records.* So now they only have the car to go on. Takes *a lot of temperature,* he says, *a lot of equipment,* to destroy a car beyond recognition. Even when doused in petrol. So that still gives them something to go on. Then he tells me that further to their inquiries it transpired that the car was registered to one Dennie Harper. *And being as how,* he says, *being as how the individual found in the boot may or may not be Dennie Harper*, it follows that they would like to speak to Dennie Harper, to find him then speak to him in connection with the car and, obviously, he says, in connection with the fire and, obviously, he says, the torso. He tells me they need to do this in order to rule him out. Or not. Because one way or another, he says, one way or another they're treating it as murder. With the victim yet to be identified.

He's telling me there's to be an incident room. *Notices are to be circulated around the community*. Crimestoppers number goes without saying, he says. They'll be talking to considerable numbers of people in this case. And of course, he reminds me, *all sources will be treated confidentially*. That's the word he uses: *sources*.

Me, half the time answering with half-truths, the other half thinking about Georgio, about what he said. Or didn't. It could be Soper in there, in the boot. He slipped. I never knew him. Now he's a torso known to me by name alone. It could be that Georgio told the truth. It could be. And if *troof be told*, then what? Then Dennie, not dead, not in the boot, responsible or not but still with his head – At some point, this point or another, I'm in the toilet, throwing up. The woman, the other's a woman officer, she sits next to me on the sofa, pats my back, tells me *nothing's totally certain*.

Then he starts again, asks me about enemies, about people, about Nathalie. I think of all the people, friends and half-friends, half-enemies and enemies and cannot name one. He reminds me of Dennie's record, asks about drugs, because *this may be drug-related*, asks about people I might have seen him with, about conversations I might have heard, must have heard, at some point. Or overheard. Even a nickname or a place or both, together. Very likely there's something I know, he says, but don't think is important *which may nevertheless reflect in a crucial way on the investigation*. Then he moves on to other questions, all beginning with the words: *would you say . . . ? Would you say your brother is violent? Would you say he has ongoing criminal connections? Would you say he has underworld associates? Would you say he has a mobile telephone*

241

number? What would you say he does for a living? Would you say he's ok for money? Would you say he's in debt? Would you say he's in trouble? Would you say he ever gave you the impression of being in any danger?

And me, I deny and deny and don't know and can't think, can't remember, don't remember. He sees, he knows, he looks at me and knows I'm sure, that there's more to tell. I think about Georgio, about what he said, what he said one time about *bruvvers an' geezers*, about how they die different deaths. High-speed, low-speed. Car-crashed or hanged. Shot or chibbed. And so on. Must be a whole load of different ways. But who's a bruvver or a geezer? Only Georgio could decide. Only Georgio could know. I could say so many things. Each one would have some consequence, one sure consequence for one person. I could pick a thing at random. Why not? Give them something. Alv and a shooting. Burston and a burglary. A saxophone. Dennie and the Stanwells. Georgio the bail bandit. I'd be waking up the herd, one of *the considerable number of people*. Like a *screamin' titty girl*. Or a trippy bint whose boyfriend scams insurance and three-piece suites. Or bruvvers who don't grass. Or geezers who follow bruvvers. Or the rest, *youths* on a playing field winding up the law for laughs. Who shall I give them?

The woman, I sense her exchanging looks with him, as if a bit of tea and sympathy would get better results, would have me *fessin' up my sins* and all the names of all the sinners. *Would you say you were close to your brother? Would you say you got on well with him?* How do I know if it's Dennie or not – At another point I'm too choked to talk, too choked to cry. *Would there be any sources you could point us to?*

Then he changes tack, asks about the TV, the little one and the big one, says the big one must get a really good picture. *Must have been expensive . . .* It was a present, I tell him. *A present, you say?* Then he changes tack again, asks how long I've lived here, comments on the view. Asks if I was in that night. Asks if I could have seen it from up here, the fire. Jodie reckoned I might have been able to see it from here. But there's no way. You can't see everything from up here. So he's asking if I know the field. All I know is it's a playing field sometimes used by Kensal Grove. The rugby posts are twisted because the field slopes. It gets waterlogged in winter, cracks up in summer. Apart from a patch of scorched grass, it's still just a playing field like any other. Only one day, next term, if there is a next term, people will talk about it. They'll tell the story of the car on the playing field, the fire, the body, the head and the hands. They'll all have their theories. And it'll take them no time at all to reach conclusions. *Who did what to whom? Hands up, one at a time . . .*

Me, I'm tired. So tired. Like I've travelled all the way from being a *fishfanny* via *stupid bitch* to being a *clued-up chick*. Wherever. All clued-up and nowhere to go. Because I'm waiting for him to turn up. And that's what this is all about, the working out of the waiting.

He's been telling me, if there's anything else, anything I can think of . . . He wants to say something else but he's just run out of stuff. And the other one, she's run out of sympathetic looks and pats on the back. So they go, leaving nothing clear, nothing definite, leaving none of us any the wiser. I could have said something about Georgio, and then what? They'll find a car registered in his name, and a mobile phone. But he'll be gone, ducked out to Cyprus or just ducked out, gone, leaving nothing else in his wake.

Then again, looking out the window, maybe if I looked hard enough down through the buildings, through the streets, through the crowds, through the traffic, I'd catch a glimpse of Georgio as he zupped by, mouth open wide, well sorted, laughing, loaded, *darin' fings uvver bruvver don't*, on his way to another burglary. And if I looked harder into the streets beyond, the sidestreets, maybe I'd see Dennie too, out there living the life like a *for real bruvver.*

MISS THING

after is another thing

—No listen listen my Dad reckons iss easy to be a bus driver,
Ridge is saying. All you go'a do righ' is six week trainin', coupla
time round the Chiswick skid pan, an' you're out there, drivin'
like a bastard.

—Nah, I ain't gonna do no such thing.

—Why not?

—Cos I don't wanna sit in no mobile armchair all day. I wanna
live *max power* innit.

—Yeah? So wha' you turn up here for B?

—First day's the lick, y'na mean star.

—Yeah, iss true, goes W. Iss one mega surf innit. Do anything.

—*Anything*, goes B. Cos day one's just for firin' up.

—Innit. Like day one is when God just *created* the word innit,
goes W.

—Yeah, by day two it was all verbal abuse, goes B. You get me?
After day one is *anuvver ting* innit . . .

Yeah right. This was Stanky, *hangin' an' scopin'* at the gate, first
day, last term. This was the beginning of term, when everyone was
psyched up to go to school, when everyone was psyched up to get
their kids to school, and all of them had firm intentions to stay in

245

school, to make sure their kids stayed in school. First day: *it's the lick*. At least for them it is.

I could say I'm there, register in hand, ticking all the people who have yet to go missing. I could say me an' Marcus, Alv an' Sabine, Dennie an' Nathalie are sat in deckchairs sipping cocktails on an undisclosed island in the Caribbean. Or I could say that Alv and Sabine aren't speaking to each other right now. Or that me and Marcus went to Sainsbury's for the first time together. Or that Nathalie's a hair designer now. Or that I gave Burston the saxophone, got it to him, anonymously, through Carl. I could say all kinds of things but there's not much left to say.

Two months on, the day before the first day, I still don't know whether I'm going to set my alarm. Everyone tells me, keeps telling me, that he'll turn up, that he couldn't have done it, couldn't have done what Georgio said. They tell me to stop thinking about it, to close it off in my head. But that's Sabine talking, trying to make the most of things without changing them; that's Alv talking, Marcus talking. Mum, she didn't say that. She didn't say nearly enough. Like if she had, she'd've said, she'd've asked me why I didn't know any more than I did, why I couldn't, didn't, do anything, why I waited so long, why I didn't see the signs. But Mum never said these things to me. And maybe that's worse.

Weird thing is, I forget for minutes at a time. About Dennie I mean. And then I feel guilty about forgetting, even for a minute. I forgot when Marcus came across the invite to Geoff's thirty-three-and-a-third. We almost went, looked in through the door, got close enough to hear Geoff, microphone in hand, on stage, coming to the end of his speech, saying: *it's taken years to have a reliable social life*. Then he danced the lambada with Samantha Day.

Us, we turned and split there and then, laughing, couldn't face going in. But somehow, looking back, it was enough. Their reliable social lives, their certainties, their sanity, their clear view of everything. These were enough. And that's why, one way or another, now that it's cooler, with a drizzle misting up the air, I will be back at school. And that's that.